James Craig has worked as a journalist and consultant for more tha~~n thirty years. He lives in London with his family. His previ~~o~~us~~

We hope you enjoy this book. Please return or renew it by the due date.

You can renew it at www.norfolk.gov.uk/libraries or by using our free library app.

Otherwise you can phone 0344 800 8020 - please have your library card and PIN ready.

You can sign up for email reminders too.

D0334684

NORFOLK ITEM

30129 084 465 609

NORFOLK COUNTY COUNCIL
LIBRARY AND INFORMATION SERVICE

Also by James Craig

Novels
London Calling
Never Apologise, Never Explain
Buckingham Palace Blues
The Circus
Then We Die
A Man of Sorrows
Shoot to Kill
Sins of the Fathers
Nobody's Hero
Acts of Violence
All Kinds of Dead
This is Where I Say Goodbye
Dying Days

Short Stories
The Enemy Within
What Dies Inside
The Hand of God

JAMES CRAIG

INTO THE VALLEY

CONSTABLE

CONSTABLE

First published in Great Britain in 2020 by Constable

Copyright © James Craig, 2020

1 3 5 7 9 10 8 6 4 2

The moral right of the author has been asserted.

*All characters and events in this publication, other than those clearly in the
public domain, are fictitious and any resemblance to real persons,
living or dead, is purely coincidental.*

All rights reserved.
No part of this publication may be reproduced, stored in a retrieval system, or
transmitted, in any form, or by any means, without the prior permission in writing
of the publisher, nor be otherwise circulated in any form of binding or cover other
than that in which it is published and without a similar condition including this
condition being imposed on the subsequent purchaser.

A CIP catalogue record for this book is available from the British Library.

ISBN: 978-1-47212-224-7

Typeset in Times New Roman by Initial Typesetting Services, Edinburgh
Printed and bound in Great Britain by Clays Ltd, Elcograf S.p.A.

Papers used by Constable are from well-managed forests
and other responsible sources.

MIX
Paper from
responsible sources
FSC® C104740

Constable
An imprint of
Little, Brown Book Group
Carmelite House
50 Victoria Embankment
London EC4Y 0DZ

An Hachette UK Company
www.hachette.co.uk

www.littlebrown.co.uk

For Catherine and Cate

This is the fourteenth Carlyle novel.
Thanks for getting it done go to
Michael Doggart, Krystyna Green,
Rebecca Sheppard and Hazel Orme.

*'There are hills and there are valleys.
You find out who you are in the valleys.'*

Count Basie

ONE

Just past dawn, the sky was blue, cloudless, the air chilled. Obeid Idris slipped on a pair of sunglasses and contemplated the copse standing on a small hill in front of him. It was like looking at one of the landscape paintings in the National Gallery, and he was reminded of an exhibition he had promised his girlfriend they would visit. Making a mental note to book some tickets, he let his gaze drift towards the narrow road that snaked between the fields. Their quarry was somewhere on the other side of the hill, heading towards them.

Now was the time for maximum calm. Soothed by the autumnal colours, Idris heard the words of Moshe Izaki, his Kendo instructor, in his ear: *'You are not fighting your opponent.'*

'You are fighting yourself.' Idris ran a palm across his bald head. His breathing was shallow and regular. Closing his eyes, he let all distractions fall from his mind.

A burst of static was followed by the familiar voice of Fuad Samater: *'They're here.'*

A murmur of anticipation rose among the assembled team.

'Six cars in the convoy. We want the penultimate vehicle. The people-carrier.'

Idris slowly opened his eyes and spoke into his radio. 'Understood.'

'*They should be with you in three minutes. We will be ninety seconds behind them. Over and out.*'

'Over and out.' Reaching for the pistol in the waistband of his jeans, Idris scanned the expectant faces in front of him, six heavily built young men armed with serious expressions and Heckler & Koch submachine guns. Each one had been recruited by Fuad, based on word-of-mouth recommendations from trusted associates. These were not the kind of guys you found at the Job Centre.

Idris pulled on a pair of gloves in almost ceremonial fashion before addressing the crew: 'Remember, the guns are just for show. No one will put up any resistance. There will be no need for any shooting, no need for any violence at all.'

He determinedly ignored the disappointed looks. 'Let's do this thing right – no drama. If we're calm and professional, it'll take less than five minutes.' Taking their silence as agreement, he began picking his way across the freshly ploughed earth, heading towards the road.

Biggin Hill, 5 miles. Standing beside the road sign, Idris checked his watch. One minute to go. He watched impassively as a trio of red BMWs, stolen from a garage in Manchester two days ago, rolled into place, blocking the junction in front of him. As the target convoy approached, another two cars – also red – would block off the rear, trapping the target on the narrow road.

'*You should be able to see them now.*'

Right on cue, the first of the black Mercedes vehicles that made up the convoy rolled around the corner, travelling at a cautious thirty miles an hour.

'We have them in sight.'

'*Perfect. See you in a couple of minutes. Over.*'

Idris tossed the radio to one of his men and began marching towards the roadblock.

The convoy came to an obedient halt, the drivers patiently awaiting developments, their engines still running. Somewhere overhead a couple of crows squawked noisily. Stepping in front of the first Merc, Idris counted seven in the convoy. Fucking Fuad, he never was any good at maths. At least there was only one people-carrier. It was easy enough to spot, sitting a good four feet higher on the road than the vehicles in front and behind. He signalled for the team to move forward.

The driver in the first Merc watched impassively as the heavily armed men took up their positions on either side of the road. The sound of boots on tarmac was obliterated by the throaty roar of Fuad's team approaching from the rear, cutting off any chance of retreat. As their cars screeched to a halt, the doors flew open and another six men jumped out. They were identical to the guys already deployed, right down to the brand of gum they chewed. Not for the first time, Idris wondered idly if they might have been cloned.

The driver in the first Merc was a small Asian guy with a thin moustache. He kept his eyes firmly on an imaginary spot in the middle distance, his hands still on the wheel in the classic ten-two position. Beside him, in the front passenger seat, a bodyguard glared at Idris from behind a pair of tinted sunglasses. The guy was ex-Saudi Special Forces, as were his colleagues in the remaining cars. His hands remained below the dashboard, doubtless cradling a Glock handgun, wondering if he would get the chance to use it.

Slipping past the first car, Idris continued at a casual pace, eyeballing each driver in turn. The exhaust fumes were beginning to irritate his throat, but he tried to ignore them. In the back of each vehicle, behind the tinted glass, he knew that some very important people would be cursing their phones when they realised that out here – in the middle of nowhere – there was no cellular coverage.

3

Reaching the people-carrier, Idris glared at Fuad. 'You can't bloody count.' He pointed at the line of expensive motors. 'There's seven vehicles, not six.'

Fuad's gaze dropped to the tarmac. 'Does it matter?'

'Not as long as we get what we came for.' Idris pointed at the people-carrier. 'Is this the one?'

'Yeah.'

'For sure?'

'For sure.'

From behind the bulletproof glass, the driver eyed them both with an air of professional detachment. Like all of his colleagues, he came from the Ashkona neighbourhood of Dhaka. To all intents and purposes indentured labour, the Bangladeshi earned barely five hundred dollars a month, in return for being on call seven days a week, with two weeks off each year to return home to see his family. Small and skinny, his leathery skin stretched across prominent cheekbones, the driver was almost invisible inside his ill-fitting suit. Not someone who was used to being centre stage – an extra in the drama of his own life – he wasn't going to try to play the hero.

Idris locked eyes with him for a few seconds, then turned back to Fuad. 'How many people inside?'

'Four in the back, plus the two in the front.'

'All right.' Stepping over to the driver's door, Idris tapped on the window with the barrel of his pistol. Showing considerable force of will, the man kept his eyes front. Idris counted to three and hit the glass again, harder this time. 'Open the window,' he barked. 'Nothing is going to happen to you if you do what I say.'

After several moments, the driver's right hand moved slowly from the steering wheel. There was an audible click and the whir of an electric motor as the window opened.

Idris placed a hand on the rim of the door and leaned forward. The inside of the vehicle smelled of stale cigarettes and citrus

4

air-freshener. The driver put his hand back on the steering wheel and resumed staring at the car in front. In the passenger seat beside him, the bodyguard had sensibly placed both hands on the dashboard, palms down. The passengers in the rear were hidden behind a partition of tinted glass.

'How many in the back?'

The driver weighed his answer carefully. 'Four.'

At least Fuad got that right.

'All women.'

The bodyguard muttered something to the driver. Idris missed the words, but the sentiment was clear: *Shut up.*

'Don't worry. We're not here to steal your women.' Idris waved his gun at the driver. 'Get out of the car.'

The driver hesitated.

Taking a step back from the door, Idris glanced towards the front of the convoy. There was no sign of trouble. None of the bodyguards were trying to make a name for themselves. Everything was going according to plan. It's almost as if they were expecting us. Discarding the thought, he jerked open the door. 'Quickly.' Under his T-shirt, he felt a bead of sweat roll down his spine. 'We are simply taking the car. Neither you nor your passengers will be hurt.'

The driver released his seatbelt.

'Step out.'

The driver obliged. Shivering on the tarmac, the top of his head barely reached Idris's shoulder.

'What's your name?'

The man looked thrown by the question. Lifting his gaze, he squinted against the glare of the early-morning sun.

'Your name,' Idris repeated.

'Niaz. Niaz Hom.'

'Okay, Niaz.' Idris pointed at the final vehicle in the convoy. 'Tell your colleague to put his car in the ditch so we can get

5

out of here.' He led Niaz towards the last Mercedes while Fuad and two of their crew emptied the people-carrier of its passengers. Relieved of his weapon, the bodyguard stood sullenly on the grass verge, head bowed, hands carefully positioned behind his back. Out of the back spilled four figures, each wearing a full black chador. One, at least three inches taller than her companions, was complaining violently in Arabic, jabbing an angry finger at the bodyguard, who pretended not to notice. Only when Fuad waved his Heckler & Koch directly under her nose, did the woman finally fall silent. Following her companions to the far side of the road, she took up a position as far from the hapless bodyguard as possible.

Fuad ducked into the back of the vehicle.

'Have we got what we came for?' Idris asked.

'Yeah.' Fuad gave him a thumbs-up.

'Good.' Idris watched as the driver in the final car lowered his window slightly and exchanged a few words with Niaz in Bengali. Niaz stepped away from the vehicle and gave Idris a small nod. The two men watched as the Mercedes was carefully manoeuvred off the road, leaving enough space to allow Fuad to jump behind the wheel of the people-carrier and reverse it back towards the BMWs. The roadblock opened to let him pass through.

'There you go. It's over.' Idris gave Niaz a gentle pat on the back. 'No harm done.' Reaching into his pocket, he pulled out three identical keys. He held them up for Niaz to inspect before pointing down the road. 'For the cars at the front.' He placed the keys in the driver's hand. 'Move them out of the way and you will be at the airport in ten minutes. Give His Highness my apologies for any inconvenience caused by the delay but reassure him that he still has plenty of time to make his flight.'

Idris began walking towards the waiting people-carrier, fifty metres back along the road. Fuad had thrown open the passenger seat and was gesturing to him to hurry up. Idris, however, would not be rushed. With everyone watching, his relaxed stride would leave a lasting impression. Off to his left, a flock of starlings swooped across the sky. Conscious of his elevated heart rate, he upped pace slightly as he approached the vehicle.

There was a shout, followed by a loud crack and a sharp tug at his sleeve. Idris looked down and saw that the fabric of his jacket had been torn. Soft white feathers were cascading out, leaving a trail on the tarmac. Idris turned in slow motion. Niaz Hom was lying face down, a pool of blood expanding from underneath him. Further down the road, the bodyguard from the first Merc was taking aim for a second shot. Just as he was about to squeeze the trigger, a controlled burst of fire sent the man jerking across the tarmac, the gun falling from his hand. Instinctively, Idris sought out the second bodyguard, but he had dropped into the ditch, having no desire to get involved in a gun fight.

'The woman,' Fuad screamed, 'to your left.' Idris spun around in time to see the tall woman in the chador walking towards him, a pistol aimed at his head. A second burst of fire almost cut her in half. 'Come on. Before anyone else tries to be a hero.' Leaning across the bonnet of the people-carrier, Fuad squeezed off more rounds from his Heckler & Koch into the sky, sending the other women diving for cover.

Idris jumped into the passenger seat and reached for his seat-belt. 'Good to see your aim's improving.'

His sidekick's reply came in the form of squealing tyres as they shot off down the road.

TWO

'We should go after them.' Jamal Alsukait pointed in the direction that the carjackers had fled. 'Once they reach the motorway,' he waved his hand helplessly in the air, 'they'll be gone.'

Khaldoon Ghosn shook his head. 'We're not chasing after anyone, Jamal. We're on a deadline. His Highness does not like delays,' he ran his fingers over his moustache as he watched the bodies being unceremoniously deposited in the boot of one of the abandoned BMWs, 'for any reason.'

'But we must retaliate.'

The youth has a lot to learn. And such a bad attitude, too. Why should I be the one stuck with the job of teaching him? As the trunk slammed shut, it crossed Ghosn's mind that things might have been easier if Jamal had been one of the fatalities.

Jamal Alsukait was a new addition to the prince's security detail. Like so many youngsters these days, he didn't know his place. Jamal imagined he should be in charge because he *wanted* to be in charge. The fact that Khaldoon Ghosn had almost thirty years of practical experience when it came to protecting royalty was something that Jamal discounted completely. In his underdeveloped mind, Ghosn's years on the job counted for nothing compared to a degree from some second-rate American university and the backing of an uncle on the National Security Council.

Given the choice, Ghosn wouldn't have hired the kid in a million years. But Jamal wasn't the first hire imposed upon him. He wouldn't be the last, either. That's the problem with our country, he reflected sadly. In Saudi Arabia, nepotism trumped everything. Talent, experience and endeavour counted for nothing compared to family ties and connections. There was absolutely nothing he – or anyone else – could do about it, but it still irritated Ghosn immensely.

'Who did this?' Jamal scratched his head furiously. 'What did they steal?'

None of your damn business. 'I know who did this. Don't worry, I know where to find them. I will take care of it I can assure you.'

'When you catch them, make sure I'm there.' Unable to stand still, Jamal pirouetted on one leg and spat into the ditch. 'Payback for Carlos will be a total bitch.'

It was all a pose. Ghosn was surprised that Jamal could even remember the dead bodyguard's name. 'Carlos should have stayed in the vehicle,' he pointed out. 'He deviated from the standard operating protocol and got two people killed. Not to mention himself.'

Jamal kicked a small stone down the road. 'At least he tried to do something.'

'That's not how we operate. We're professionals.'

'And professionals do nothing?' Jamal scoffed.

'Sometimes.' The more agitated his colleague became, the calmer Ghosn felt. 'Sometimes you need to concede the game and wait for the next one.'

'I suppose you'll have to find a replacement for Carlos.'

'In due course,' Ghosn replied warily.

'Because I have a cousin—'

'In due course,' Ghosn repeated. He glanced at the three women still standing by the side of the road, each puffing on a cigarette. 'Get everyone back in the cars and make sure the scene has been cleaned up as much as possible. It's time to get moving.'

An adolescent scowl crossed Jamal's face. He stalked off, muttering to himself.

I'll have to deal with that one before he causes too much trouble. Approaching the back door of a Mercedes, Ghosn bowed his head and waited patiently as the darkened window slowly opened.

Sitting in the back seat, Mansour Hayek looked up from his newspaper. 'Hard work?'

Ghosn frowned. 'Sorry?'

'Thirty-four down.' Affecting an air of casual detachment from the morning's events, the special adviser to Prince Bader Goyalan tapped the crossword puzzle with his gold pen. 'Hard work – T, something, something, L.'

Buying himself a couple of seconds, Ghosn scratched his nose. 'Toil.'

'That fits.' Hayek jotted down the missing letters. 'Is everything finally under control?'

'Yes.' Ghosn glanced at the prince, sitting next to Hayek. His Highness, engrossed in a game on his iPhone, did not look up. 'My sincere apologies for the delay.'

'We can discuss it on the flight. This should never have happened, Khaldoon. There will be repercussions – *serious* repercussions.'

'I will deal with it.'

Irritated, Hayek pushed his spectacles up his nose.

'That remains to be seen. Now, are we ready to resume our journey?'

Ghosn nodded. 'We will be on our way in the next few minutes.'

The prince's phone started bleeping. 'I've reached level a

hundred and four.' His Highness let out a squeal of delight. 'A new personal best.'

'Congratulations, sir,' the two men muttered in unison.

The window slid closed. Taking a step backwards, Ghosn scanned the horizon. The blue sky had been replaced by a blanket of cloud, promising rain. A shower would be good, washing away any further trace evidence of the shootings. No evidence, no witnesses. It could have been a lot worse. If they had been hijacked in central London, the shitstorm would have been impossible to control. For that, at least, he should be grateful. As the convoy moved off, Ghosn waited for the final car, plotting his next move. Whatever Hayek imagined, he would be the one to deal with this.

Mike Stoner switched off the engine of his tractor. For a while there was nothing other than the sound of the wind in the trees. Then came a staccato burst of gunfire.

Automatic weapons.

Unmistakable.

Stoner had spent the best part of fifteen years in the Royal Marines, including more than a decade on active service in various trouble spots around the world. It was a sound that he hadn't expected to encounter while working on the family farm in Kent.

Another burst of fire. Stoner calculated that it was coming from the far side of a cluster of trees, maybe three-quarters of a mile away. Jumping from the cab of the tractor, he made his way across the heavy ground at a steady pace.

Reaching the trees, he paused to catch his breath. A black people-carrier and two red vehicles moved through his field of vision, heading away from the airport at speed. Stoner tracked the cars until they disappeared. Retracing their path, his gaze fell on a larger, stationary convoy at the Biggin Hill junction. It was hard to make out what was going on in any detail, but the farmer could detect the signs of frantic activity. His gaze fell on two figures, standing away from the main group, having an animated discussion, maybe arguing. The sound of engines encouraged the duo slowly to return to their respective cars. Watching the convoy pull away, Stoner ran through all the things he needed to get done today. It was a long list. Tearing it up, he set off down the hill, heading for the junction.

The blue skies were gone. It had turned into a typically filthy English day with rain bouncing off the vehicle's windscreen. This was basically how things would be for at least the next six months, Idris reflected. England was a good place to do business but a terrible place to live. Thank God he and Gabriella were heading to Miami. Temperatures in the thirties and guaranteed sunshine. Perfect.

A sign by the side of the motorway announced, *London 32 miles*. Idris lifted the jacket lying on his lap and stuck a finger into the hole that had been torn in the arm, searching, in vain, for traces of blood or soft tissue. What had the driver been called? Niaz something. The luckless sod had been doing his job one minute and completely out of the game the next.

Idris imagined the bullet had gone straight through poor Niaz's brain before clipping the arm of his own padded jacket. A couple of centimetres to the left and the round would have hit Idris in the back. In the event, he had escaped without so much as a scratch. That was the difference between life and death.

Poor old Niaz would end up in some unmarked grave, his fate not recorded. Idris remembered a thin wedding band on his finger. He wondered about the man's wife and kids. When had he last seen them? How long had he ever been able to spend at home?

'That jacket's ruined.' From behind the driving wheel, Fuad Samater expressed his approval of the brand, which was insanely expensive. 'At least you can afford to buy a new one.'

12

'That idiot bodyguard had to try to be a hero, didn't he?' Idris tossed the jacket onto the back seat and turned his attention to the small holdall that had been underneath.

'We should have used the explosives. A big bang always gets people's attention. It would have focused their minds nicely.'

Idris shook his head. 'That would have been way over the top. Apart from anything else, we'd have blown the money to bits.' Unzipping the bag, he flicked through the contents: underneath the thick stacks of euro notes was a selection of bearer bonds that could be easily redeemed at almost any bank in the world. Better than cash. Better than he'd expected.

All in all, the raid had netted more than forty million dollars in cash and cash equivalents. Everyone would be very well paid for this job. His own share could be as high as ten million. Not bad for a morning's work. 'We didn't want to leave a mess.'

'Three bodies.' Fuad giggled. 'That looks like a mess to me.' Swerving into the outside lane, he accelerated past a van advertising health-food supplements.

'The Saudis'll clean it up. They don't want an investigation any more than we do.'

Fuad's expression grew serious. 'They'll come after us.'

'Someone will, but we can handle that. Always have, always will.' Digging into the bottom of the bag, Idris pulled out one last piece of booty: a diamond-studded phone. His first instinct was to open the car window and toss the gaudy bauble under the wheels of an onrushing vehicle. Instead, he powered it up. The screen sprang into life. 'No password protection. How stupid is that?' He began flicking through the different functions until he came to a cache of photographs. 'Urgh.'

'What is it?' Fuad asked eagerly. 'Porn?'

'Never mind.' Idris hastily switched off the phone and dropped it back into the bag. 'Keep your eyes on the road.'

'Good stuff?'

'Not your kind of thing.' Zipping up the bag, Idris tossed it onto the back seat with the jacket.

'Since when did you become such a prude?'

'I'm not a prude.' Idris watched the display on the dashboard tick up past ninety miles per hour. 'Slow down,' he commanded, 'we don't want to get done for breaking the speed limit.'

'Don't be such a chicken.'

'Imagine if we got stopped right now.' Idris jerked a thumb at the booty on the back seat. 'How would you explain all that lot?'

'The cops are dumb,' Fuad declared. 'We just jabber away in Arabic and they'll give us a ticket and move on.'

Not as dumb as you. 'We just jabber away in Arabic,' Idris replied, 'and they'll arrest us on the spot for being terrorists.'

'In this motor? They'll think we're off on a shopping trip to Harrods or something.'

'Hardly.' Of the different stereotypes on offer, Idris knew which one he would prefer to live up to.

'We can yammer away in French, then.'

'Same difference.'

'Spanish?'

'Why can't you just do what you're told for once? Just slow the fuck down.'

Muttering to himself, Fuad signalled left and moved back into the middle lane. Idris relaxed slightly as he saw their speed falling back towards sixty.

'Pick any language you like, but if we get stopped, we're heading straight to the cells.'

Fuad watched a Porsche muscle past them and disappear into the distance as if they were standing still. 'Now there's a man who's speeding,' he cooed.

'He's probably not driving a stolen car with a bunch of guns and shit.'

'Chill out, will you?' Fuad slapped a palm against the steering wheel. 'By the time anyone catches up with this piece of crap, it'll be a burned-out wreck.'

Let's hope so. Idris was beginning to think that the heist had gone *too* well. He glanced at the rear-view mirror, but the rain was so bad he could hardly make out the vehicle behind.

'Relax, man.' Fuad gave him a friendly punch on the arm. 'The boys'll be on their way to France by now, enjoying a drink on the Eurostar.'

Idris wasn't concerned about their crew. They had completed the job and gone their separate ways. All very professional. In the unlikely event that the authorities – any authorities – ever managed to catch up with them, there was no way they could possibly lead the cops back to Idris or Fuad. The only person who could mess this up now was Fuad himself, the Lewis Hamilton wannabe sitting next to him.

'Slow down a bit more,' Idris insisted. 'Move back into the inside lane and keep it around fifty.'

'Yes, *Dad*.' With a heavy sigh, Fuad once again hit the indicator and eased his way into the left-hand lane. 'It's gonna take us for ever to get back at this rate, though. Once we hit the M25, it'll be totally jammed.'

'Don't worry. We're not under any time pressure.'

'Speak for yourself.' Fuad snorted. 'I've got a hot date tonight.' He pushed the people-carrier back up towards sixty. 'I need to get back.'

'Keep it at fifty.' Idris tried to recall the name of Fuad's latest squeeze. 'It's not even lunchtime, how can you possibly be late?'

'It's drinks,' Fuad whined. 'I need time to get ready.'

'Drinks?' Idris teased. 'Nice. I'm sure Susan will be really grateful for all the time and effort you're putting in.'

'Sarah.'

'Yeah, right.' Susan, Sarah, Idris mused, they're all the same.

15

'Or, rather, it was. I ditched her weeks ago.'

'Hm.' Idris wasn't surprised. Fuad had yet to find a girl who would put up with him for more than a month.

'I'm dating a MILF now.' Fuad chuckled. 'Well, she's not exactly a mum, but she's married.'

'She's not a MILF, then, is she?'

Fuad considered that for a moment. 'She would be a MILF – if she had a kid.'

'The clue's in the name, idiot.'

'She's a sophisticated older woman – you know what I mean.' Fuad struggled to come up with the word. 'A *cougar*.'

Idris laughed. 'A cougar?'

'Yeah.' Fuad frowned. 'That's the word, isn't it?'

'No woman with an ounce of experience or sophistication would look at you twice, Fuad. You're totally full of shit.'

'Niamh is thirty-six. I met her at a club last week. She's an accountant.'

'A married accountant?' Idris tried to think of a less obvious potential match for his friend.

'Separated.'

'Makes all the difference.'

'Her husband videoed himself fucking a prostitute while he was on a business trip. Niamh found it on his phone and ditched him.'

'Sounds reasonable.'

'The thing that really pissed her off was that the hooker was such a tart.'

'I suppose that wouldn't do much for your self-esteem.'

'She showed me the video.' Fuad shuddered. 'Gross. You see, the guy—'

'Too much information.'

'Yeah, well, anyway. Niamh isn't the kind to forgive and forget. She sees me as her revenge. Wants to fuck all the time.'

'Lucky you,' Idris said.

'You're just jealous.'

'Yeah, right. What you really need is to find a nice girl your own age, start acting like a grown-up and settle down.'

Fuad let out a hoot of derision. 'You make it sound *sooooo* boring.'

'Don't knock it till you've tried it.'

'Niamh is very sophisticated. Gabriella would like her.'

'Leave Gabriella out of this.'

'Just saying.' Coming up behind an ancient VW, Fuad waved an arm in exasperation. 'Can I at least overtake this guy?'

'If you must,' Idris muttered. 'If you must.'

THREE

Ensconced in Paddington Green police station, John Carlyle contemplated the framed photograph sitting on his desk. His daughter Alice, resplendent in a faded Rage Against the Machine T-shirt, was waving the letter confirming his promotion to the rank of commander. It had pride of place at home, taped to the fridge.

A seagull hovered outside his window. From the streets below, the sound of multiple sirens rose to a mild crescendo, then fell away. Carlyle stifled a yawn and shook himself into the here and now.

'Linda!'

After a couple of moments, Linda Sanderson appeared in the office doorway. A slender woman in her late thirties, Sanderson wore the permanently exhausted look of someone who had been juggling work and family commitments for more than a decade. Carlyle hoped he wasn't adding too much to her obvious burden.

'Yes, Commander?'

You don't have to call me that. Carlyle still felt somewhat bemused by his new rank, even more so by others' reaction to it. 'Sorry to be a pain.' He waved a hand at his blank computer screen. 'I've locked myself out of the system again.'

Linda didn't seem surprised. 'I'll get IT to reset your password.'

Carlyle contemplated his reflection in the dark screen. 'What have I got on today?'

'I'll print off your diary. First up is the budget sub-committee. That's due to start in the Warnock Room, downstairs, in fifteen minutes.'

A look of dismay crossed Carlyle's face. 'The Warnock Room? Isn't that the one that smells?'

'I think Facilities had it cleaned.'

'That's not much good if you can't open a bloody window,' Carlyle muttered. You couldn't open any of the windows in Paddington Green – presumably the architects had been worried that too many cops might decide to jump out of them.

'DAC Mara would like a word before you go down there.'

Great. Carlyle now reported to Deputy Assistant Commissioner Michelle Mara. Given that she had almost eighty direct reports, he had assumed – hoped – that the practical extent of her oversight would be severely limited. Sadly, so far at least, that had not proved to be the case. 'What does she want?' he whined, at least managing to avoid adding 'now'.

Linda ignored his scowl. 'I don't know, something to do with an ongoing investigation, I think.'

'That narrows it down.' Carlyle wondered which case might have caught the DAC's eye. One of the problems, he was discovering, was that when you reached this level of seniority, nothing much stood out from the general morass.

'Do you want me to get her on the line?'

'I'd better get dressed, then give her a call.' His uniform, freshly dry-cleaned, hung on the back of the door, still in its polythene bag. Carlyle rubbed at a stain on his Clash T-shirt. 'I don't think this is suitable attire for the budget sub-committee, do you?'

'Not really.' Linda disappeared back into her own office.

Slumped in his seat, Carlyle listened to his brain telling him to get on with it. After almost six months in the job, he was still suffering from imposter syndrome. Not a sniff of a promotion for more than twenty years and then, almost out of nowhere, he was kicked four rungs up the ladder in one go. He was smart enough to realise that this strange turn of events had had very little to do with him. A combination of factors – the patronage of his predecessor, Carole Simpson, internal police politics and the rapid retirement of a group of apparently more qualified officers in the wake of one of the Met's periodic scandals – had left him as the last man standing when it came to the Promotions Board.

Not surprisingly, his good fortune had created a lot of bad feeling among colleagues who had been eyeing the job for themselves. Never one to court popularity, Carlyle wasn't worried about their bitching. What *did* trouble him, however, was the uncomfortable feeling in his gut that the job wasn't for him. The reality – which he was reluctant to acknowledge – was that he was no longer a cop. Rather, he had become an administrator, the kind of man who filled his days with meetings, trying to avoid making decisions. It was something he should have considered before taking the post.

Ten minutes to go till the budget meeting. He'd better find out what Mara wanted, or the matter would hang over him all day. With a profound sigh, he found his phone and pulled up the DAC's number. With his thumb hovering over the call button, he felt the handset start to vibrate in his hand. Without thinking about it, he hit receive.

'Carlyle.'

'Is that *Commander* John Carlyle?' From down the line there came something that sounded very much like a chuckle. 'London's top cop?'

'Yes and no.' Carlyle laughed, pathetically grateful for the sound of a friendly voice.

'Long time no speak.' Despite the relatively early hour, the noisy backdrop suggested Dominic Silver was out and about. Carlyle imagined that he might be waiting for a client to turn up for a meeting at the Wolseley, his favoured breakfast venue.

'You're so important these days,' Dom teased. 'I guess you don't have much time for your friends any more.'

'Hardly. What can I do for you?'

'I'm going to be in your neighbourhood later and was wondering if you might fancy a bit of lunch.'

Carlyle looked up in time to see Linda reappear in front of his desk. Handing him a sheet of A4, she pointed at her watch. Nodding, he scanned the list of the day's appointments as she retreated from the room.

'I'd love to,' he groaned, 'but it looks like I'm already down for a sandwich lunch with the Victims of Crime liaison group.'

'This is important.' Dom's voice turned a couple of degrees colder. 'Maybe you could make your apologies and see them another time.'

'I'm not so sure about that.'

'I'll be at the Lisson at twelve thirty – the gallery on the north side of Bell Street. I'll see you in there. We can have a chat, then go and get something to eat. There's a nice pub at the end of the road that does a decent lunch menu.' Dom rang off.

Carlyle glanced at the clock on the wall. It told him he had just over six minutes to get into his uniform and head downstairs for the budget sub-committee.

'This is where it happened.' Mike Stoner took a moment to re-adjust his tweed cap. The rain had stopped but the sky promised more to come. 'The robbers held them up at the junction.'

Daniel Hunter dropped to his haunches and scanned the tarmac. 'How do you know it was a heist?'

'I don't,' the farmer admitted. 'But thinking about what I saw – and what I heard – I can't see what else went down.'

The questions started backing up in Hunter's brain. Resting his forearms on his thighs, he looked up at his friend. 'Was there an exchange of fire? Or was there only one side doing the shooting?'

'Hard to say. It sounded like different weapons were discharged, but I can't be sure of that. The carjackers took what they wanted and legged it. The whole thing only took five minutes, max. I'm fairly sure that no one shot at them as they left.'

'Casualties?'

'Not able to confirm that. But there was certainly a significant delay before the convoy that was robbed headed off. Perhaps they were cleaning up.'

'Well, the rain's done a good job of washing away any evidence left behind.' Hunter heard his knees crack as he stood up. After living in warmer climes, the crappy English weather did him no favours. 'Why would anyone be driving around here in convoy anyway?'

Stoner pointed at the road sign for Biggin Hill. 'Private flights. All sorts of VIPs come and go from the airport. You see quite a few top-end vehicles on the roads, not the kind of thing the locals drive.'

'Hm.' It was a long time since Hunter had been a cop. But he still felt a familiar frisson of excitement as a line of enquiry appeared before him. 'Could we check today's flight list?'

'The police could,' Stoner said, 'but I didn't think you'd want me calling nine-nine-nine.'

'No. Good point.' Technically speaking, Hunter was a fugitive from British justice. He was going to deal with that soon enough – it was the reason he'd come back to Blighty, after all – but didn't need to put himself in front of a bunch of provincial police in the interim. 'This isn't something a local cop would be allowed to run with anyway, even if he knew what he was looking at.'

'But you would.'

'In my past life, maybe.'

'You were a cop.'

'I was a military policeman.'

'Same thing. What do you see?'

'Not a lot,' Hunter admitted. 'Your take on it seems perfectly plausible but, as things stand, it's just a theory.' The sound of an approaching car caused him to step to the side of the road. A white Nissan hatchback appeared at the junction. The driver, a grey-haired woman, nodded at Stoner as she rolled past.

The farmer gave her a friendly wave. 'Mrs Harrington,' he explained. 'Runs the Dog and Duck. The best pub around here for miles. They do a great Sunday roast. I'll take you there for lunch next weekend.'

'Sounds good.' Hunter knew that wouldn't happen. He had been exploiting his old comrade's hospitality for over a week already. It was time for him to head to London and face the music.

'Are we done?' Stoner started towards his Range Rover, ten yards back along the road.

'Sure.' As he turned towards the car, Hunter caught a glimpse of something metallic in the grass. 'Hold on.' Pulling a tissue from his pocket, he stepped into the ditch.

'Found something?'

'Looks like it.' Bending down, Hunter retrieved the small brass shell casing and held it up for Stoner to inspect.

A look of triumph passed across the farmer's face. 'I was right.'

Hunter wrapped the casing in the tissue and slipped it into his pocket. 'Whatever happened here, someone tried to clear it up.'

'But they missed one.'

Hunter jumped out of the ditch and began marching towards the car. 'What time's the next train to London? I need you to drop me at the station.'

Obeid Idris crossed the waste ground, retreating a sensible distance as the flames took hold of the stolen people-carrier.

'Can I have this?' Fuad Samater flashed the crystal-encrusted phone that was part of their booty. 'I could do with a new phone. It's not even locked.'

'I need it.' Idris grabbed the handset and shoved it into the back pocket of his jeans. 'You haven't deleted those pictures, have you?'

'I should have done. They're, like, perverted, man. Totally sick.' Fuad scrunched up his face in disgust. 'You're not into that kind of thing, are you?'

'No,' Idris frowned, 'definitely not.'

'What do you want them for, then?'

Leverage. 'I'll explain later.'

'You sure you ain't got something to tell me?'

Idris responded by smacking the top of Fuad's head with the flat of his palm.

Fuad danced away in delight. 'No need to be ashamed about it. Everyone has *needs* they got to attend to.'

'C'mon. Let's get going.' Idris started towards the black taxi that would take them home. Stealing the vehicle had been one of his comrade's better ideas – no one would give them a second glance in a London cab. 'Gabriella's waiting for me.'

Fuad's interest in the phone vanished in an instant. 'I'll drive,' he stated. 'I can't have you pottering around at thirty miles an hour. Gabriella might be waiting for you, but *I've* got a date.'

'You mentioned it.' Idris could feel the adrenalin leaching from his body. He was looking forward to a long bath, followed by a restorative nap. When Gabriella finished work they would go for an early dinner at her favourite Italian, just off Ladbroke Grove.

'Come on, bro.'

'Relax. We've got plenty of time. Another five minutes isn't going to hurt your chances of getting laid.'

'You can say that again.'

There was a pop as the windscreen of the people-carrier started to crack and buckle. 'It's important that this is done properly. That car has got to *burn*. No clues.' Standing by the passenger door of the taxi, Idris folded his arms and watched the glass blow out.

'Don't worry about it,' Fuad scoffed. 'The police aren't going to find anything.'

It wasn't the police Idris was worried about. The guys they'd ripped off would be coming after them soon enough. There was no need to hasten the process by being sloppy.

'C'mon, it's time to go.' Fuad unlocked the doors of the taxi. 'When the fire reaches the petrol tank – kaboom.'

'Just keep it nice and slow.' Idris slipped into the back seat. 'Remember, the meter's supposed to be running and taxi drivers are never in a hurry to get anywhere.'

Fuad settled into the driver's seat and flicked on the intercom. 'Where to then, guv?'

It was the worst attempt at a Cockney accent that Idris had ever heard. 'Home,' he commanded. 'And, remember, take it easy.'

'All righty.' Fuad started up the engine and slowly turned onto the road. They had gone less than a hundred yards when the people-carrier exploded with a satisfying roar.

FOUR

'This isn't valid.' The ticket inspector waved Daniel Hunter's ticket in front of his face. 'This is an off-peak super saver,' she snapped. 'You can't use it on this service.' She looked around the carriage, challenging any of the other passengers to contradict her.

'It's what they sold me at the station.' Hunter was conscious of the faces turned in his direction as people tuned into his conversation. If there was going to be an argument, his fellow travellers didn't want to miss out on the entertainment.

The inspector dismissed his feeble explanation with a shake of the head. 'You're on the wrong train, *sir*. That ticket's only valid on the stopping service, the *slow* service.'

Hunter resisted the temptation to remind her that the so-called fast service had barely strayed above twenty miles an hour since he had joined it at the previous stop. The last garbled update from the guard had them almost forty minutes behind schedule and they were currently at a standstill. He gazed out of the window at a couple of depressed-looking horses standing in the corner of a waterlogged field.

'You'll have to pay the full fare or take a penalty notice.' The woman tapped the side of the ticket machine hanging from a strap around her neck, inviting him to choose his punishment.

Stifling a groan, Hunter shoved a hand deep into the pocket of his trousers. 'How much is a ticket?'

'Single or return?'

'Single.'

The woman tapped the screen of her machine with a small biro. 'That'll be fifty-one pounds and seventy pence.' She sounded disappointed that it wasn't more. *'Please.'*

Jesus. Hunter fished out a thin wad of notes from his pocket. After this unexpected raid on his funds, he was going to arrive in London with barely enough to cover the cost of a cup of coffee and a sandwich. Handing over two twenties and a ten, he took some coins out of his jacket and counted out the correct amount.

The inspector printed out a ticket, defaced it with a flourish of her biro and dropped it onto the table, along with Hunter's redundant off-peak super saver. 'Next time, get the right ticket,' she suggested smugly, then scuttled off to the next carriage in the hope of finding another unfortunate to scalp.

A teenage girl on the other side of the carriage gave him an amused smirk. 'They're bastards, aren't they?'

Ignoring her, Hunter picked up the tickets and shoved them into his pocket. As a consolation, the train finally resumed its forward motion.

'Total bastards,' the girl muttered, talking to herself now.

The train slowly began to pick up speed. Hunter closed his eyes, considering his options if things didn't start going to plan when he finally made it to the city. What the hell would he do if they didn't arrest him on the spot?

Sunshine flooded in through the skylight. Bouncing off the white walls, it made the room so bright that you could almost fancy you were in Barcelona or, perhaps, Lisbon, rather than grey old London. Squinting against the glare, Carlyle listened to the rubber soles of his footwear squeak on the wooden flooring. Off to his left, a young woman was standing in front of a series of black-and-white photographs, busily scribbling in a Moleskine notebook. Looking up, she shot him a quizzical glance before drifting into the room next door.

'This guy's really good.' Sitting on a low bench in the middle of the room, Dominic Silver pointed towards the massive photograph dominating the wall in front of him. It was a colour image of a rickshaw parked in a grimy alleyway just off Oxford Street, a bunch of drooping pink carnations tied to its handlebars. 'I've tried a couple of times to get him to exhibit with me.' Silver owned a small gallery in the West End, nothing like the Lisson in terms of size or prestige, but, as far as Carlyle could see, it did well enough.

Carlyle stared at the picture, which went by the title *I ♥ London*. Belatedly, he realised that the rickshaw wasn't empty, as he had first imagined. Someone – presumably the driver – was asleep on the back seat, as evidenced by a pair of dirty feet sticking out from under a blanket. On the ground, by the back wheel, a pair of pigeons pecked at a crust of bread. At the end of the alleyway, you could make out the blur of a red bus. 'That's one way to solve the housing crisis.'

'I used to walk past that guy quite regularly, on the way to the gallery. He's not there now, though.'

'People come and go,' Carlyle mused. The image had been blown up to something like ten feet by twelve, giving it a pixilated, slightly surreal quality. The commander resisted the temptation to ask how much it would cost. 'You could never show this,' he ventured. 'You'd never get it through the front door at Cork Street.'

'He does other things – his prices are going through the roof. Collectors are coming from all over the world to snap his stuff up.'

'Ah, I see.' With Dom it always came down to money in the end.

'I'll get him, one day.'

'You always get your man.'

'Something like that.' Dom placed a hand on Carlyle's shoulder. 'Anyway, thanks for making the time to meet up. I appreciate it.'

'No problem. Apparently, the Victims of Crime liaison group were very understanding about my late no-show.'

Dom seemed tired and drawn. His hair was greyer, and he'd put on a little weight. Not looking so good, Carlyle decided. Then again, I don't suppose I look that great myself. He self-consciously ran a hand across his stomach. Six months behind a desk wasn't exactly doing much to keep him svelte.

'It's been a while.'

Carlyle scratched his chin. 'A year or so?'

'More like nine months – we went to the Emirates not so long after your dad's funeral.'

'Yeah.' Carlyle recalled struggling through a boring nil–nil draw, surrounded by moaning Arsenal fans. At least the corporate hospitality had been good.

'Sorry to hear about Carole Simpson, by the way.' Carlyle's former boss was another who had gone.

'Yeah, that was a real bummer.' Shifting on the bench, Carlyle unbuttoned his overcoat. 'She deserved better.'

'Cancer?'

'Yeah. She lasted barely three months after retiring and half of that was in a hospice.'

'Jesus.'

'I don't think he had much to do with it,' Carlyle replied. 'The day is long, as they say, but life is short.'

For several moments, they sat in silence, contemplating the fickleness of Fate.

'Were you surprised to get her job?' Dom asked finally.

'Surprised would be something of an understatement.'

'You were always going to get there in the end.'

29

They both knew that was bollocks.

Carlyle pushed his lips together.

'Better late than never,' Dom opined. 'What does Helen make of it?'

'My dear wife is even more suspicious about the motives of the powers that be than I am. She thinks they've kicked me upstairs to beef up my pension in the hope that I'll retire sooner rather than later.'

'There are worse fates that can befall a man.'

'I know, but the commander's job is just so fucking *boring*.' Carlyle was conscious that he sounded like a whining teenager, but he didn't care. 'I mean, there was a lot of crap to deal with before, but now it's just *all* crap. I'm not sure I can put up with being stuck in an office.'

'You've just got to fake it,' Dom advised. 'That's life. You fake it till you make it and then you fake it some more.'

'I never was much good at faking it.'

'Well, now's the perfect time to learn.'

'Maybe.' Carlyle hadn't come here to discuss his career angst. 'What did you want to see me about?'

'Not what, who.' Dom glanced over his shoulder, then concentrated his gaze on Carlyle. 'Bernie Gilmore.'

'Now there's a blast from the past.' Over the years, Carlyle had occasionally swapped information with Bernie. He was a journalist who was always prepared to deal. Likewise, Carlyle was perfectly willing to share information when he considered it in their mutual self-interest for Bernie to run a story. 'I haven't seen him for ages. I can't even recall the last time I saw his name in the paper. He could be dead now, for all I know.'

'Sadly, Bernie is still very much alive. He joined an online outfit called the Investigation Unit. It's basically a bunch of old-school hacks who go around digging up stories that the newspapers don't have the resources or the bottle to go after, these days.'

Carlyle looked at his watch. Where was this going? And why couldn't they discuss it over lunch?

'Freed from the tyranny of rolling news deadlines and crazy owners, Bernie has too much time on his hands.' Dom grimaced. 'And now he's coming after us.'

'Us?' Carlyle rose to his feet and started pacing in front of the bench. The girl with the notebook reappeared and got busy making a sketch of a small sculpture in the corner of the room. 'What d'ya mean?'

'The Investigation Unit,' Dom explained, keeping his voice low, 'is funded by Francesca Culverhouse, the wife of a guy who made a fortune in the last financial crash. She was a journalist herself, back in the day.' He mentioned a couple of BBC current-affairs shows, well regarded by the chattering classes perhaps forty years ago. 'Culverhouse's thesis is that investigative journalism has been eviscerated by commercial pressures, twenty-four/seven rolling news and the rise of the internet and social media. It's all celebrity crap and trolling.'

'She's got a point.' Carlyle watched the woman with the notebook sketching away. 'Whether she can do anything about it is another matter entirely.'

'Yeah, well, I think you should be more focused on what she could specifically do to you and me. One of Ms Culverhouse's particular areas of interest is police corruption. The Unit broke the Carstairs story.'

'In that case, I owe them one.' Carlyle tapped the lapel of the commander's uniform beneath his overcoat. 'That helped me get this.' Chief Superintendent Stanley Carstairs had been at the head of the queue for Carole Simpson's job until his finances were leaked to the media. The Met was bounced into an investigation, which outed Carstairs as leader of a group of officers involved in dodgy schemes ranging from providing security at high-end golf courses in Surrey to operating a couple of brothels in Notting Hill. Seventeen colleagues ended up taking very early retirement. Five, including Carstairs himself, were awaiting trial on a range of criminal charges, including embezzlement, living off immoral earnings, money-laundering and tax evasion.

Carlyle ran a hand across his chin. 'Didn't *The Times* break that story?'

'They *ran* the story. Bernie, working for the Unit, was the one who actually dug it up. He was very pissed off when he didn't get all the credit he felt he was due.'

'I bet. It was a good story.'

Dom pointed towards Carlyle's feet. 'Nice shoes, by the way.'

Carlyle looked down at his tatty trainers. 'Had a bit of a wardrobe malfunction this morning. I left my proper shoes at home.'

Dom pointed the toe of an immaculately polished brogue at him. 'Get yourself down to Oliver Sweeney's, my son. You should be able to afford it, these days.'

'Thanks for the tip. To get back to Bernie, though . . .'

Dom's face darkened. 'The fat wanker is trying to repeat the Carstairs scoop. He's spent the best part of the last year compiling the mother of all exposés into corruption and malpractice in the Met. As if people don't know all this shit already. He reckons he's going to turn it into a book. Plus a series on BBC4, or whatever.'

Carlyle waited patiently for his mate to finish his rant.

'As part of all this, good old Bernie's decided we'd make a nice case study.' Dom waggled a finger between them. 'You and me.'

'The cop and the drug dealer.'

'Ex-drug dealer.'

'Yes, quite.' Dom had retired from the drugs game a while ago. At the same time, he wouldn't have been able to reinvent himself as a moderately successful art dealer had it not been for the tsunami of cash that had washed over him during his highly lucrative years in the black economy.

Dom pushed himself to his feet. 'Not good.'

'Not necessarily that bad, though,' Carlyle reasoned. 'I mean, it's not like it's much of a secret. Everybody knows we go back a long way – all the way to Hendon. So what?' It was true enough. Dominic Silver was a legend in the Met. The latest recruit from a family of cops, he had decided that being a plod was a mug's game, packed it in and gone over to the dark side. 'People've dug around in the past. If necessary, I've always presented you as a CI.'

They chuckled in unison. The relationship had always been far more complicated than that of cop and informant. On the other side of the room, the woman looked up from her notebook then went back to her drawing.

'You're much more high-profile now,' Dom said. 'I don't think Bernie would have bothered with any of this if you hadn't been promoted.'

'Still, I can't see how it could be a big deal.'

'Bernie called me two days ago. We talked about nothing for a while.' Dom paused. 'Then he asked me about Tuco Martinez.'

FIVE

The train staggered into London Bridge more than an hour late. Dipping into his meagre funds, Hunter bought a filter coffee and a tube ticket. A combination of the Northern and Bakerloo lines got him to Charing Cross. Five minutes later, he was standing in Charing Cross police station, trying to engage with a disinterested civilian worker on the other side of a bulletproof window. The woman's name badge identified her as Sharon Simpkins. She had a round, featureless face, largely hidden behind an outsized pair of spectacles. Hunter guessed she was somewhere in her mid-twenties. After his run-in with authority on the train, he tried to adopt a suitably deferential tone. 'I'm looking for an inspector called John Carlyle, please.'

Simpkins blinked twice. 'C-A-R . . .' Hunter spelled out the name. Staring at her computer screen, the woman bit her upper lip. 'We don't have any Carlyle,' she declared.

'John Carlyle. He's an inspector, worked here for years.'

The woman shook her head. 'I'm sorry.' She lifted her gaze past Hunter, towards her next customer. 'There is no Carlyle listed.'

Hunter frowned. Could he have retired? Not likely. 'Maybe he's moved to another station.'

Simpkins pushed her spectacles up her nose. 'I can only access details regarding staff in this station. If you want to speak to the duty officer, I can book you an appointment for the day after tomorrow.'

'No, no. It's fine. It's Carlyle I was looking for.' Hunter turned away from the counter and straight into a woman walking past. 'Sorry.'

'Careful.' Sergeant Alison Roche scowled as she continued on her way.

Hunter thought the exhausted-looking redhead was vaguely familiar. 'Excuse me,' he called after her, 'but I was looking for Inspector John Carlyle.'

'You'll find him at Paddington Green,' Roche announced over her shoulder. 'He moved a while back.'

His appetite had vanished. Apart from a couple of business-men at a corner table, the pub was empty. Picking a table as far removed from their fellow diners as possible, Carlyle scanned the menu. 'Deep fried calamari and char-grilled halloumi.'

'They do a nice roast,' Dom ventured.

Carlyle was beginning to understand where his friend's extra padding came from.

'Or we do a range of sandwiches.' A hipster waiter, complete with bushy beard and neck tattoo, appeared at the table with a basket of artisan bread and a small bowl of olive oil. Flipping over Carlyle's menu, he pointed at a range of options.

Scanning the list, Carlyle let out a disapproving cluck. *Eight quid fifty for a bloody sandwich. Four quid for an orange juice.* Dom would be picking up the tab but, even so, it was outrageous. 'Is the orange juice freshly squeezed?'

'Yes, sir.' The waiter looked mildly affronted by the question.

Carlyle ordered a juice and the closest approximation to a straightforward cheese sandwich on offer.

'Thank God we managed to sort that out.' Dom ordered roast beef and Yorkshire pudding, with a large glass of Merlot.

The waiter tapped the order into his terminal and scuttled off.

Carlyle glanced at the clock above the bar. It was already almost one thirty. He tried to recall his schedule for the afternoon. He was sure that there was some meeting or other in the diary for two, even if he couldn't remember what it was. 'I'm going to have to get back soon.'

Dom shot him an irritated look. 'Surely this is more important than the latest paperclip initiative.'

The sudden recall of the contents of his diary for the afternoon prompted Carlyle to groan. 'I think it's the Body Positive Initiative this afternoon.' Dom looked at him blankly. 'Basically, it's a group that was set up to lobby against sacking officers just because they're fat.'

'What a load of old bollocks.'

'It's the modern world we live in.'

'It's still bollocks,' Dom insisted. 'And nowhere near as important as dealing with Bernie.'

'Let's not get carried away. Bernie always talks a good game. In reality, what has he got that could hurt us?'

'"Hope for the best, prepare for the worst." That's our motto,' Dom reminded him. 'That's how you stay in the game – *prepare for the fucking worst*. And Tuco Martinez coming back to fuck us from beyond the grave could be the worst of the worst.'

Stuffing a chunk of bread into his mouth, Carlyle chewed thoughtfully. Dom had hooked up with Tuco towards the end of his drug-dealing days. The French gangster had proved a very poor choice of associate and their disastrous partnership had been a major reason why Dom had decided to get out of the business for good.

For his part, Tuco had responded badly when Dom had sought to terminate their relationship. Caught in the fallout, Carlyle had been forced to deal with Tuco coming after his family. That had meant a three-man hit squad gunning Tuco down in his remote

French farmhouse. Two members of that hit squad now eyed each other warily as the waiter placed their drinks on the table. Dom took a sip of his wine and signalled his approval. The waiter nodded and retreated behind the bar.

'What's Gideon up to, these days?' Carlyle asked softly. Gideon Spanner had been the third member of their team.

'Good question.' Dom weighed his glass in his hand. 'After I had my . . . what you might call my career change, I didn't have the same staff requirements. I was quite happy to keep Gideon on the payroll, but he got bored very quickly. And, fair dos, he didn't want to just take the money for sitting around doing nothing.'

'Gideon always seemed a decent enough guy to me,' Carlyle offered blandly. 'I couldn't really see him sitting behind a desk at the gallery handing out catalogues to rich Americans.'

'Yeah. Like so many guys, after he left the army he just needed a bit of direction. Something to do.' Dom took a mouthful of wine. 'I gave him that – for a while. But he was always restless and, frankly, after I set up the gallery, I didn't think I'd have any interesting work for him.'

'No.' Carlyle didn't need to ask what kind of 'interesting' work Dom was referring to.

'Sometimes I struggled with the rather mundane nature of the art business myself,' Dom mused, 'in the beginning, at least.'

'That was before Lucio Spargo,' Carlyle muttered, recalling another nutter who'd crossed their path. Spargo, although not Tuco-league crazy, was a thoroughly nasty piece of work, a ruthless property developer who'd tried to force Dom out of Cork Street. 'Gideon would have been useful in dealing with him.'

'I had you for that.'

Carlyle didn't want to be reminded of another time he had crossed the line to take a villain off the streets.

'What happened to Spargo?' Dom asked.

Carlyle pushed his lips out. 'Still in jail, as far as I know.'

Dom nodded. 'Best place for him. Hopefully he'll die in there.'

'Amen to that.'

'Anyway, Gideon. I gave him a severance payment – nothing massive but a decent amount. Enough to live on for a while – he was always a frugal type of guy. We went our separate ways. The last time I spoke to him, he was talking about going off travelling. That was a few years ago now. I literally haven't heard from him since.'

'You think he's back in town?'

'It's possible. I've put a few feelers out, but I haven't heard anything yet.'

'Gideon's the only other person who knew about Tuco.' Carlyle sought to keep the edge from his voice. The more he considered it, the more nervous he felt. Whichever way you cut it, *Police Commander Executed Criminal on Foreign Soil* was one hell of a story.

'Gideon Spanner's the most tight-lipped man you could ever meet. And utterly dependable. We worked together for a long time. I can't see him being Bernie's source.'

'Someone must've put Tuco's name out there.' Carlyle made a face as he downed his orange juice. Freshly squeezed, my arse. 'What else has Bernie got?'

'Dunno,' Dom admitted. 'When he dropped Tuco's name into the conversation, I just played it cool. If I'd started pumping him for information, it would have been too suspicious. He would have known he was on to something.'

'Makes sense.' Carlyle watched their food arrive.

'Would you like another juice?' the waiter asked, placing Carlyle's sandwich in front of him.

Carlyle shook his head. 'I'm good.'

'Some water?'

'No, thanks.'

Retrieving the empty glass, the waiter stalked off.

Dom hacked at a slice of beef, stuck it into his mouth and chewed carefully.

Carlyle made no effort to touch his sandwich. 'What exactly did Bernie say?'

'He came on and asked me about you and your promotion. Was I surprised? Yada, yada, yada. I pointed out I wasn't that close to what went on inside the Met but that you were widely recognised as a very good cop and that a promotion was long overdue.'

'You're too kind.' Uncomfortable with any sort of praise, Carlyle felt himself redden slightly.

'Bernie asked about our relationship. I said I know lots of cops, which is true enough.' Dom cut another slice of beef and held it in front of his mouth. 'He *implied* that he knew about my CV but didn't come straight out and ask me about dealing drugs. And then he asked about Tuco.' Putting the food into his mouth, he chewed and swallowed. Then he continued, 'It was more than a fishing expedition – you don't pluck the name out of thin air, right? – but I got the impression that Bernie's still at quite an early stage of his research. He just wanted to see if I'd cough up something to help him drag the story over the line.'

'I'll talk to Bernie, see what he has. If he has enough to trade with, I'll trade. Bernie's completely pragmatic.' Carlyle hoped that was still the case. 'The bottom line is he'll kill the Tuco story – no pun intended – in exchange for a better one.'

'Christ, what would be a better story than Tuco?'

Bloody good question. 'I'll come up with something,' Carlyle promised.

'If money would help,' Dom waved his fork across the table, 'I can always make a sizeable donation to the Bernie Gilmore retirement fund.'

39

'I don't think that would work. Knowing Bernie, he'd just go off and write a story about you trying to bribe him.'

'Bloody journalists.' Dom began attacking his Yorkshire pudding. 'I hate people who think they've got principles.'

'He'll trade,' Carlyle insisted. 'Plus, he'll understand the importance of the longer-term relationship. Now I've moved up in the world, I'll be a much more useful contact for him.'

Finishing his food, Dom placed his knife and fork on the plate and reached for his wine. 'In that case, I'll leave it with you. Plan A is to trade.'

'Agreed.' Carlyle hoped his faith in Bernie would prove justified.

'Plan B is to offer the man some fuck-off money.'

'If things get that far, we're in trouble.'

'In that case,' from behind his glass, Dom arched an eyebrow, 'there's always Plan C.'

Carlyle felt his stomach take a further lurch downwards. 'I don't know about that.' He lowered his voice to barely a whisper. 'We can't—'

'If it comes to it, Plan C's not a problem.' Dom signalled to the waiter for another glass of wine. As he turned back to Carlyle, his face hardened. 'We haven't come all this way to be laid low by some fat fucking journalist. If Bernie won't play the game, we'll show him the door – same as with Tuco.'

SIX

Hopelessly late, he hurried past his PA's desk. Linda Sanderson waved her phone at him in a threatening manner. 'I've got Deputy Assistant Commissioner Mara on the phone for you,' she trilled.

Failing to come up with a decent excuse for not taking the call, Carlyle admitted defeat. 'I suppose you'd better put her through.'

Linda gestured towards the ceiling with the receiver. 'And you were due upstairs twenty minutes ago.'

Reaching the relative sanctuary of his office, Carlyle slumped into his chair, taking a deep breath and slowly counting to three before reaching for the phone blinking on his desk.

'Michelle.'

'John, I've been trying to get hold of you all day.' The deputy assistant commissioner made no attempt to hide her profound irritation.

'Sorry,' he muttered. 'I've been stuck in meetings.' How, in such a male-dominated environment, he had managed to bounce from one female boss to another was a mystery. Carlyle didn't have a problem with women managers, per se. He had a problem with authority, full stop.

Issuing a dismissive grunt, Mara didn't probe any further. 'What's your diary looking like tomorrow afternoon?'

'Well . . .' He took a wild guess. 'Pretty terrible, I'm afraid.

I'm back to back with, erm, different things.' He was struck by a sudden pang of nostalgia for his previous life as a humble plod. What he wouldn't do right now to be landed with a nice murder or a humble robbery.

'I need you to make some space for a Project Scimitar meeting. It's with the head of security at the ICBRS, so a priority determined by the commissioner himself.'

Project Scimitar? ICBRS? Carlyle didn't have a clue what his boss was talking about.

'I was supposed to host it but now I've got to go over to the Palace about this Royal Protection Unit thing.' At least Carlyle understood *that* reference. Oblivious to the cuts being imposed on the Met from every angle, the lesser royals were once again moaning about proposed reductions in their bodyguard teams. He remembered reading something about it in the latest Federation newsletter. The police union had been scathing about the way in which scarce resources were deployed. It was a view Carlyle had considerable sympathy with. On the other hand, he knew that the rich and powerful would get what they wanted in the end – that was just a basic law of nature – so why fight for a lost cause?

'That must be quite tricky.' He tried to sound sympathetic. 'I know that the RPU is a pretty delicate issue.' If Mara handled it badly, her MBE might never materialise. That was another thing about the rich and powerful: they had long memories.

'It's just one of those things.' Mara had no interest in the half-hearted sympathy of an underling. 'I'm perfectly happy to do it but I hate it when things like that get dropped into my diary at the last minute. Even I can't be in two places at once.'

'No, I suppose not.' Carlyle imagined there was nothing the DAC would like more than to be able to defeat the basic laws of time and space. A classic fast-tracked high flyer – Cheltenham Ladies' College, King's, inspector at twenty-seven, DAC by the time she had just turned forty – Mara had none of the street-level experience needed to be a good cop, and all of the inbred self-assurance required not to let that bother her in the slightest. Carlyle had no idea what she made of his own promotion, but he doubted very much that she was a fan. Apart from anything else, the two of them simply had no points of common reference.

'I'll get my office to send over the details,' Mara continued. 'Make sure you give my apologies to all concerned.'

Within seconds of the call ending, Linda was standing in front of his desk. Carlyle didn't know whether to be impressed by her efficiency or appalled at her snooping. He explained Mara's latest instructions.

'I'm going to have to reschedule *more* meetings.' The PA groaned. 'That's going to cause a lot of problems.'

Carlyle tried to look contrite. 'The DAC was very firm.'

'Maybe we need to send you on a time-management course.'

'Don't you dare.' Carlyle shot her a hard stare. 'Anyway, no time-management course can stop other people dropping things on you at the last minute.'

'Well, you still need to do something,' Linda chided. 'Your diary is a complete shambles. Whatever did you do when you were at Charing Cross?'

'I didn't have a diary,' Carlyle told her, 'and I didn't have a secretary.' He was about to add, 'Back then, I was a cop,' but managed to bite his tongue, asking instead, 'What's Project Scimitar? I need some information on that, please. Also, some background on the head of security at the ICBRS – whatever that is – would be helpful.

'What about the meeting you're supposed to be in now?'

'Better reschedule that as well.' Carlyle jabbed at the *on* button of his PC. 'Did IT fix this?'

'They unlocked it, yes.'

'Good.'

43

'You need to reset your password to something you can remember.'

'Yes, yes.'

'And tell me what it is this time, so we don't have the same problem again.' She turned towards the door. 'Oh, and there's a man downstairs to see you.'

'No visitors.' Carlyle needed some quiet time to ponder the Tuco Martinez situation. Bernie Gilmore would need to be approached with considerable caution. If the commander got his opening gambit wrong, things with the journalist could quickly spin out of control.

'He says it's important.'

'Take a message.'

'He says he knows you,' Linda persisted.

Fucking hell, how many times? 'I'm busy.' The computer was prompting him to come up with a new password. His fingers hovering over the keyboard, Carlyle tried to think of something he might reasonably expect to remember for more than a day.

'A Mr Hunter.'

It took his brain a second to process the name. Then it hit him like a punch between the shoulder blades. Carlyle looked enquiringly at Linda, who was hovering in the doorway.

'Mr Hunter,' she repeated. 'Daniel Hunter.'

'Sorry just to turn up unannounced.' Sitting in front of the commander's desk, Daniel Hunter cradled a mug bearing the legend *MAKING LONDON A SAFER PLACE.* Radiating health and energy, he made Carlyle feel positively ill. Dressed in jeans and a woollen shirt, tanned and relaxed, he looked more like a catalogue model than a fugitive.

'It's certainly turning into a memorable day.' First Tuco Martinez, and now Danny Hunter. Who else'll be making a return from the dead before teatime? Carlyle wondered.

44

'You must be surprised to see me.'

'Just a little bit.' Carlyle glanced at his computer screen. Miraculously, he had managed to reset his password without locking himself out again. Peering under his glasses, he carefully picked out the correct letters on his keyboard with two fingers.

Helen&Alice

He hit return and watched the screen come to life.

'I didn't know how to contact you. Even this morning, when I turned up at Charing Cross, they claimed not to know you.'

'How quickly they forget,' Carlyle sighed. 'I moved here earlier this year.'

'Your secretary told me about the promotion. Congratulations.'

'A last chance to beef up my pension before they finally show me the door.' Carlyle clicked onto the National Police Archives, only to be confronted by a request for another username and password. Bollocks. Unable to access the database without Linda's assistance, he turned his attention back to Hunter. 'How're you doing?'

'I'm good, all things considered.'

'Glad to hear it.' It was true. Carlyle had worked with Hunter for a short time – only a few days – but he respected the man and had a lot of sympathy for the situation he had ended up in.

'That's why I'm back. It's been only recently that I felt I could cope with all the hoopla.'

'I can understand that. How long's it been?'

Hunter pushed out his bottom lip. 'I did my five years in the Legion.'

Five years ago, Jesus. It felt like two, max. 'And they took you in, no questions asked?' Carlyle was genuinely curious.

'More or less. When I signed up, there were no red flags and, given my CV, well, I was whisked straight through. After I left the UK, I went straight to a recruitment centre near Paris. Arrived at eleven o'clock at night and by three in the morning all the paperwork was done.'

'Impressive.'

'The French can get their finger out when they want to. I was in before there was any chance of an Interpol warrant out for my arrest. After that, I don't suppose they checked again.'

'Interesting approach.'

'Maybe they looked the other way, maybe they didn't. Once I was in, I was in. I don't feel the need to apologise for what happened. Apart from anything else, there are plenty of guys there who've done far worse than I ever did.'

'I'm sure.'

'Bottom line, I've a lot of respect for the Legion. As long as you can do the job, they can give you a second chance.' Hunter scratched his chin. 'It saved me, really.'

'When did you leave?'

'My contract ended a fortnight ago. I walked out with my new French passport.' Hunter reached into his pocket. 'Which I will happily surrender to you.'

'No need for that just yet.' A French citizen. Carlyle recoiled at the prospect of the additional paperwork that arresting a foreigner would entail. 'When did you get back?'

'I arrived in England ten days ago. I spent a bit of time with an ex-comrade who runs a farm in Kent, just to get reacclimatised, so to speak, before coming to London to see you.'

'You want to hand yourself in?' Carlyle struggled to keep the incredulity from his voice. Hunter had endured his own personal Year Zero and, somehow, managed to rebuild his life. Why was he going to throw it all away now?

'There's no statute of limitations on murder.' Hunter slurped the last of his coffee. 'Not in this country, at least. I always knew that if I wanted to come back – and I did want to come back – I'd have to surrender myself to the authorities. To you.'

'You could have just stayed away,' Carlyle suggested. 'I think that would have been my preferred option.'

'You can't run away from things for ever. I knew that I'd have to come back and face the music if I was going to have any chance of getting on with my life.' Hunter stared into his empty mug. '*Really* get on with it.'

'That makes sense, I suppose.'

'I think I've done a reasonable job of, you know, dealing with what happened.'

Carlyle had to agree. Hunter didn't seem like a man haunted by his past at all.

'It's like anything, I suppose, time dulls the pain. You begin to forget.'

'I suppose so.' Despite the man's calm demeanour, Carlyle assumed that the horrors residing in Hunter's brain must still give him regular sleepless nights.

'I mean, you never let it go completely. You wouldn't want to. But it doesn't stop you functioning. Or, at least, it hasn't stopped me functioning.'

'From what I recall, you functioned pretty well. Plus, I don't imagine you get into the French Foreign Legion if you're not up to scratch.'

'In the Legion, I performed satisfactorily. I wasn't that great with the language, but English gets you quite a bit further than the French would like to admit. Anyway, when it came down to it, I could have signed on for another couple of years, probably longer. But I'm not getting any younger. Soon I wouldn't be able to hack it. The guys they get now, they're *machines*. Total beasts. The writing was on the wall.' Hunter tapped at his temple with an index finger. 'I knew up here that the crunch would come when I retired from the Legion. And the longer I left it, the harder it would be. I want to have my reckoning now.' He was talking to Carlyle, but his eyes were focused on some invisible spot on the wall. 'Even if you put me away for, say, ten years, I'll still be a reasonably young man when I get out. Fit and healthy.'

47

Carlyle did not disagree.

'And then there's the question of Andrew Carson's family.'

'Given what happened, you did them a big favour, taking out that bastard.' Andrew Carson, a soldier-turned-criminal, had killed Hunter's wife and kids during a joint Royal Military Police/Metropolitan Police Service investigation. While Carlyle had been left floundering, Hunter had exacted swift and brutal revenge, killing Carson, then taking a ferry across the Channel and joining the Legion.

'They deserve justice, too.'

'I don't know about that.' Carlyle drummed his fingers on the desk as it all came back to him. 'From what I recall, Carson's wife gave him up. The man was an animal. He got what he deserved. The only shame – and it was a real shame – was that someone didn't do it earlier.'

'I've made my decision.'

Carlyle didn't have the time or the inclination for an extended debate on the ethics of the situation. 'What do you want me to do?'

'Well, I was expecting you to arrest me, for a start.'

'It's not necessarily that simple.'

'It's not?' Hunter shot him a quizzical look.

'Does anyone know you're here?'

'Other than Border Security? Only Mike Stoner. He's the guy I mentioned, the farmer I've been staying with the last few days.'

'Okay. Well, I'd leave him out of it for a start. I'm sure he doesn't want to find himself dragged into an old murder case.'

'No.' Hunter took out his passport, along with a balled-up tissue. Reaching forward, he carefully placed both items on the table. 'There's this other thing, though.'

Carlyle looked at the small brass cylinder in dismay.

'A spent 9mm casing,' Hunter explained. 'I found it by the side of the road near Biggin Hill airport.' He quickly ran through the story of the apparent heist in Kent.

Fucking hell, what's this got to do with anything? Carlyle placed the casing, still in its tissue wrapping, in the top drawer of his desk. 'I'll add it to my to-do list. Let's try and get you sorted out first.'

'Sounds like a plan,' Hunter agreed.

'Let me find out if anyone's still working on the Carson investigation and then we can work out the best way to deal with this little problem. In the meantime, you can have a last night of freedom.' It was a strange offer, but Carlyle knew that, having decided to return, Hunter would not disappear a second time. 'Come back here tomorrow.'

Hunter remained in his seat. 'I would, but I don't have anywhere else to stay. And I don't have any cash.'

Carlyle frowned. 'Don't you get a pension from the Legion?'

'To be honest, I didn't expect to be needing much cash.' Hunter pointed at the window and the city beyond. 'If you send me back out there, I'd have to sleep in a doorway somewhere.'

Irritated, Carlyle tried to come up with an alternative plan. The truth was, it would have been better for everyone if the guy had just stayed in France. Reopening the Carson case would generate a ton of paperwork. And then there was this alleged shootout thing in Kent. Someone would need to investigate that as well. 'Wouldn't it be better if you gave yourself up to the army?' he asked hopefully.

Hunter shook his head. 'I want to deal with someone I know, at least in the first instance, someone who knows what happened. I tried to get hold of my old CO, Trevor Naylor, but he's retired to Cyprus.'

'Good for him.'

'That leaves you.'

'Once you go into the system,' the commander was trying to play the bureaucracy card, 'you won't be getting out for a while. Don't you have anyone you need to see tonight?'

'I just want to get on with it.'

'All right.' Carlyle reluctantly accepted that it was time for him to stop trying to wriggle off the hook. 'What about a lawyer?'

'No need.'

What about a shrink? Carlyle didn't go there. Instead he asked: 'Do I need to read you your rights?'

'No. Taken as read.'

'Fine. Let me make a few calls, see how we can sort this out. Why don't you wait in Linda's office? She can get you some more coffee and maybe something to eat.'

'I appreciate it.' Getting to his feet, Hunter extended a hand across the desk.

Lifting himself out of his chair, Carlyle shook the man's hand. 'It's good to see you, despite the circumstances.'

'You too.'

'You didn't need to come back, you know.'

'In the end, you just have to stop moving forward.' Hunter's shoulders slumped and suddenly he appeared very weary. 'You run out of gas.'

SEVEN

Andrew Carson had departed this life while playing a computer game in the living room of a holiday home called Monkey Beach Cottage. After executing Daniel Hunter's family, he had fled to Mersea Island to lie low. His wife, however, had refused to go along with the plan: determined to protect her children and herself from the consequences of her husband's actions, Becky Carson had decided to bring her spouse's criminal career to a suitably brutal end. A phone call to Daniel Hunter effectively sealed Carson's death warrant. The military policeman duly put two bullets into Carson's face, caught a ferry at Felixstowe and sailed across the North Sea to Zeebrugge. By the time the body was found, Hunter had disappeared. From the outset, it was clear that the investigation into Carson's death was going nowhere. And that, as far as one Inspector J. Carlyle had been concerned, was *case closed*.

Until now.

Sitting in his office, Carlyle considered Hunter's unwelcome reappearance. How much of this was really his problem? Over the years, he had become better at giving things time to sort themselves out. As a younger man, he had invariably felt impelled, when confronted with an issue, to jump straight in and try to solve it immediately. Often, failure and frustration were the result. With experience, he had learned to pace himself. Just as important, he had become adept at the art of delegation.

Who could he delegate Daniel Hunter to?

Trying to empty his mind, Carlyle contemplated the crack that ran across the entire length of the ceiling. Surely he could get someone to fix it. Come to think of it, the whole place could do with a bit of redecoration.

After a while, wondering about the chances of having the beige walls painted over, maybe with a nice off-white, his subconscious threw out a name.

'Sarah Ward, come on down.'

Technically speaking, the Andrew Carson shooting had never been Carlyle's case. Mersea Island was more than sixty miles to the north and the local cops had caught the murder. An inspector from West End Central called Sarah Ward was given responsibility for handling the London end of things. Slowly, Carlyle pieced together his memories of her. 'Young', 'blonde' and 'brittle' were the words that came to mind. He remembered that their working relationship had been strained. To his mind, Ward had been a shameless careerist, more interested in networking at Women in Policing events than in solving actual crimes. A woman in a hurry, she had made no attempt to disguise her dislike of a mid-level bumbler like Carlyle.

The prospect of picking up the phone after all this time hardly filled him with enthusiasm. On the other hand, if Ward could take Hunter off his hands, he could get back to worrying about Tuco Martinez and Bernie Gilmour, not to mention his seemingly endless backlog of meetings. He called West End Central. After some toing and froing, it was established that Ward was still there, still an inspector. 'Remember,' Carlyle muttered to himself, as he waited patiently to be connected, 'you're the boss.'

Having worked himself up to having the conversation, he was rather deflated when he was finally put through to Ward's voicemail. Helpfully, however, the inspector had included a mobile number in her recorded message. Repeating the number to himself, Carlyle scribbled it down on a Post-it. Hanging up, he immediately dialled the new number, being rather nonplussed when the woman herself picked up after barely the second ring.

'I heard you got kicked upstairs.' Ward made the news of his promotion sound as credible as Elvis being found alive or the Loch Ness monster finally surfacing. She didn't offer any congratulations.

'Yes.'

'Well, I suppose you've hung around long enough. In my experience, the Met always goes for the easy option.'

'That's one way of looking at it.' Irritated by her refusal even to pretend to suck up to him, Carlyle got straight down to business. 'Daniel Hunter.'

Ward was silent. Children were squealing in the background.

'The Andrew Carson shooting,' he added, trying to prompt her memory.

'Yes, yes,' Ward snapped. 'Daniel Hunter. The Military Police guy who lost the plot. I remember. What about him?'

'I have him in custody, here at Paddington Green.' Through the open door, he could see Hunter sitting in the outer office reading one of Linda's magazines. Not quite in custody in the traditional sense, he reflected, but he's here.

Ward greeted the news with silence. Then she asked, 'You've arrested him?'

'Seeing as it was – is – your case, I presumed you might like the honour.'

'I've not really got time for this.'

'But—'

'You'd be better off talking to someone in the Essex Police. I think the investigation was run by someone out of Colchester.' The childish squeals were getting louder, quickly mutating into

53

screams. 'Look, I've got to run. It's all very interesting, about Hunter and so on, but I'm just about to go on maternity leave again so we'll have to catch up some other time. Good luck with Hunter, Commander. And good luck with the new job.'

With that she hung up.

Carlyle looked at the phone in disbelief. Between the cops who were sacked, the cops who couldn't give a fuck, the cops who were off sick, and the cops who were on maternity or paternity leave, he wondered if he was just about the only damn policeman left in London who actually worked full-time.

'Colchester,' he grumbled. 'Maybe the buggers up there are interested in closing a murder case.' First, however, he needed to do something about Hunter. After searching through various pockets, he found his phone and pulled up a number. Hitting call, he listened to the phone ring for what seemed like an eternity before being picked up.

'To what do I owe this honour?'

'Where are you?' Carlyle was never one for trying to pretend there was a social aspect to a business call.

'I'm at home.' A touch of wariness immediately crept into Sergeant Alison Roche's voice.

'Is Shaggy there?'

'*Alex* should be home in an hour or so.' Roche had given up trying to get Carlyle to stop calling her partner 'Shaggy', based on his alleged similarities to the *Scooby Doo* character. On the plus side, not many people under the age of fifty got the alleged gag.

'Good. When Sha– I mean, when *Alex* gets home, could you come and meet me at Charing Cross?'

All he got by way of reply was a long sigh.

'It's about a development in one of our old cases. Daniel Hunter.'

She was silent, clearly trying to place the name.

'The military cop.'

'Oh, God, yes. I remember. The poor guy.'

Carlyle lowered his voice. 'He's come back. He turned up at my office.'

'He has?' Roche mentioned the man asking for Carlyle at Charing Cross.

'That was him.'

'I didn't give him a second glance,' Roche admitted blithely. 'I imagined he'd done a runner for good.'

'Didn't we all? Anyway, I spoke to Sarah Ward about it—'

'That useless cow,' Roche scoffed. 'What did she have to say for herself?'

'Not a lot. She's going off on maternity leave and doesn't want to know basically.'

'That sounds like Ward.'

'Yes.' The prospect of Roche deciding to drop sprog number two suddenly crossed his mind, but he knew better than to raise the question.

'Where's Hunter now?' she asked.

'He's still here, in Paddington Green, but I want to park him in Charing Cross for a while, if I can.'

'Why?'

'It's a long story. I'll explain when I see you.'

Roche hesitated. 'I had plans.'

'I'll owe you one.'

'You'll owe me *another* one.'

'Fair enough. I trust you're keeping count.'

'I sure am. You're not the only one who deserves a promotion, you know.'

Carlyle readily agreed.

'Gimme a couple of hours. I'll call you when I'm on my way in.'

'Great. Oh, and Alison?'

'Yes?'

'In the meantime, will you give the station a shout and see if you can get Hunter a cell for the night?'

'Is this all we've got?' The smell of paint was beginning to give Carlyle a headache. Nudging a plastic bucket out of the way with the toe of his shoe, he stepped inside the cell.

'They should've finished redecorating last week,' Alison Roche explained. 'There've been a few delays.'

'Now there's a surprise.' The commander contemplated the walls, deciding the light grey hue was exactly what he wanted for his own office. Peering at the label on a five-litre tin of paint sitting on the floor, he made a mental note of the name – Cool Grey Silk. 'Don't you have anything else?'

Standing in the doorway, Roche shrugged. 'I'm afraid not. Three of the cells have been turned into meeting rooms, so we've only got five to start with and the others are all occupied.'

Carlyle looked at Hunter, who was hovering in the corridor.

'It's fine. I can sleep anywhere.' Hunter pointed towards the small window, high up on the far wall, which had been opened to try to dissipate the smell. 'And at least there's some fresh air.'

'Better than Wormwood Scrubs,' Roche told him.

'It'll do for tonight,' Carlyle concluded. 'Let's see where we are tomorrow.'

Leaving Hunter to settle in to his new digs, Carlyle and Roche repaired to the Trafalgar Tavern, a small bar located down a grimy alley, close to the Theatre Royal. Stuck somewhere in the late 1970s, the Trafalgar had never been too high on the commander's list of favourite hostelries but at least it wasn't too much of a tourist trap. Pushing his way through the doors, Carlyle spied an empty table near the unlit fireplace. 'You grab a seat,' he told Roche, 'and I'll get the drinks in.'

Roche split left to secure their space. 'I'll have a Jameson's,' she instructed over her shoulder. 'In fact, make it a double.'

The commander raised an eyebrow. 'Since when did you start on the hard stuff?'

'Since I had to start surviving on four hours' sleep a night.' Falling into a chair, Roche dropped her bag onto the filthy carpet. Instantly thinking better of it, she lifted it onto the table. Fishing a packet of wet wipes from her pocket, she began wiping down the surface. 'David's never managed to sleep through the night.'

From behind the bar, the landlady, Janice, eyed the sergeant coolly. Carlyle held up two fingers. 'Two Jamesons, please. Make them doubles.'

'Ice?' Janice's glare was a welcome of sorts. They knew each other well enough – Janice's old man had been no stranger to Charing Cross nick in the days before he had run off with a girl doing some shifts behind the bar – but Roche's act of aggression with the wet wipes had put paid to the possibility of any small-talk.

The commander looked at Roche, who shook her head. 'Just straight,' he confirmed. 'No ice.'

'It's just relentless,' Roche complained, once the first mouthful of whiskey had warmed her throat. 'Alice wasn't that bad when it came to sleeping through the night, was she?'

'You get through it.' The truth was, more than a decade and a half on, Carlyle couldn't really remember. That part of being a parent was a hazy, faintly unreal memory.

'Nothing's worked.' Roche lowered her voice. 'I have to admit, I even tried dipping the teat of his bottle in a little whiskey once or twice. He wasn't having it, but I developed quite a taste for the stuff.' She glanced over at the bar. 'Something to eat would be good, as well. Maybe some vegetable crisps.'

'Might be a bit exotic for this place,' Carlyle ventured, after checking that Janice was out of earshot, 'but I'll see what they've got.'

Janice watched his speedy return to the bar with suspicion bordering on hostility. As expected, the crisps options were limited: ready salted or cheese and onion. After plumping for the former, Carlyle made the mistake of trying a little small-talk. 'Any word on Pete?'

'That bastard.' A torrent of abuse spewed from Janice's mouth as she laid into her ex-husband. From what Carlyle could make out between the curses, he had last been heard of in Thailand. 'The good news,' Janice cackled maliciously as she tossed a couple of packets of ready salted on to the bar, 'is that the stupid bimbo dumped him.'

'What goes around comes around,' Carlyle mused.

'I tell you what, though, he'd better not come crawling back here if he knows what's good for him.'

'No, I suppose that would be somewhat unwise.' Carlyle noticed that the sell-by dates on the crisps had passed a couple of months earlier but decided to let it slide. Janice was stressed enough already and, anyway, how could some fried potato chips in a vacuum-sealed bag possibly go off? Retreating to the table, he handed a packet to Roche.

'Ta.' The sergeant ripped it open and began shovelling crisps into her mouth with impressive efficiency.

Daintily sipping his drink, Carlyle looked on in amusement.

'Well,' she offered, through a mouthful of crumbs, 'I didn't get the chance to have any tea, did I?'

'No, sorry. Thanks for coming back in. And thanks to Shaggy for stepping into the breach.'

Roche gave him a gentle punch on the arm. 'You've got to stop calling him that.'

'Yes, sorry.'

'And stop saying "sorry".'

'Sorr– er, okay.'

Finishing her crisps, Roche eyed the second packet sitting on the table. 'Are you going to eat those?'

It sounded more like a threat than a question. Carlyle pushed the bag towards her. 'You go ahead.'

'Thanks.'

As Roche started on her second course, he asked, 'How're things going?'

'Work or home?' Tiring of the snacks, Roche wiped a crumb from the corner of her mouth and reached for her glass.

'Both.'

'Things at home are fine. Alex and I are a good team. We're making it up as we go along, but that's what all first-time parents do, isn't it? He's a good dad, and David seems a happy little soul, even if he doesn't sleep much.'

'And work?'

'It's good to be back in Charing Cross. I think if I'd remained stuck in Limehouse I might very well have packed it in by now.'

'I'm glad I was able to sort that out.' Carlyle was pleased that Roche had raised the matter of her unhappy stint working at the Limehouse station. That he had been able to manoeuvre her return to Charing Cross meant that he should have some credit in the bank.

'If anything, things have been a bit on the boring side,' Roche admitted. 'Without you around, getting us into trouble all the time, it's not as much fun as I remember it.' Lifting the glass to her mouth, she downed the remainder of her drink in a single smooth gulp. 'But, then again, there was only ever one Inspector Carlyle, thank God.'

Not sure if that was a compliment or a criticism, he stared at his drink.

'What about you?' Roche asked.

'What about me?'

'How's the big job going? Is it fun?'

'It's a lot of meetings.'

'I wouldn't have imagined that's your thing.'

'It's not,' Carlyle acknowledged. Suddenly feeling rather warm, he unbuttoned his jacket.

Roche looked at his threadbare T-shirt and made a face. 'Not in uniform?'

'Too conspicuous. I tend to leave it at work.'

'Sounds like you're struggling to come to terms with the new realities.' Roche's face was starting to show the first signs of the alcohol. 'The pressures of command.'

'It's definitely a change.' Not wishing to dwell on his circumstances, he moved the conversation along. 'Who're you working with at the moment?'

'Thomson.'

Carlyle stuck out his lower lip, signalling that the name did not resonate.

'Inspector Nayla Thomson. Arrived at Charing Cross a couple of months ago. She's okay. A bit dull maybe. But, then again, not much interesting has come up, so far.' Roche contemplated her empty glass. 'Which is a good thing, really, what with my schedule. I have to try to fit in with David's routine.'

'Yes.' Carlyle looked at his own glass, which still had half an inch of whiskey in it. 'Want another drink?'

'Maybe just one more. Then I should be getting home. Get ready for the night shift.' She rolled her eyes. 'Alex isn't very good at getting out of bed when David starts crying.'

'No.' Carlyle didn't remember being much good at that himself. He got to his feet. 'Won't be a sec.'

Avoiding engaging Janice in any further conversation, he ordered a double and a single. Back at the table, he handed Roche her double and dumped his single whiskey into the remains of his first drink.

'What about Daniel Hunter?' Roche asked. 'Is he nuts or what?'

Carlyle considered his glass. 'That's one way to look at it.'

'I mean, why come back?'

It was a question that the commander had been kicking around in his head since Hunter had first appeared in his office. 'I don't know. It's hard for us to put ourselves in his position. Think of all the things he's gone through. You'd expect his brain to be working in unusual ways.'

'That's one way of looking at it.' Roche assaulted her second whiskey, leaving the thinnest coating possible in the bottom of the glass.

'I suppose, if you were a shrink, you'd say he needs closure.'

'And what about you?' Roche asked.

'Me?' Carlyle arched an eyebrow. 'Whaddaya mean?'

'Why are you treating Hunter with kid gloves? If it was me, I would have whisked him straight down to the cells in Paddington Green, processed him straight away. None of this Charing Cross B-and-B business. We're not running an accommodation service.'

'No.' Carlyle imagined Hunter sitting in his cell amid the paint pots. It was hardly top-quality lodgings. Belatedly, he wondered whether he might have called in a favour from the concierge of the Garden Hotel – one of his local contacts – and wangled a complimentary room for his unexpected guest.

'You should have just dropped him into the system and let someone else sort it out.' Roche looked at Carlyle like he was being a bit of a berk. 'You're going out on a limb, here. Couldn't you come a bit of a cropper?'

'I dunno. Maybe. I just think I owe him more than to throw him to the wolves.' Carlyle checked his phone for a message from the Colchester station. He had called Essex about the Carson investigation before bringing Hunter to Charing Cross, but no one seemed in any hurry to get back to him.

'You don't owe him anything,' Roche persisted.

'I know that,' Carlyle replied, slightly irked by her attitude. 'But we were comrades in arms, if only for a short while.'

'You're not responsible for what happened to his family.' Her voice was louder than he would have liked, and he was conscious of Janice and some of the others at the bar beginning to tune in to their conversation. 'It wasn't your fault. You shouldn't feel guilty.'

'I don't feel guilty.'

'It wasn't your fault,' Roche repeated.

Time to be going. Carlyle downed the remainder of his drink. 'Let me make a couple of calls, see how the land lies. Then we can work out what to do with our guest in the morning.'

'All right.' Taking her cue from Carlyle, Roche got up. 'I'm on an early shift, so I'll babysit your man, first thing.'

'Thanks.'

'No problem.' Slinging her bag over her shoulder, she moved rather unsteadily towards the door. 'Hopefully, with a couple of drinks inside me, I can finally get a decent night's sleep.'

EIGHT

A look of deep suspicion crossed Helen's face as he appeared in the doorway. 'I was wondering when you'd turn up.' His wife kept one eye on the television while giving him the once-over. 'Have you been drinking?'

Carlyle dropped onto the sofa. 'I had a quick one with Alison Roche.'

'How's she getting on? How's David?'

'The kid's doing well but she's finding it a bit of a struggle, I think. Not surprising, really, having to juggle home and work.' He knew better than to mention that he had dragged Roche back to the station when she had been off-shift.

'The poor mite must spend his whole time in nursery.' Helen had made a determined effort to spend as much time at home as possible during Alice's pre-school years. It had proved to be an inspired decision. 'I wonder how much time he gets to spend with his mother. Not much, I suspect.'

'Can't be helped, I suppose. Both parents work. And you can't work from home if you're a cop.'

'And I don't suppose her boyfriend is proving much help,' Helen scoffed.

'According to Roche, he's rolling his sleeves up. I think they're making a decent stab at it.' Shuffling closer, he slipped an arm around her. 'It's always a chaotic time. You remember what it was like for us.'

'I think they'll be fine.' Helen returned her full attention to the television.

Sensing an easing of her initial hostility, he ran a finger past her earlobe. Helen swatted it away with an exasperated sigh.

'They're just getting on with it.'

'Good for them,' Helen grunted. 'What was so important that it required you to ply poor Sergeant Roche with alcohol?'

Poor Sergeant Roche had seemed quite happy throwing the whiskey down her neck, Carlyle recalled. 'You remember a guy called Daniel Hunter?'

Helen gave it a nanosecond's thought. 'The name doesn't ring a bell.'

'An old case.' He gave her a brief run-through of Hunter's back story.

'Nasty,' was Helen's only comment.

Given her clear disinterest, they sat in silence until the TV show went to a commercial break.

'I had a call from Eva this afternoon.' Eva Hollander, a.k.a. Mrs Dominic Silver.

'What did she want?'

'She just wanted to catch up. We haven't spoken for ages. They're all doing well.'

'Uh-huh.'

'We're having lunch in a couple of weeks.'

'Good.' Eva and Helen went way back, almost as far back as Dom and Carlyle. There was no reason why they shouldn't have lunch, even if the timing was deeply suspect.

Helen scratched her knee. 'She told me you and Dom are doing some work together.'

'I wouldn't say that.' Carlyle chose his words carefully. 'I saw Dom at lunchtime.' He forced out a yawn as a proxy for insouciance. 'We went to this crappy gastropub place near the Lisson

Gallery.' The meeting seemed days ago now, pushed into the background by the Hunter business.

Helen wasn't interested in a restaurant review. 'What did you talk about?'

'Nothing in particular. He seemed on good form. Put a bit of weight on, though.'

'Eva says the gallery's doing well,' Helen offered. 'Apparently, Dom's making almost as much money as he did before.'

When he was a drug dealer? Carlyle found that hard to believe.

'She says there's an endless stream of foreigners who seem only too happy to pay top dollar for the type of stuff they have in the gallery.'

'It doesn't really matter what Dom's selling, he's always good at getting a top price.'

'Shame he didn't make the career change earlier, then,' Helen ventured.

'You can't micro-manage these things. He did very well to get out and then move on to something else.'

Helen returned to her probing. 'What did he want to talk to you about?'

Why do I think you know all about this anyway? Carlyle waited for the spasm of irritation at Helen's artless fishing to pass. 'He's worried that some journalist is trying to dig up a story about his past.'

'*His* past?' Helen shot him a sideways glance.

'Our past,' Carlyle admitted.

She shook her head. 'Oh, John.'

Oh, John? Carlyle bristled. She'd made it sound like he'd somehow fucked things up. 'What did I do?'

'After all this time – decades – you finally get a promotion and now some journalist is trying to take you down?' The alarm in her voice was unsettling.

65

'He's just trying to fill some column inches by rehashing old rumours about Dom.'

'More than rumours.' Helen snorted.

'Yes and no. Dominic Silver may be something of a legend among Met old-timers like me, but he's never been jailed for anything. Never even been charged, for that matter.'

'He was bloody lucky.'

'Lucky or smart, it doesn't really matter now, does it?'

'Who's the journalist?'

'A guy called Bernie Gilmore. I know him. He's better than most. I'll speak to him and sort it out.'

'Sort it out how?'

'I'll give him something else. Trade.'

'Trade what?'

'TBC,' he admitted.

Shrugging off his arm, she turned to look him in the face. 'And just when did you think you were going to mention it to me?'

He cursed Eva for dropping this on Helen before he'd had a chance to talk to his wife. 'I only found out about it myself earlier on today.' The commercial break had come to an end. He looked at the TV screen hopefully, willing Helen to go back to watching her programme. When her gaze didn't waver, he added, 'It's Dom they're interested in and, anyway, as you know, it's several years too late.' When Helen looked less than convinced, Carlyle again tried to play down the threat. 'It's not a big deal. I can get it sorted. Dom's been a respectable businessman for quite a while now. We haven't really done much together for ages. There's no story.'

'Then why is this journalist chasing it?'

'Because that's what they do.'

'What does he have?'

'Nothing.' The lie was out of his mouth before he'd even had

66

time to reflect on it. Carlyle tried to recall whether Helen knew the name Tuco Martinez. The loon had caused a certain amount of chaos – including blowing up one of their elderly neighbours with a parcel bomb addressed to Carlyle – but he had shielded his wife from the true nature of the threat against the family. As far as he could remember, Helen had never heard of Tuco. There had been no point in raising it then and there was certainly no point in raising it now.

Whatever happened, Tuco wasn't about to come back from the dead. Hold on to that fact, Carlyle told himself, because it justifies everything you did. 'Bernie has nothing,' he repeated, 'just a few old rumours from years back. There's no story.'

'That's what people say when they've got something to hide,' Helen muttered darkly.

'It's true,' Carlyle protested.

Alice appeared in the doorway, sparing her father from further cross-examination. Skipping across the room, she dropped a glossy colour brochure into his lap.

'What's this?' Picking it up, Carlyle began flicking through the pages.

'It's the Imperial College prospectus.'

'Imperial?' Carlyle's heart leaped at the prospect of his only child staying in London for university.

'There's an open day next week. I want to go.' Alice shot her father a winning smile. 'And I want *you* to come with me.'

'Sure,' Carlyle replied, delighted to be asked and even more delighted to have moved off the subject of Tuco and Bernie.

'Good.' Alice disappeared back down the hallway.

'When did she decide on this?' Carlyle asked, holding up the prospectus.

'Just now, I suppose.'

'Aeronautical engineering, geophysics, nuclear engineering.' Scanning the list of available courses, Carlyle had the horrible realisation that his daughter, whatever she chose to do, was on the brink of leaving him far, far behind. 'Do you want to come, too?'

'Doesn't look like I'm invited.' Folding her arms, Helen returned her attention to the TV.

'Maybe we can all grab a bite to eat afterwards.'

'I'll leave it to you. It's about time you did a bit of father-daughter bonding.' Extending a leg, Helen pointed at the coffee-table with her foot. 'Your phone's ringing.'

Carlyle watched it vibrating across the table.

'Aren't you going to answer it?'

'I suppose so.' Leaning forward, he grabbed the handset. 'Hello?' Conscious of Helen scowling at him, he skulked out of the living room.

'Commander Carlyle?'

Still not used to the title, he had to think about it for a moment before answering in the affirmative.

'This is Detective Inspector Tommy Plant.'

From the gravelly voice, Carlyle imagined Plant as a veteran detective, fraying at the edges, counting down the days to retirement. 'What can I do for you?' Reaching the kitchen, he pulled open the fridge and helped himself to a beer.

'You called me,' Plant asserted.

I did? Making a noncommittal response, Carlyle pulled open a drawer, looking for something to open the bottle with.

'I'm calling from Colchester,' Plant explained. 'I led the Andrew Carson investigation.'

'Ah, yes, good.' Locating a bottle-opener under a mound of takeaway napkins, Carlyle wedged the phone between ear and shoulder. Flipping off the lid with a flick of the wrist, he watched as it spun in the air before bouncing across the worktop and into the sink. Nice shot. Lifting the bottle to his lips, he took a long drag.

'I suppose you're ringing about Kurt Zerlkderik,' the DI offered.

'Who?'

'Kurt Zerlkderik.' A hint of doubt crept into Plant's voice.

'Who's Kurt . . . Whatsisname?' Carlyle took another mouthful of beer.

'Kurt *Zerlkderik*.' Plant adopted the weary but wary tone of an officer dealing with a not-quite-up-to-speed superior. 'The guy who shot Andrew Carson in the face.'

'Uh-huh.' Choking on his beer, Carlyle suddenly found himself engulfed in a violent coughing fit.

Daniel Hunter sat on the edge of his bed and stared at the cell floor. Standing in the doorway, Carlyle tapped his phone, trying to work out which meeting he was going to be late for that morning.

'We need to get out of here.'

'What was the guy called?' The expression on Hunter's face was one of discomfort rather than relief.

'His name was . . .' Carlyle recovered a scrap of paper from his pocket, squinting at it under the bottom of his glasses '. . . Kurt Zerlkderik.'

He gave a nod of approval at his own pronunciation before slowly enunciating each individual letter in turn. Tommy Plant had spelled it out for him three times over the phone to make sure that he got it right.

'What kind of name is that?' Hunter wondered.

'No idea,' Carlyle admitted. Pronouncing it was one thing, explaining its origins quite another. 'The DI in charge of the case said he originally came from Ipswich.'

'Never heard of him.'

'There's no reason you should.' Carlyle crumpled the slip of paper in his hand and shoved it back into his pocket. Hopefully

69

he would never need it again. 'Looks like he did you a big favour, whoever he was.'

'They fitted him up for the murder of Andy Carson?'

'Yes, well, there is that.'

'The guy you spoke to, is he bent?'

'Tommy Plant?' Carlyle scratched his chin. 'Dunno. There's a big difference between being bent and taking the easy option. Once they had a suspect, the local cops didn't look too hard for another.' The commander watched a spider scamper up the wall, unsure whether the DI's shortcomings should leave him pleased or displeased. 'Then again, why would they?'

The police had responded to a 999 call from a neighbour, reporting suspected gunshots at Monkey Beach Cottage. The first responders were a couple of uniforms who found Kurt Zerlkderik covered with Andrew Carson's blood, a games console in his hands, muttering incomprehensibly to himself. When the officers tried to arrest him, Zerlkderik smacked one of them on the jaw and tried to leg it. He made it two hundred yards down the road – still carrying the console – before being apprehended by Plant coming the other way in his new BMW.

'I remember it well,' Plant recalled. 'I'd only picked it up from the dealer that afternoon.'

'Uh-huh.' Carlyle's interest in cars was less than nil.

'Still got it. Runs like a dream.' He paused, apparently to consider his infinite good fortune. 'Well, the Germans know how to make motors, don't they?'

'You came across Kurt,' Carlyle offered, trying to get the conversation back on track.

'Almost ran the stupid bugger over,' Plant told him. 'He ended up on his arse but there was no real damage done – he escaped with a few cuts and bruises. I had a quick word with him in private and got a confession before the uniforms arrived.'

A quick word? Carlyle imagined how a few slaps might have encouraged the guy to confess to something he hadn't done.

'They took him off to the station and I went home to bed. We got the paperwork done in the morning. All in all, it was a good result, that one. A great result, in fact. Saved us all the time and effort of a long investigation. And a trial.'

Carlyle started to say something, then thought better of it. This thing was turning into a terrible mess: a blatant miscarriage of justice on top of the original crime. How the hell was he going to sort it all out?

'Kurt really did the taxpayer a favour on that one,' Plant mused.

'How long did he get?'

'Indefinite sentence in a secure medical facility.' Plant mentioned a place that Carlyle had heard of – a notorious establishment located near the coast – then let out a harsh laugh. 'When his lawyer put in a plea of insanity, no one was going to contest it.'

'Is he still there?'

'Nah. They took him out in a box after less than six months.'

'Sorry?'

'The silly bugger stopped taking his meds. He sneaked up on the roof one day and threw himself off.'

'You're kidding.' Carlyle's surprise was genuine. A secure facility was just that: you didn't wander onto the roof and jump.

If Plant shared the commander's scepticism, he didn't let it show. 'The guy thought he was a hawk or something. He imagined he was going to fly right out of there. You couldn't make it up.'

'No, I suppose not.' Carlyle pondered the implications of Zerlkderik's failure to take flight. It looked very much like his problem had resolved itself. Plant had not mentioned Daniel Hunter during their conversation. At the time, he must have been aware of the name. Under the circumstances, however, it would have been all too easy to push Hunter to the outer edges of the investigation. Like any cop, Plant would have played the percentages. He wasn't going to look beyond Kurt Zerlkderik for a suspect in the murder of Andrew Carson. Open and shut cases were rare enough. When you lucked across one, you slammed it closed and kept it closed.

'Sarah Ward didn't exactly cover herself in glory, either,' Carlyle mumbled to himself.

'What?'

'Erm, nothing.'

'Why are you interested, anyway?' Plant's voice had cooled several degrees. 'This was all done and dusted a long time ago.'

'Well, as you probably recall, Carson was a person of interest to us down here for various reasons.'

'He was of interest to a lot of people. A right bastard. He got what was coming to him, by all accounts.'

'Yes.' There was a pause. The commander realised that he was still on the hook for the original question. 'I was just clearing out some old files and came across a stack of papers relating to Carson and realised I never discovered how the investigation played out.'

It wasn't much of an explanation, but Plant seemed happy enough to take it at face value.

'Why do you think he did it?' Carlyle asked.

'Huh?'

'Why do you think Kurt killed Carson?'

'He wanted the games console. He was still holding on to it after I ran him over.'

'Not much of a motive,' Carlyle mumbled.

'He was a classic basket case,' Plant added, 'an only child from a broken home. Never knew his father. His mother killed herself when he was six. She jumped off Clacton pier – maybe that's what gave him the idea.'

'Maybe.' Carlyle felt uncomfortable dismissing the poor bloke as a freak.

'Little Kurt lived in a succession of institutions and foster homes. He had educational difficulties – no surprise there – and basically dropped out of school when he was thirteen. After almost a decade of living rough around parts of Essex and East Anglia, he had built up a criminal record, with a long list of arrests for drunkenness and vagrancy, bookended by a couple of violent assaults, which had led to him being jailed for eight months and two years respectively.'

Carlyle gave a silent apology to the spirit of poor Kurt Zerlkderik, if such a thing existed. Still, he couldn't get too worked up about Plant's behaviour. After all, he had done much worse himself, over the years. When an image of the bloody corpse of Tuco Martinez floated into his brain he quickly pushed it away. 'Thanks for bringing me up to speed. Sorry to take up so much of your time but I was genuinely curious.'

'That's fine, Commander.' Plant's mood brightened as it became clear that his cross-examination was at an end. 'Always happy to help.'

'Just one final question.'

'Yes?'

'Did you ever recover the murder weapon?'

The silence at the other end of the line was so long that Carlyle wondered if he'd lost the connection. It was finally broken by the sound of Plant clearing his throat. 'We searched for it for ages, but it never turned up. What we suspect happened was that Kurt must have thrown it into the sea when he tried to make his escape.'

'That would explain it,' Carlyle agreed, reasonableness personified. 'Could've ended up anywhere.'

A more perfect patsy than Kurt Zerlkderik would have been almost impossible to find. The lack of a motive – or a murder weapon – hadn't got in the way of the stampede for a conviction. And with the poor sod crashing on take-off after his incarceration, any chance of the case being reviewed had died with him. Hunter, it seemed, was in the clear.

'The guy must have turned up after I left the cottage.' Hunter's face took on a faraway expression as he went back to the night in question. 'I didn't see anyone.'

'He was probably just looking for a place to kip,' Carlyle agreed. 'Anyway, the timing was perfect.'

'Not for him,' Hunter responded. 'What a mess.'

'Not as much of a mess as it might have been.'

Hunter looked at him blankly.

'I don't want to sound too blasé about it,' the commander coughed, 'but these things do happen. Sometimes. Well, very occasionally. Like once in a blue moon.'

'He didn't do it.'

'That doesn't really matter much now, does it?'

'But it's the truth.' Rocking backwards and forwards, Hunter began mumbling to himself. Carlyle wondered if maybe the guy had gone a bit loopy, too. After all that had happened, it would be perfectly understandable. After a while, Hunter rose from the bed. 'Is he coming down here?'

'Eh?'

'DI Plant. Is he coming down here to take my statement? Or do I have to go up there?'

'The investigation is closed. And it's going to remain closed. The last thing that Tommy Plant – or anyone else for that matter – wants is for you to appear in front of him and try to reopen an old murder case that has long since been solved.'

'But—'

'But nothing. You won the lottery here. Just take it and move on.'

Shoving his hands into his pockets, Hunter didn't look

like a man who had miraculously dodged a lengthy custodial sentence.

'We need to get you out of here.' Carlyle edged out of the cell. 'You're not under arrest. You're free to go.'

Reaching for his coat, Hunter finally snapped out of his funk. 'All right.'

'Good.' Realising he had been holding his breath, Carlyle exhaled. 'What will you do now?'

'I'll head up to Peterborough.' Hunter pulled on his coat. 'I might have dodged the murder charge but there's still the question of going AWOL from the army.'

The guy seemed absolutely determined to find someone to put him behind bars. 'If there's anything I can do to help on that score,' Carlyle offered, confident that the answer would be in the negative, 'just let me know.'

Hunter scratched his ear. 'Like what?'

'I dunno.' Carlyle tried to think of something remotely credible. 'When this is finally all over, if you need help getting back on your feet, you know, with a job or something, there's always people I can talk to.'

'There is one thing.' Hunter looked embarrassed.

'Yes?' Carlyle's heart sank.

'I could do with some help with the train fare.'

NINE

Hands on hips, Inspector Nayla Thomson scanned the desolate patch of empty ground covering almost an entire city block. The site had been cleared, with a fifteen-foot wooden fence ringing the perimeter. A trio of diggers stood thirty yards away, in anticipation of getting started on the foundations of a new building.

Thomson remembered the time, more than ten years ago now, when she had flirted with the idea of becoming an architect, just one of a random selection of career choices thrown up by her teenage self. I should have stuck with that, she reflected, rather than joining the police.

Feeling vaguely regretful, she watched Alison Roche walking towards her. The sergeant's arrival only served to make Thomson doubt her career choice even more. A tough, no-nonsense officer, dressed in jeans and a battered leather jacket, Roche was Thomson's idea of what a cop *should* look like. By comparison, the inspector felt like an M&S management trainee.

Not only did Roche look the part, she was well-respected as a solid, hard-working officer. Most galling of all, she even had her private life sorted – shacked up with a cute lawyer who worked for the Police Federation. They had a young kid and a place somewhere in north London. Thomson felt a bubble of jealousy, acidic in her stomach. She acknowledged the sergeant's arrival with a question: 'What's this place going to be?'

Roche pointed towards an advertising hoarding standing in one corner of the site. 'It's supposed to be part of a new mixed-use development.'

'Mixed use,' Thomson grumbled, 'as in offices and more flats for rich foreigners who never live in them?'

'Something like that.'

'I bet they cost a fortune.'

Roche mentioned a number in the not-so-low seven figures. 'I think that's for the penthouses, though.'

Thomson let out a hollow laugh. 'Maybe I'll put in an offer.' The inspector had only recently managed to find a place of her own, allowing her finally to move out of her mother's back room. Even then, all she could afford was a tiny shared-ownership studio located so far from the centre of the city that it was almost off the tube map. There was more chance of her making commissioner than of her ever being able to afford somewhere to live around here.

The sergeant eyed her superior suspiciously. A small, elfin creature, Thomson had been parachuted into the Charing Cross station to replace John Carlyle when the latter, amazingly, had been promoted and, disappointingly, sent into exile at Paddington Green. Roche, very much of the better-the-devil-you-know persuasion, was ready to be underwhelmed from the off. Thomson's CV – St Paul's, Exeter University, Met graduate trainee scheme – had been debated at length before the woman had even walked through the front door. The consensus was that she would be just the kind of over-rewarded, underachieving bureaucrat, who would happily trample over her fellow officers as she climbed the greasy pole, ruthlessly taking advantage of the Met's desire to be seen to embrace contemporary standards of diversity and equality.

In the event, Roche had found Thomson to be rather shy and

insecure. The woman seemed almost embarrassed to have made inspector before she had even reached thirty. Now, standing in the middle of a building site watching each breath disappear into the chill of the morning sky, Roche would have switched places with Thomson in an instant. No commitments and a proper career. The woman had it made.

'The site manager's asking how long it'll be before he can get his guys back to work.' Roche shook her head in disgust. 'I told him it'll take as long as it takes.'

'As long as it takes,' Thomson repeated. 'What've we got?'

Roche glanced over at the small white tent sitting in the middle of the site and recited what Chris Hallam, the pathologist, had told her minutes earlier. 'White female, in her thirties, shot twice in the chest.'

The gloomy expression on Thomson's face darkened further. 'How long has she been here?'

'Hallam reckons six to eight hours.'

'Is this the primary?'

'Looks like it. Hallam estimates that she was killed here.'

'There were no reports of any shots?'

'No. The body was found by one of the workmen this morning when he came in to start his shift.' Roche waited patiently for her instructions. This was Thomson's first murder and doubtless the inspector was going to do things by the book. That was fair enough.

'We'll need to canvass the neighbours.'

'Sure.' The buildings that overlooked the site were mostly offices, which would have been empty in the middle of the night. That would speed things up.

'What about CCTV?'

'Only on the perimeter but it's being checked as we speak.'

'Good.'

Roche watched the pathologist emerge from the tent and

begin walking towards them. In his hand was a clear plastic evidence bag. As he came closer, she could see that the bag contained a purse.

'Seems we've got an ID.' Hallam carefully picked his way through the mud. 'The victim's name is Karen Jansen.' He offered the bag to Roche. 'And it looks like she knew some interesting people.'

'You've got to be kidding me.' Dominic Silver looked despairingly at the guy from the security company, then stalked into the gallery, crunching broken glass underfoot.

'I managed to switch the alarm off,' the guard pointed out. 'And the emergency glazing firm are on their way.'

Dom tore his gaze away from the shattered front window and looked around the empty walls. Not everything had been taken: the raiders had left the largest pieces, going instead for the more portable items, which also happened to be the most valuable. He counted a dozen missing canvases. Off the top of his head, their retail value was somewhere in the region of three million pounds. 'The insurance company's going to love this,' he groaned. Thank God his premiums were up to date.

'We've seen a couple of these in the last year or so, the security guy said. 'The same gang, probably. They nick stuff to order. It's all pre-sold.'

Dom vaguely recalled reading an article about a robbery at a gallery in the East End. Stepping carefully over to the receptionist's desk, he picked up a catalogue and began flicking through the pages. After a further review of the inventory of stolen paintings, he revised the cost up, towards four mil.

How much was his excess? The details of the policy should be in the back. He pointed towards his office. 'They didn't go in there, did they?'

'Nah.' The security guy gestured at an empty space on the

wall to his left. 'They didn't go for anything else, just the pictures. Who's the artist, anyway?'

Mentioning the name of a highly strung Canadian, Dom made a mental note to call the guy's agent to tell him what had happened. For his fifteen per cent, the agent could be the bearer of bad news. And this was *very* bad news. Apart from anything else, each painting represented something like six months' work for his client. The artist was now in his seventies and was known to be in poor health; the main reason his prices had been going up in recent years was that collectors were expecting a nice little bump in valuations when he snuffed it.

'Popular, is he?' the security guard asked, not pretending to recognise the name.

Dom contemplated the mess at their feet. 'Popular enough, it seems, for someone to do this.'

The security guard pushed at a shard of glass with his toe. 'The stuff'll be out of the country by teatime. In the hands of some private collector within forty-eight hours. Could be anywhere in the world.' He sounded impressed by the efficiency of the criminal operation. 'There's not a lot you can do about it, really.'

Dom felt long-forgotten anger flare in his breast. 'We'll see about that.'

In his office, he pulled a bottle of Talisker and a shot glass from his desk drawer. He needed a stiffener ahead of what would be a difficult morning. Pouring an inch of the amber liquid into the bottom of the glass, he took a healthy swig, letting the spirit roll across his tongue and down the back of his throat. 'Aaah.' He placed the bottle back in the drawer and slammed it shut. Reaching for his phone, he pulled up a familiar number and hit call.

Carlyle had just made it into his office, when he felt his phone start to vibrate. Pulling it from the breast pocket of his jacket, he glanced at the screen. 'No, I haven't spoken to Bernie Gilmore yet,' he grumbled. 'Gimme a chance.' Declining Dom's call, he tossed the phone on top of a green file sitting on his desk and turned to Linda, who had shuffled into the room behind him.

'What am I late for?' he asked wearily. It was barely nine in the morning but already he felt like he'd put in a full shift. At least the Daniel Hunter situation had been sorted out. Carlyle had handed the military policeman a hundred quid to get to Peterborough – money well spent under the circumstances. Hopefully the army would put him behind bars for a short spell – just long enough to purge him of his guilt – and then the poor bugger could get on with his life.

'Nothing,' Linda replied, 'so far.'

Slipping behind his desk, Carlyle sat down. 'No meetings?' he asked, not quite able to believe it.

'No.' Linda shook her head. 'Steve Morrison cancelled your eight thirty. We'll try to get it rescheduled for next week.'

'Great.' Carlyle gave silent thanks to Steve Morrison, who-ever he was. 'So, what's next?'

'You're relatively free now until three.'

Carlyle ignored the word 'relatively' and contemplated how best to use this windfall. 'What's at three?'

'DAC Mara's Project Scimitar meeting.' Linda pointed at the green file. 'The background information is in there.'

'I'll take a look.'

'Then there's the review of the performance stats and you've got the commissioner's reception at six thirty.'

Brushing aside the performance statistics, Carlyle asked, 'What's the reception?'

'It's the annual media drinks,' Linda explained.

Media drinks. Carlyle wondered if Bernie Gilmore would be there. The only thing Bernie liked more than a drink was a free drink. 'Can I have a list of the journalists attending?'

'I'll get it for you right now.' Turning on her heel, Linda headed from the room.

'Thanks.' Carlyle sat back in his chair and watched his phone start to vibrate again.

'Fuck off, Dom.'

He picked it up anyway.

'I hear your mate had a bit of trouble last night.'

Immediately recognising the caller, Carlyle sat upright in his chair. 'Good morning to you, too.'

'Sorry to be so abrupt,' Bernie Gilmore let out a low cackle, 'but it's a miracle if you ever pick up. When I manage to get you on the phone, I have to go straight to the point.'

'How are things?' The commander tried to sound business-like but friendly.

'Same old, same old. You know what it's like, the clowns may change but the circus stays the same. There's always someone trying to fuck you over, one way or another.'

'Tell me about it.'

'By the way, do you know Andy Wick?'

'Indeed I do.' Chief Inspector Andy Wick was one of Carlyle's more memorable colleagues. Twenty-three years on the force had yielded sixteen complaints, five disciplinary hearings and two official warnings. To be fair, it had also yielded three commendations, a bravery award and an OBE, in recognition of the four years working on royal protection. Wick's private life was pretty colourful, too: four wives, seven kids by five different women, a string of office romances and various run-ins with alcohol and drug abuse. There was even a rumour that Wick had been banging a lady-in-waiting while working at the Palace, although Carlyle found that hard to believe, given that all the ladies-in-waiting seemed to be in their seventies, at least.

Despite everything, Wick had managed to keep his job. Until now. A week ago, he was found slumped over the wheel of his

Audi outside a kebab shop on the Edgware Road at two o'clock in the morning. When a couple of uniforms searched his car, they'd found a dozen small packets of heroin and cocaine in the glove compartment. Arrested on suspicion of possessing class-A drugs with intent to supply, Wick was suspended ahead of his inevitable sacking. With grim inevitability, the story had appeared in the press a couple of days later.

Carlyle had already started looking for a replacement.

'I hear he worked for you.'

'A lot of people work for me, these days.'

'Yeah, yeah, of course. Congrats on the promotion. Very well deserved and all that.'

Fuck off, Bernie. Carlyle appreciated the journalist's disdain for such things.

'It's a bit of a shocker,' Bernie remarked cheerily, always happy to discuss the shortcomings of Met staff. 'Top cop arrested on suspicion of dealing class A.' The hack talked, as he wrote, in staccato, sugar-rush sentences. 'It's unbelievable what you boys get up to.'

'Not all of us,' Carlyle pointed out. '*I* haven't chased the dragon for a while, to be honest.'

'Well, it looks like your Mr Wick is the guy to see if you want to score.'

'I'll bear it in mind,' Carlyle joked, 'for when things get too much.'

'Really, you couldn't make it up. What did the guy think he was up to?'

'I'm not across the detail,' Carlyle replied, sensing where their conversation was going.

'Well, the chief inspector's certainly in the shit,' the hack pronounced sagely. 'He might even have to give his OBE back,' he mused. 'They don't like it when you embarrass the Queen.'

'If I ever get a gong, I'll remember not to misbehave.'

'There's a suggestion that Wick was stitched up.'

'There's always a suggestion that someone's been stitched up.' The commander wasn't particularly interested in conspiracy theories. 'It's a pretty standard line of defence.'

'Someone with a grudge.'

'It usually is.' Carlyle was not going to rise to the bait.

'Yes, well, if you hear anything, let me know.'

'Sure.'

'Similarly on this Dominic Silver thing.'

Carlyle wished now he had taken Dom's earlier call. 'What Dominic Silver thing?'

'Your mate's gallery on Cork Street got done over last night. A gang smashed their way through the front window and nicked a bunch of Sigmund Kessling paintings. They got away with a nice little haul. Worth as much as ten million, apparently.'

'Uh-huh.'

'It's amazing what Kessling's stuff goes for these days,' Bernie added. 'Personally, I'm not a great fan. I'm rather more of a Colin Menzies man myself.'

'I didn't know you were an art critic . . . as well as everything else.'

'I know what I like. Kessling's not really my cup of tea. In my humble opinion, he's just riding the current fashion for Canadian artists, stimulated by the likes of Buckland and Napier.'

'Right.'

'Someone clearly likes him, though. The word is that the stuff was stolen to order. And the robbery itself was a very professional job. You should see the CCTV pictures. They're quite something.'

With a sigh, the commander fired up the computer on his desk. 'I suppose I can see all this on your website, can I?'

'Nah. That's not really our thing. We don't do news, we do *investigations*.'

'Pardon me.'

'Which brings me to the real reason for the call. We're doing a deep dive into police corruption in London and—'

Carlyle cut him off. 'Are you going to the drinks thing tonight?'

'The commissioner's bash? Sadly not. I'm double-booked this evening – got to meet up with an important source.'

An important source regarding the killing of Tuco Martinez? Carlyle didn't much care for *that* possibility. On the other hand, Bernie was an inveterate bullshitter: he could just as easily be going round to his mum's for tea.

'Which is a shame. It's normally a good do,' Bernie said.

'Why don't we meet up?' the commander suggested.

'When will you be free?'

Might as well get on with it, Carlyle decided. 'This morning's good.' After agreeing a time and a place with Bernie, he rang Dom, leaving a quick voicemail when his friend didn't pick up. Dropping the phone back onto the desk, he watched in disbelief as it immediately started to vibrate. Scooping it up, Carlyle lifted the handset to his ear.

'That was quick. I just left you a message.'

'You did?' Roche sounded nonplussed at the commander's opening gambit.

'S-sorry,' Carlyle stammered. 'I thought you were somebody else.'

'It's okay.' Over the years, Roche had become accustomed to Carlyle's inability to master the basics of telephone etiquette.

Carlyle quickly recovered his composure. 'Where were you this morning?' he demanded. 'You were supposed to look after Daniel Hunter for me.'

'I had to go out with Inspector Thomson,' Roche explained. 'We caught a nasty one.'

'Unlucky,' was as much consolation as the commander could offer. 'The good news, however, is that the Hunter problem is solved.' He started explaining about Hunter, Andy Carson and the hapless Kurt Zerlkderik when the sergeant unceremoniously cut him off.

'I'm still at the scene.' Roche gave him an address just north of Oxford Street. 'You need to come down here.'

The location was on the way to his meeting with Bernie or, at least, it *could* be. On the other hand, Carlyle didn't like the idea of more of his 'free' morning disappearing in front of his eyes. 'I'm a bit busy,' he said, trying to adopt the persona of the toiling pen-pusher.

Roche muttered something under her breath that might have questioned both his intelligence and parentage. Then she asked, 'Do you remember a woman called Karen Jansen?'

TEN

One of the perks of his new rank was access to a car and a driver. In London, however, a motor was about as much use as free sand in the desert. Carlyle had only made use of his ride a handful of times, normally to get home after events that spilled into the early hours of the morning. Telling Linda he would be back after lunch, he left Paddington Green and headed for the tube. Fifteen minutes later, he was standing in the middle of a building site, watching the all-too-familiar activity of a recently identified crime scene as it played out around him.

'This used to be a hospital, you know.' Finding a small stone at his feet, he couldn't resist the temptation to kick it into a nearby puddle.

'Yeah, well, it's going to be luxury flats now.'

'That's progress, I suppose.' Carlyle eyed the small bag in Roche's hand.

She lifted it up so he could get a better view. 'Your business card – it was in Karen Jansen's purse.'

Carlyle nodded. 'I remember giving it to her.' He was surprised that she had kept it, but maybe not that surprised.

Roche let her arm drop to her side. 'Did she ever call you?'

'Nope.'

'She was all right.' Roche stared at the mud on her boots. 'What a bummer.'

'It is for Karen.'

'Ever the cynic.'

Carlyle regretted his quip. He could try too hard to play up to the stereotype of the hard-bitten cop. 'It's a shame. She seemed an interesting character, certainly not your run-of-the-mill victim.'

'I'm sure that will be a lot of comfort to her parents.'

The commander didn't argue the point. 'I hoped she'd be smart enough to get out,' was all he could come up with.

'Easy to say, harder to do.'

'Yeah, yeah, I know. But she had a plan.'

'They all have plans,' Roche observed drily.

'She had the chance to go home.' Carlyle felt a sense of profound frustration as he watched an ambulance pull up at the gates of the construction site. 'A fresh start.'

A couple of paramedics jumped out of the vehicle and began bouncing a gurney across the uneven ground. 'You'd have thought Vernon Holder could have been more discreet about it,' Roche mused.

'If it was Vernon.'

'Who else would it be?' Roche gave him a lingering look. 'This wasn't a mugging that went wrong.'

'We knew the woman for about five minutes,' Carlyle countered. 'Who knows what she might have been involved in? Maybe she wasn't as smart as she looked. Maybe she was just unlucky.'

'Maybe.' Roche stared vacantly into the middle distance, clearly not buying it.

'Although I accept that Vernon Holder is the name that jumps out at you.' Vernon bloody Holder was an old-school East End gangster, pimp and all-round piece of work. Liked to think of himself as a cross between the Krays and one of those businessmen off *Dragon's Den*. Karen Jansen had worked for Holder

– more successfully than most – managing his collection of girls for an international clientele. 'I guess he doesn't care whether we know about it or not.'

'No.' A hard look settled on Roche's face. Transported back to the days when they had first worked together, Carlyle couldn't help but smile.

'What's so funny?'

'Nothing.'

'If it is Vernon,' Roche said, 'he'll be waiting for us to come after him.'

He'll waiting for *me* to come after him. Since the Tuco Martinez thing, however, Carlyle's vigilante days were over. He had been lucky to get away with killing Tuco – if, indeed, he *had* got away with it. Holder, he vowed, would be handled strictly above board.

The paramedics arrived at the tent that had been set up around the body. One of them waited with the gurney while the other disappeared inside. Moments later, a small woman emerged, a phone clamped to her ear.

'Is that Thomson?' Carlyle asked. 'She looks about twelve.'

'Keep that opinion to yourself,' Roche advised. 'You don't want to find yourself up on a sexual-harassment charge.'

How is that sexual harassment? 'I'm not another Umar.' Roche's predecessor, Sergeant Umar Sligo, had left the job under a cloud after developing a penchant for sending pictures of his knob to unfortunate female colleagues.

'You don't have to send people pictures of your willy to get into hot water, these days.'

'I suppose not.' Carlyle knew she was right. He should keep his smart-arse comments to himself, especially when dealing with a new colleague. One of the things that had become pain-fully obvious over the years was that his sense of humour was an acquired taste – one that not many people cared to acquire.

He watched Thomson end her call and begin walking towards them. 'How are you two getting on?' he asked.

'She'll be all right. Better than Wrench.' Inspector Jay Wrench had been Roche's boss at Limehouse. 'She'll go far but she's still a bit unsure of herself. She needs to act the part, needs to trust her own judgement a bit more.'

'What've you told her?'

'About Jansen and Holder? Nothing, so far.'

'That's good.' A knowing look passed between them. 'Let me do the talking.' Carlyle lowered his voice as the inspector approached. 'I don't want this turning into a right old mess.'

'Remember, this is Thomson's first murder,' Roche whispered. 'She'll want to be thorough, cross all the *t*s, dot all the *i*s. Be patient with her.'

'I'm always patient.' Carlyle extended a hand. 'Inspector Thomson, I'm Commander Carlyle.'

'Ah, yes, my predecessor. Sergeant Roche has told me all about you.' A thin smile wriggled across the inspector's lips as she shook his hand.

'Has she now?'

'Only the good things,' Roche assured him.

'That would be a rather short story, then.' The commander signalled towards the tent. 'What happened?'

Clearing her throat, Thomson adopted the dry tone of an officer briefing her superior. 'A woman who has been provisionally identified as Karen Jansen was fatally shot in the chest last night. So far, we have no witnesses. We're still checking the relevant CCTV.' Thomson gestured towards the perimeter fencing. 'It's all on the outside but there's a possibility that one of the cameras on the neighbouring buildings will give us some images of the site itself.'

Carlyle gave a nod to show that he was paying full attention.

'There are no signs of a struggle,' Thomson continued, 'and the victim was not sexually assaulted.'

Carlyle glanced at Roche before turning his attention back to the inspector. 'Was she robbed?'

Thomson shook her head. 'In her purse, we found a couple of credit cards and more than two hundred pounds in cash.'

'Motive?'

'Nothing yet. It's early days.' Thomson paused. 'She had one of your business cards.'

Carlyle nodded. 'Sergeant Roche told me.' Thomson looked irked that her revelation had been leaked. 'Why else would I be here?'

'Yes, Commander.' Thomson's face darkened further. 'Thank you for giving us some of your precious time.' Her tone contained a whiff of sarcasm.

'If I can be of any assistance, I'm at your disposal. But I have other commitments.' Out of the corner of his eye, Carlyle could see Roche smirking. 'One thing I've learned in the last few months is that a commander's diary is not his own. I have to keep a lot of balls in the air at once.'

'Playing the big I am' was what his father used to call it. He recalled his parents, both deceased. Neither of them had been happy when he became a cop but, maybe, they would have been proud of him now. Would it have pleased him if they were? He hadn't thought about it.

'How did you know Karen Jansen?'

Carlyle parked his parents and eased into the brief monologue he'd just rehearsed in his head on the way over to the site. 'Jansen was indirectly involved in a case of mine, when I was at Charing Cross. She was quite helpful, as I recall.'

Thomson wanted more than that. 'What was the case?'

'There were several overlapping cases, actually.' Carlyle looked to Roche for help. He had tried to review the details before leaving the office, but his computer wouldn't play ball and his memory of what had happened was hazy, at best.

Roche's expression suggested her recollection wasn't much better, but she said, 'We interviewed one of Jansen's, erm, colleagues, a woman called Melody Rainbow, in connection with the death of a businessman called Balthazar Quant.'

Melody Rainbow. How could he ever have forgotten a name like that? Not to mention the girl's shocking pink hair. Carlyle tried to remember whether he had completed all the required paperwork at the time.

'Mr Quant,' Roche continued, 'was found on a building site – part of the Crossrail works for Canary Wharf station – stuffed into a concrete-making machine. Perhaps you remember it. There was a bit of coverage in the papers.'

'Doesn't ring any bells,' Thomson admitted.

'We got the guys responsible for Balthazar,' Carlyle mentioned casually, 'so the case was closed.'

Roche knew that was considerably less than the whole story but restricted her comments to 'Jansen was very helpful. She helped get Melody to talk to us.'

'What about Jansen's friends and family?' Thomson asked.

'Friends,' Carlyle scratched his nose, 'no idea. As far as family goes, she was from Australia – her parents are over there, I suppose. And I believe she wasn't married, no kids.'

'There was no wedding ring,' Thomson said, 'but that doesn't mean she didn't have a boyfriend. Might her death be connected to your previous investigation?'

Carlyle pretended to give the theory some consideration. 'Her work may well have had something to do with it, assuming she was still in the same line of business.'

'And what line of business was that?' Annoyed at having to drag the information out of him, Thomson was struggling to show the commander due deference.

'She was a madam, basically.' Carlyle checked his watch. He

needed to be on his way. Time and Bernie Gilmore waited for no man.

'Jansen worked for a pimp called Vernon Holder,' Roche explained. 'She ran his girls for him.'

'Her death's more than likely connected to that,' was Thomson's initial verdict.

'What's the plan?' Carlyle listened patiently while Thomson ran through the standard checklist, as taught at Hendon. 'Good.' He started for the exit. 'Keep me informed. And make sure you give her parents my condolences.' He nodded at Roche. 'I'll call you later.'

Thomson watched the commander disappear through the gate. 'So that's the famous John Carlyle. Not exactly helpful, was he?'

'The commander's pretty uncommunicative at the best of times – he's not much of a team player. It's just his style. Idiosyncratic. Moves to the beat of his own drum and all that. I wouldn't read too much into it.'

'Could there be more to his relationship with Jansen than he was letting on?'

'Oh, no.' Roche was genuinely shocked by the suggestion. 'Never in a million years would he play away. He's just not that type of guy.'

'All men are that type,' Thomson muttered.

How would you know? Roche wondered. 'Not Carlyle,' she insisted. 'I've known him a long time. He's a family man. One hundred per cent.'

'Karen Jansen was a good-looking woman.'

'She was only a minor character in our investigation,' Roche reminded her. 'What we were looking at back then is probably unconnected to this.'

Thomson was clearly unconvinced. 'That remains to be seen.

I expect to see all the reports. In the meantime, let's go and hear what the neighbours have to say.'

Sliding into the booth at the back of Morgan's Café, a seedy seventies dive located down an alley round the back of Golden Square, Carlyle did a double-take. 'What the hell happened to you?'

Lounging on the banquette, Bernie Gilmore looked hurt by the commander's reaction to his new look. 'I've been on a bit of a health kick.' He sounded slightly embarrassed by the admission. 'They've had me on a strict diet for the last couple of years.'

The commander didn't bother to enquire as to who 'they' might be.

'I even joined Weight Watchers.'

'Good for you,' Carlyle replied, stifling a laugh.

'I've had to develop my powers of self-control.'

'I can imagine.'

'I call it the anything-you-like diet,' the journalist deadpanned. 'If it's anything you like, you have to give it a miss.' He slurped noisily from a mug of green tea. 'It's been a bugger, but it's worked. I've lost quite a bit of weight.'

'A bit of weight?' Carlyle parroted, incredulous. The man looked like a shadow of his former self. With a bit of luck, he might starve to death before he could write anything about Tuco Martinez.

A waitress appeared at the table, but the commander waved her away. The wasted figure in front of him had temporarily put him off the idea of food. 'You look like you've been on the Nigel Lawson diet.'

'Who?'

'The former Chancellor of the Exchequer. Father of the celebrity cook.'

'Uh-huh.'

'One of Thatcher's cronies. Goes by the title of Baron something or other, these days. One of those Brexit-supporting cretins who prefers to live in France.'

'That's rich people for you,' Bernie declared. 'They think the rules don't apply to them. Which, to be fair, they don't.'

'Well, Lawson's more famous for losing five stone than for anything he ever did as a politician. He even wrote a diet book, I think. Anyway, it made him look weird – his face never caught up with the rest of him. He looked like he was melting.'

'You're saying my face looks weird?'

That's a monster fucking understatement. 'No, no. Just a bit . . .' Carlyle tried to come up with an alternative to 'emaciated' '. . . gaunt.' Realising that the conversation wasn't going particularly well, he added, 'You're looking good. Very fit.'

The belated endorsement seemed to cheer the hack up somewhat. Leaning across the table, he lowered his voice even further. 'I've lost almost nine stone.'

From *The Blob*, to *The Night of the Living Dead* was Carlyle's ultimate verdict. 'Impressive.'

'As well as Weight Watchers, I had a gastric band fitted. It's worked a treat.'

'Hm.' Carlyle didn't want to contemplate Bernie's stomach – on the inside or the outside. 'That must have been expensive,' was all he could think of to say.

'It cost a few bob,' Bernie admitted. 'I could have had it done on the NHS, but the waiting lists were enormous.'

'I can imagine.'

'Almost two-thirds of people in Britain are classified as obese or overweight.'

Right on cue, Carlyle watched a particularly fat couple waddle past the window. 'I'm surprised it's not more.'

'The numbers are going up all the time.' Bernie patted his shrunken belly. 'Soon, everybody's gonna need to have one of these.'

No wonder the health service is buggered, the commander reflected. We're all just a bunch of lazy fat bastards drowning in junk food.

'My GP said I was a heart attack waiting to happen if I didn't do something about it. I tried some drugs for a while, but they didn't work so I booked myself into a clinic in Hammersmith. There was no real alternative. I could have spent five years on the NHS waiting list, wondering when I was going to keel over.' He snapped his fingers. 'Just like that.'

Carlyle tried to inject some empathy into his voice. 'I could see how that would be stressful.'

'I booked myself in on the Wednesday and I had it done on the Monday. It was so much easier, going private.'

'I can imagine.'

'After my initial recovery, I took a week's R-and-R on a beach in Greece and I was back at work in just over a fortnight.'

'It's clearly worked.'

'Yeah. It's like I'm a new man.'

What a shame. A nice – fatal – heart attack for Bernie Gilmore would have been just the job. 'So how does it work?' Carlyle couldn't resist asking. 'Does it suppress your appetite or what?'

'Basically, it makes your stomach smaller, so you feel full quicker.' The hack looked Carlyle up and down. 'Something to keep in mind.'

Carlyle stared at him blankly.

'If you keep on putting on the pounds, I mean.'

'Fuck off,' Carlyle hissed. 'I'm not fat.' Sitting up straight, he pulled in his stomach.

Bernie took another mouthful of tea. 'How's the new job going?'

'Meetings, meetings, meetings,' Carlyle complained. 'Most of the time it's not like being a cop at all.'

'That's what happens when you climb the management

ladder,' Bernie mused. 'It won't help you keep the weight off, either.'

'Thanks for pointing that out.'

'Look on the bright side, you're doing better than Andy Wick. Not to mention Stan Carstairs.'

Carlyle conceded the point with a grunt.

'Last time I heard, the disgraced chief superintendent was under sedation for stress in the medical wing of Aberdeen prison.' Bernie shook his head sadly. 'The guy's a total zombie, apparently. And his case isn't even due to be heard until the back end of next year.'

'Keeping Stanley in on remand is very harsh,' Carlyle said. Could that happen to him if the Tuco thing came out? It didn't bear thinking about. 'It's only embezzlement, after all. It's not like he killed anyone.' Did he really say that? He felt himself blushing slightly.

Bernie didn't seem to notice. 'They have to make an example,' he intoned solemnly. 'If they let Stan out, the civil-liberties mob would go nuts – special treatment for bent cops and all that. Plus there were concerns about the possibility of witness intimidation.'

'Fair point,' Carlyle conceded. Even doped up to the eyeballs, Chief Superintendent Stanley Carstairs was a hard nut. He would have no qualms about nobbling anyone prepared to give evidence against him.

'Anyway, every cloud and all that. I hear that Stan the man would have been in the frame for your job if he hadn't come a cropper.'

'He's welcome to it.'

'You sound like you're pining for the old days.'

'Just edging towards the exit.' The waitress reappeared, giving Carlyle the chance to order a double espresso. Bernie asked for another green tea. Ignoring the woman's obvious scorn for such a modest order, the commander decided it was time to get down to business. 'Dom said you wanted to talk to me about Tuco Martinez.'

'A very interesting character by all accounts.' An expression of professional detachment settled on the reporter's hollowed face. 'What can you tell me about him?'

Carlyle eyed the iPhone sitting on the table. 'You recording this?'

'No.' Bernie put the phone away. 'Everything here is between you and me. Off the record. The usual rules apply.'

'Fair enough.' In their previous dealings, Bernie had respected the basis of their conversations. Even so, Carlyle had absolutely no intention of saying anything that would help the hack write his story. 'Tuco Martinez is a pretty serious French crim. His son got arrested in London a few years ago. There was some shooting at St Pancras – you probably remember it.'

'I do. Nasty business.'

'I can't remember the son's name, but he escaped from custody. We recaptured him – obviously – but Tuco was fairly pissed off about it, from what I remember.'

'Not as pissed off as he must have been when someone shot him dead,' Bernie suggested.

Carlyle made no effort to look surprised. 'Live by the sword and all that.'

'The case is still open, though. The French police have never made any arrests.'

'These things happen,' was Carlyle's only observation.

Bernie kept probing. 'How did you know Tuco Martinez?'

'I knew *about* him through the thing with the son.'

'Tuco wanted Dom Silver to work for him, dealing drugs.'

'I don't know anything about that.'

'But you knew what Dom was up to.'

Carlyle kept his irritation in check. 'My relationship with Dominic Silver is well documented, but I'm not his keeper. What he might have got up to is his business, but it would surprise nobody if he sometimes operated in a few grey areas.' There was no point in trying to deny Dom's past. The trick was to focus on his present.

'And you condone that?'

'I don't condone anything that involves breaking the law.' Carlyle kept a straight face. 'Anyway, this is all a while ago, right? *Old* news. Dom has always had various strings to his bow, but he's been pretty much exclusively focused on his gallery for some years now. To the best of my knowledge, he's been completely straight for some time.'

'Talking about the gallery, do you know any more about what happened last night?'

'Only what you told me.'

'You haven't spoken to Dom about it?'

'No. I suppose he's been quite busy this morning.'

'You two go back a long way.'

'We started out on the force together.'

'Long time ago.'

'Almost forty years.'

'And are you still in touch with anyone else from Hendon?'

'One or two people.'

'Silver didn't stay on the force long, did he?'

'No. I think the miners' strike put him off. Straight after Hendon we had the dubious pleasure of being sent up north to do hand-to-hand combat with the NUM.'

'Ah, yes, picket-line duty. That must have been a formative experience.'

Don't try to psychoanalyse me, sunshine. 'It wasn't what we signed up for.'

'So, he packed it in when you got back to London?'

'You're better off talking to him about that.' The waitress finally arrived with their drinks, unceremoniously slapping the bill on the table before leaving. The message was clear: *It's*

99

coming up to the lunchtime rush, so drink up and be off with you.

'I'll get this,' Bernie offered.

Carlyle almost choked on his coffee. 'There's a first time for everything, I suppose.'

Ignoring the barb, the journalist reached for the bill. 'I'm old enough to remember the miners' strike, Arthur Scargill and all that. It can't have been much fun having to deal with that shower.'

'It was a kind of civil war,' Carlyle reflected, 'the boys in blue versus the enemy within.'

'And Dom didn't agree with using cops to break the strike?'

'I don't think he was making any kind of political statement.' Carlyle was happy to let the conversation meander through the valleys of ancient political history. 'To be honest, I think he was just a bit bored as a constable. He wasn't sure what he wanted to do, but he knew he wanted to do something different. And he wanted to be his own boss.'

'Was Silver already dealing drugs at that time?'

Carlyle started to push out his lips, then stopped himself, fearing it was becoming an indicator of a lie slipping from his mouth. 'No idea.'

Bernie lifted an eyebrow. 'You never did drugs?'

'Once or twice.' A little truth sprinkled among the lies.

'Was Dom your dealer?'

'I never had a dealer. I was just a kid, experimenting. The usual kind of stuff. It was no big deal, like trying a cigarette. I never really got into it.' He remembered Bernie's fondness for dope. 'Not like you, anyway.'

The reporter looked mildly pained. 'I've given that up, too.'

'Jesus, you must have no vices left.'

'Getting back to *you*. According to Dom Silver—'

'Look,' Carlyle snapped, 'don't try to play us off against each other. Just put your cards on the table and we'll see where we go

100

from there.' When Bernie didn't immediately respond, he added, 'I'm out of here in five minutes. This is the only chance you're going to get.'

'Righty-ho, cards on the table.' Bernie took a deep breath. 'I know that Dominic Silver killed Tuco Martinez. And I know you helped him.'

ELEVEN

A decade on, there was a limit to what he could remember. There was a limit to what he wanted to remember. They had crossed the Channel on a sailboat hired under a fake name. Renaissance man Dom was quite the sailor, as it turned out. Dom's reptilian sidekick, Gideon Spanner, was also very capable on the high seas. Carlyle, for his part, got drunk and tried not to be sick.

Standing near the stern of the yacht, Dom and Gideon were pulling on what looked like black jumpsuits. A third lay crumpled at their feet. Dom looked at Carlyle. 'Get this on.'

A beacon of light appeared overhead, briefly illuminated the sky, then disappeared. 'What's that?' Carlyle asked.

'The lighthouse. Nothing to worry about.' Dom picked through a selection of weapons.

Gideon nodded at Carlyle. 'What about him?'

Dom tossed Carlyle a gun. 'Here.'

Carlyle caught it by the barrel, relieved that it hadn't gone off. 'What is it?'

'A Beretta. Why? Do you have a preference?'

'No,' the inspector admitted sheepishly.

Dom looked him up and down. 'Have you ever used a gun before?'

Carlyle acknowledged that he had not.

'Jesus.' Dom shook his head. 'What kind of a cop are you?'

The lair of Tuco Martinez was a long, low building that radiated decay and malevolence. To his relief, Carlyle was ordered to stay outside while Dom and Gideon headed in. After what seemed like an eternity, there was a muzzle flash from a darkened window, followed by another.

When it was clear no one was coming out, Carlyle reluctantly approached the house. Inside, he found his comrades in a filthy room, chained to a metal ring driven into the floor. Standing over them, grinning like a lunatic, Tuco Martinez was wielding a machete.

'Shoot the fucker,' Dom demanded.

Taking the Beretta in both hands, Carlyle planted his feet apart, like they did in the movies, pointing the gun at a spot he hoped was somewhere near the middle of Tuco's chest.

Unperturbed by the new arrival, Tuco turned to Dom. 'So you brought your bastard flic, too, huh?'

'Put down your weapons and lie face down on the floor.'

'You're not in London now, you metrosexual ponce,' Dom wailed. 'Fucking do him.'

'Okay, okay, just stay calm.' Tuco lifted his hands in the air and took a careful sideways step away from his prisoners.

'Throw your weapons towards me,' Carlyle commanded.

'Sure. Anything you say, Mr Policeman.' Arching his back, Tuco heaved the machete towards Carlyle's head. The throw was wild, high and wide. Standing his ground, the inspector kept his weapon trained on the Frenchman.

'John, for fuck's sake, get on with it.'

Carlyle heard the pure, unadulterated fear in Dom's voice. 'Don't worry, I've got it all under control.' As the words stumbled across his lips, Tuco reached for the gun stuck in the waistband of *his trousers. A jolt of adrenalin surged through Carlyle's chest. Gripping the gun as tightly as he could, he pulled the trigger.*

Nothing happened.

Fuck. What now?

'The safety!' Dom screamed. 'The fucking safety!'

'Shit.' As he fiddled with the switch above the grip, Tuco aimed for his head. Flinching, Carlyle closed his eyes and yanked the Beretta's trigger once, twice, three times.

What's gone and what's past help should be past caring. Carlyle watched Bernie reappear from the insalubrious confines of the café's tiny lavatory. The old Bernie wouldn't have managed to squeeze inside but the new slimmed-down version had just about managed it. After paying at the till, the journalist returned to the table and dropped back into his seat. The place was pretty much full now and the look of anguish on the waitress's face at their reluctance to leave spoke volumes.

'You looked like you were deep in contemplation.'

'Just thinking about universities,' Carlyle lied. 'My daughter wants to go to Imperial. I'm taking her for a look round next week.'

'Good choice,' was Bernie's verdict. 'My brother went there.'

'Oh?' Sensing internship possibilities for Alice – or, at least, a reference for her course application – Carlyle's ears pricked up.

'Yeah. He's an honest-to-God nuclear physicist. The black sheep of the family. Works in the States.'

Bugger. So much for that plan.

'I couldn't really tell you what he does.'

'No.'

The waitress appeared at the table and scooped up their empty cups. 'Will you be having lunch?' she asked pointedly.

'We're just leaving,' the two men announced in unison.

Hardly mollified, the woman stalked off.

'Cheeky cow,' Bernie muttered. 'I left her a big bloody tip as well.'

It was time for the commander to speak up. 'You were asking about Andy Wick?'

'From what I hear, the chief inspector was quite a character. As things stand, he's shaping up to be a whole article in this series on his own.'

'Series?'

'Yes. Francesca, the woman who set up the Investigation Unit, wants to do a multi-part series on the corruption and conflicts of interest at the heart of modern-day policing. Basically, a compilation of all the bad behaviour we can find. Fran's had a bit of a hard-on for you lot ever since her eldest son got arrested on some demo. He got a month in Pentonville for pissing on a police dog.'

'Nice.'

'The lad was high as a kite at the time.'

'Obviously.'

'He ended up doing a week inside but, according to Fran, the poor snowflake has been traumatised for life. I think she had to send him to the Priory in the end. Anyway, you can't have any kind of conversation with her, these days, without the subject of police brutality coming up. Not that it's all bad news – she's commissioned me to do half a dozen articles. It's gonna take me the best part of a year.'

Jesus fucking Christ. The commander contemplated the prospect of being brought down as a direct consequence of some doped-up little wanker relieving himself on a K9 officer. You just couldn't make this shit up. 'I can help you with Wick.'

'Thanks, but that one's going to write itself.' Bernie rummaged in his pocket and came up with a packet of fags. You've still got some bad habits then, Carlyle noted. 'The Dalai Lama story is my favourite.'

'I haven't heard that one,' Carlyle admitted.

'When the Dalai Lama came to town, Wick oversaw his security. While His Holiness was in powwowing with the Prime Minister, our hero slipped into the bogs to do a couple of cheeky lines of Charlie with one of the catering staff at Number 10. He gave the guy half a gram in exchange for a blow-job.'

'Allegedly.'

'Allegedly.' Bernie's tone suggested that the ultimate truth of the tale didn't much bother him, one way or another. 'It's guys like that who keep me in business.'

'What does the man himself say?'

'He's keeping schtum. Gone to ground.'

'Maybe I can track him down for you.'

'Maybe.' Bernie looked less than convinced.

Before the commander could say anything further, the wait-ress reappeared. Behind her stood a couple of hungry-looking hipsters, each of whom had a laminated menu in their hands.

'Time to go, gentlemen.'

'All right, all right.' Bernie pushed himself up. 'But this is no way to treat a loyal customer, not to mention a generous tipper.' Sticking a cigarette between his lips, he sauntered towards the door. The waitress glared at him as she ran a wet cloth across the top of the table.

Slinking away, Carlyle followed Bernie out onto the street. 'Let's keep talking,' he suggested, buttoning his coat.

'Sure.' Bernie lit his smoke and took a deep drag. 'I'll get back to you on the Tuco Martinez thing.'

The commander stepped away from the plume of smoke drift-ing towards him. 'There's nothing coming out soon?' he asked.

'Nothing planned in the short-term,' the journalist conceded, taking another puff.

That's something, at least. Noticing a plastic bottle top at his feet, Carlyle kicked it into the gutter.

Bernie glanced down the street at a line of cyclists racing

towards a red light. 'You know how these things can change, though.'

Perching on the kerb, Carlyle decided to play another card. 'One final thing. If you're sorted on Wick, there might be something else.'

Bernie looked at him through a cloud of cigarette smoke.

'I was wondering –' Carlyle coughed '– have you ever looked at a guy called Vernon Holder?'

TWELVE

What had he done? Was it murder, or self-defence? Shoving the empty whiskey bottle under his arm, Carlyle stuck his head out of the cabin and scowled at the grey morning. He had not slept a wink on the journey home. The Jameson's hadn't been able to stop his mind running in various directions all night, but at least it had helped him forget some of his physical aches and pains.

They drove back towards London in silence, stopping at a service station for some breakfast. 'Job done,' Dom pronounced, through a mouthful of doughnut. When Carlyle expressed his doubts, he added, 'I know you're worried that you've crossed the Rubicon. Gone over to the dark side, or whatever. But it's not like that. Think of all the shit you've had to deal with over the years. It's all one big grey area. This is no different.'

A very dark shade of grey, Carlyle thought.

'In difficult situations you have to make choices. Big boys live with the decisions we make. We have to.'

'Commander?'

Carlyle opened his eyes to see a worried Linda standing in front of his desk.

'Are you all right?'

'Just thinking.'

'Your visitors have arrived.'

'My visitors?'

The look of concern on his PA's face deepened. 'Mr Cosner and Mr, er, Gosh, something like that.' Flustered by her inability to pronounce the names, she quickly added, 'They're here for the Project Scimitar meeting.' Carlyle eyed the Project Scimitar file, which remained on his desk, unread. 'I've put them in Drake on the eleventh floor.'

Reaching for the file, the commander slowly got to his feet. 'I guess I'd better go and see them, then.'

Two smartly dressed men sat in the gloom of the meeting room, their conversation petering out as we walked through the door.

'I don't think things are so bad that we can't afford to pay the electricity bill.' Carlyle switched on the light.

'Commander, thank you for agreeing to see us.' The younger of the two belatedly got to his feet and extended a hand. 'I am Gregory Cosneau, head of security at the ICBRS.' He signalled to his colleague, who rose slowly from his chair. 'And this is Khaldoon Ghosn.'

Carlyle shook the hand of each man in turn. 'My apologies on behalf of my colleague, DAC Mara, for her non-appearance today.' He invited them to return to their seats. 'She was hoping to be here, but she had to take another meeting at Buckingham Palace at very short notice.' He dropped in 'Buckingham Palace' as if it was of no more note than a serviced office on Victoria Street.

'Affairs of state,' Cosneau observed.

Affairs of overtime, more like, Carlyle mused. 'I imagine so. The deputy assistant commissioner didn't share the details with me. I know, however, that she was very disappointed at her inability to avoid this most unfortunate diary clash. I will make sure that she has a full update on our meeting before the end of the day.' He had decided that an excess of honey was in order, if he was to get these gentlemen out of the building in the shortest possible time. It was also important to make it clear that this ball was being kicked straight back to Mara. As far as the commander was concerned, this was going to be two meetings in one – his first *and* last Project Scimitar gig.

'There's no need for any apologies. We are very grateful for your time.' Cosneau was somewhere in his mid-thirties, with just the slightest suggestion of grey in his anthracite hair. He had the vigorous, well-heeled look of a member of the international elite – he could have originated from just about any major metropolis around the world. 'I received a message from the deputy assistant commissioner's office last night. I know that she's incredibly busy at the best of times.'

'As are we all,' the commander pointed out.

'We appreciate you standing in for Michelle on this matter. I'm sure you will be a more than adequate stand-in.'

Michelle? 'I'll do my best.'

Ghosn theatrically looked at his watch. 'Maybe we could get started.'

'Yes, indeed.' Carlyle took a seat opposite his guests. 'Michelle made it clear to me that this is a matter of the highest priority.' Whatever it is. He wondered if he should at least have glanced at the file before making his appearance.

Cosneau passed a business card across the desk. 'It's good to know that the authorities are taking the matter very seriously.'

'As they should.' Ghosn focused on a point on the wall behind the commander's head. Considerably older than his colleague, he exuded a mix of the careworn and the experienced. Cosneau might take the lead in the meeting but Carlyle had a sense that Goshn was the more important of the two.

Picking up the business card, he confirmed that ICBRS stood for International Corporate Bank of the Red Sea. 'Perhaps you could begin by giving me a brief overview of the structure and aims of Project Scimitar and what the police service can do to help you.'

Cosneau's expression wavered slightly as he realised that the commander hadn't done any homework. Sitting back in his chair, he folded his arms. 'Project Scimitar is the informal name given to an initiative that the ICBRS has been coordinating with various interested and invested stakeholders in response to the most unfortunate upsurge of attacks on Arab citizens here in London in recent months.'

What 'upsurge' of attacks? Carlyle saw all the stats. Data flooded across his desk on a daily basis. And they told him that London was one of the safest cities in the world. There was certainly no evidence of increased anti-Arab activity. Now, however, was no time to quibble. 'We are aware of the issue and it is a priority for us.' How many times had he used the word 'priority' already? He made a mental note to revert to something else. 'This type of criminal activity is completely unacceptable, and I know that DAC Mara – that *we* want to send out a strong message that it will simply not be tolerated.'

'It is all very troubling,' Cosneau agreed, 'but, with the right action, I am sure that we can put a stop to it.'

'Only last month,' Ghosn growled, 'a senior diplomat was robbed at gunpoint, after he withdrew more than three million pounds in cash from the Edgware Road branch of the ICBRS, barely three minutes' walk from where we are sitting right now.'

'I remember that,' Carlyle lied. What kind of genius walks around with that kind of cash? he wondered. Talk about asking for trouble.

'Three masked men ambushed the man's driver as he carried the cash to his car. They put a gun to his head. It was brazen beyond belief.'

'Shocking.'

'The money belongs to Prince Bader Goyalan.' Ghosn paused

to allow the commander to appreciate the importance of the name. 'You understand who he is?'

Not a clue. 'Yes, absolutely.'

'The Diplomatic Protection Group were on the scene within minutes,' Cosneau added, 'but the robbers successfully made their getaway. They are still to be located.'

Carlyle cleared his throat. 'I'm afraid I'm not actually responsible for the DPG.'

Khaldoon Ghosn fixed the commander with an irritated stare. 'This is not simply a diplomatic issue. It is all to do with a lack of basic policing. The British police are supposed to be the best in the world. That's what we are told, time and time again. But the evidence suggests a rather different story. Whenever there is an incident, they let our people down. I have to wonder if this is not further evidence of your famous "institutional racism" in which only white people matter.'

Not at all, Carlyle reflected. We can ignore white victims too.

'Only the other day there was an even more outrageous incident where—'

Cosneau placed a calming hand on his colleague's arm. 'We are not looking to make any kind of political point, Commander. All we want is that people – our people – can have the greatest confidence in London as a place to live and work. That means having confidence in the effectiveness of the local law-enforcement agencies. As you will see from the file material, a range of cases – muggings, hotel robberies, even armed attacks – all have one thing in common. The victims are Arabs.'

Rich Arabs, Carlyle noted. This wasn't about race at all. It wasn't about cultural differences, or religion or anything else. It was about *money*. Wherever they came from, the wealthy always imagined that the police existed solely to do their bidding.

'As you can imagine, this is causing a great deal of distress to our citizens, not to mention considerable negative press in the Middle East. No one wants to feel that London is no longer safe. We have to show that all action is being taken to stop these attacks.'

'Some arrests would be a start,' Ghosn added grumpily.

'Quite.' Cosneau couldn't hide his displeasure at this latest interruption. 'But the point of Project Scimitar is wider than that. The bank, along with a small number of other sponsors, has agreed to fund the project's different workstreams, so that we can make some progress on the outstanding cases and explain to the Middle Eastern community what we're doing to make this a safe city again.'

There were so many things wrong with such an arrangement that Carlyle didn't know where to begin. 'DAC Mara is on board with all of this?'

'In principle, yes.' Cosneau waved a hand in the air. 'We're still sorting out a couple of the details, but we're hoping to launch the project formally in the next month or so.'

'What is it that I can do for you right now?' Carlyle asked politely.

'Fuad Samater and Obeid Idris,' Ghosn growled. Pulling a pen from his pocket, he scribbled the names on the back of his visitor's pass and slid it across the table. 'We are interested in speaking to these two gentlemen as a matter of some urgency.'

Carlyle picked up the slip of paper and studied the names. 'These guys stole the three mil?'

'We want to speak to them,' Ghosn repeated.

Carlyle's brow wrinkled in confusion. 'Isn't that my job? To question suspects?'

'There is a wider list of names,' Cosneau put in, 'some of which the Diplomatic Protection Group already have – individuals we feel may be involved in creating the current unfortunate situation. I will send you a copy and—'

Ghosn cut across his colleague. 'These two are the most

important. Samater and Idris are the ones I want us to locate as a matter of urgency.'

'All right.' Not wishing to find himself landed with a crappy PR job, the commander's only concern was how he might immediately escape the room. 'Let me see what I can do.'

Standing on the street, Gregory Cosneau watched Khaldoon Ghosn light a match and spark up a cigarette. 'Why did you do that?'

'Do what?' Ghosn coughed, letting the match fall to the pavement.

'Why did you tell that cop about Samater and Idris?'

'Because the bastards have gone to ground. We need all the help we can get in finding them.' Ghosn took a long drag on his cigarette. 'Our usual sources have come up with precisely nothing, so far. There's no harm in seeing if the police can turn anything up. I'd be amazed if they're any use, but you never know. That cop – what was his name?'

'Commander John Carlyle.'

'Carlyle.' Ghosn rolled the name round his tongue, clearly not liking the taste. '*He* couldn't care less – you could see it in his eyes. We should have waited until your girlfriend could take the meeting.'

'Michelle's not my girlfriend.' Cosneau eyed Khaldoon Ghosn warily. Ghosn was a legend, but he was a bitter man, well past his prime. 'And, anyway, she can't guarantee we get the money back. No one can.'

'The money is insignificant.' Ghosn took a series of rapid puffs before flicking the cigarette into the gutter. 'We're dealing with something far more important here.'

'What did these guys steal?' It was the question Cosneau had been dying to ask since members of the security services had first appeared in his office.

'Trust me, you really don't want to know.' Ghosn's phone started to ring, putting a stop to any further questions. 'Speak.' Listening to the caller, he stepped away from Cosneau. 'Are you sure about this? . . . No, I know it cannot be one hundred per cent . . . Yes, it was the right thing to tell me. If the information is correct, you will be paid well. Let me know immediately if you hear anything else . . . Yes. Indeed.'

Cosneau watched Ghosn put the phone back into his pocket. 'What was that about?'

'A tip – better late than never, as the English like to say.' Ghosn looked thoughtful. 'Maybe we can get this done ourselves, after all.' He dismissed Cosneau with a wave of his hand. 'You go back to the bank. If I need you, I will call.'

'And the prince?'

'You should be more worried about Mansour Hayek.' Mention of Prince Bader Goyalan's consigliere caused Cosneau to blanche slightly. Ghosn began walking down the street. 'If we do not retrieve the situation, he will not be in a forgiving mood.'

THIRTEEN

Sipping a glass of Merlot, Carlyle studied Peter Gabriel, *circa* 1974. 'Even I'm too young to remember that,' he muttered to himself.

Mr Gabriel was unmoved.

Feeling a presence at his shoulder, the commander turned away from the photograph.

'I wondered if I might find you here.' Michelle Mara pointed towards the throng in the adjoining room with her glass. 'On the edge of things, as usual.'

'I'm not really into these events,' Carlyle admitted, 'but I do like coming here. Apart from anything else, it's nice to know that the commissioner can still find the money in the budget to hire the National Portrait Gallery for a drinks reception.'

'I'm sure he gets a special deal.' The deputy assistant commissioner's eyes sparkled in a manner that made him wonder how many glasses of wine she'd already put away. The gossip was that Mara was a bit of a party animal, but he hadn't heard any suggestion that she had a problem with booze. Certainly, there was nothing in her face that suggested she was drinking too much as a matter of routine: she was a handsome woman with an air of solidity that you would expect – or, at least, hope for – in a senior police officer. 'After all, his sister-in-law's the director here.'

'I didn't know that,' Carlyle said.

'She's here tonight.' Mara stifled a hiccup. 'Interesting woman. I can introduce you, if you'd like.'

'It's okay.' Carlyle already had one eye on the exit. 'How was your trip to the Palace?'

'Oh, God.' Mara took a sloppy slurp from her glass. Carlyle politely looked the other way as wine splashed on the parquet flooring. 'They kept me there for more than three hours while we played out the usual pantomime. I explained the unrealistic demands being made on the Royal Protection Unit, they pretended to listen, I caved in and promised not to make any cuts in the service.'

'These people.' Carlyle gave a sympathetic cluck. 'They always get what they want.'

'That's where you're wrong, John.' Mara waved her glass in the air. 'They always want *more*.' She mentioned the name of a royal adviser. 'After I'd rolled over, this unctuous little sod, a footman or something, well, not a footman but, you know, a flunkey of some description, tabled this proposal to *increase* the RPU budget by twenty per cent next year.' She shook her head in disbelief. 'Where on earth am I supposed to find the money for that? These people – they just don't have a clue. They don't live in the real world at all.'

Carlyle was pleasantly surprised by her bluntness. He suspected that Mara was basically okay, at least when she was pissed. 'They're not supposed to, though, are they?'

Her face crumpled in confusion. 'They're not supposed to what?'

'Live in the real world.'

'Good point. They do push their luck, though. If the Federation get wind of the special treatment being meted out, they'll go bananas.'

'They'll moan,' Carlyle suggested, 'but, in the end, the union'll probably be happy about *any* budget being increased.'

'Maybe.'

117

'Will the RPU budget actually be increased?'

'Dunno,' Mara admitted. 'That's above my pay grade. The commissioner will have to decide.'

'He's still waiting for his knighthood, isn't he?'

'That's a good point,' Mara replied. 'So, I suppose the RPU will get more money. And everyone else will have to pay for it.'

A waiter appeared with a bottle in each hand. Carlyle signalled that he was fine, but Mara eagerly accepted a refill. As the man retreated, the commander tried to point her towards a buffet that had been set up at the far end of the room. 'Want to get something to eat?'

Mara watched the rows of red-faced journalists jostling in front of the trays of beef Wellington. 'I'll pass. I'm going out to dinner later. How did the Project Scimitar meeting go?'

'Fine.' Carlyle gave a quick factual summary of the discussions with Gregory Cosneau and Khaldoon Ghosn. 'Ghosn seemed quite grumpy about the whole situation, but Cosneau was more engaging. He seems a very nice guy.' Did Mara blush a little? Maybe it was the booze. What do we know? Carlyle asked himself. The pair were on first-name terms; Mara was single (divorced, twice); Cosneau hadn't been wearing a wedding band. Could Mara and Cosneau be getting it on? It was certainly possible. Carlyle liked to poke fun at Helen for jumping to conclusions about other people's relationships but that didn't mean he wasn't above doing it himself. He pushed a little more. 'How did you come across him?'

'Well,' Mara took a moment to compose her story, 'we met at a charity dinner a year or so ago. Greg also helped organise his bank's sponsorship of the COPS Children's Weekend this year.'

'A very good cause,' Carlyle agreed. Care of Police Survivors was a charity supporting the families of officers killed in the line of duty. 'What's his background?'

A look of mild concern crossed Mara's face as she was put on the spot. 'How do you mean?'

'It was hard to place him. He seemed a bit . . .' the commander struggled to find the right word '. . . *generic*.'

'He's an interesting guy.' Knowing that she couldn't feign total ignorance, Mara tossed out a few facts. 'Lebanese mother and a French father. Lived in London for most of his adult life. Very well plugged into the Middle Eastern community here. And, obviously, his job requires considerable engagement with the police service.'

'Obviously.' Again, Carlyle wondered just how far any cooperation had gone. 'And what do you know about Ghosn?'

'I don't think I've met him.' Stifling a yawn, Mara swayed slightly. 'I certainly don't remember the name.'

'Ghosn was the guy who gave me the names to check,' Carlyle growled, 'the cheeky bastard. It was like I was a private consultant and he was my client.'

Mara raised a carefully pencilled eyebrow. 'Which names?'

'Fuad Samater and Obeid Idris.' Carlyle was quite pleased with his powers of recall.

'And who are they?'

'Dunno,' Carlyle confessed. 'I haven't checked.'

'Well, get on it, first thing tomorrow.' Mara handed her glass to a passing waitress and began moving towards the door. 'Let me know what you find out, along with a memo on how you intend to execute Project Scimitar.' Smiling, she disappeared into the crowd before he could register any complaint.

'Fuck.' Carlyle scowled at Peter Gabriel. 'You don't have to put up with this kind of crap, do you?'

The singer remained silent.

Niamh gave Fuad a cheeky grin. 'Let me get another bottle from the fridge. Sort yourself out – you'll find a Durex in my bag.'

119

'But—'

Niamh put a finger to her lips, telling him to hush. 'You should know the drill, lover. No condom, no chance.' Chuckling to herself, she disappeared in the direction of the kitchen.

'Aw.' Reaching across the bed, Fuad grabbed the red leather shoulder bag sitting on the bedside table and began rooting around inside, like a five-year-old at a lucky dip.

'Are you sure they're in here?' Digging deeper, he pulled out a business card. 'What's this?' He frowned.

'What?'

'This card. It says "Niamh Sligo, Fashion Consultant".'

'That's my new business card. Do you like it?'

'Nice.' Fuad ran his thumb across the embossed gold lettering. 'But I thought your name was Grieg?'

'That's my married name. When the divorce comes in, I'm going back to Sligo. In the meantime, I need to get back into the swing of working life.'

Fuad dropped the card back into the bag. Would his sessions with Niamh be as much fun when she was no longer married? Somehow, he doubted it. Then again, chances were that their little fling would be over long before the final papers came through. Sticking his hand back into the bag, he finally came up with a packet of three Real Feels.

The blurb on the back of the packet promised 'a next generation non-latex condom for a natural skin-on-skin feeling'. Removing one of the foil-covered rubbers, he asked, 'What does a "fashion consultant" do anyway?'

'Do you really want to know?'

Fuad looked up to see Niamh framed in the doorway, a bottle of champagne in one hand, wearing nothing but a smile. Looks like she's been busy with the Lady Shaver, he noted. 'Haven't you got those boxers off yet?' Squirming across the sheets, Fuad hastily obliged.

Placing the bottle on the carpet, Niamh crawled onto the bed, taking the condom from his hand. 'Lie back.' Pushing his legs apart, she ran her carefully manicured fingernails across his scrotum before flicking at the tip of his penis with her tongue. 'Is it clean?'

'Yes,' he lied.

'Good boy.'

'Arghymhph.' As he felt her mouth encase him, Fuad closed his eyes and tried to think of something that would stop him ejaculating in embarrassingly short order. For once, his mind obliged, focusing on an image of the driver who had been shot when they had taken down the convoy. When was that? Yesterday? The day before? Longer? Already it felt like months ago, years even, like another lifetime. He visualised the driver sprawled on the road, his blood seeping across the tarmac. As the scene unfolded in a kind of slow-motion, washed-out monochrome, he registered the disgust on Obeid's face. The bullets flew past their heads, cutting through the air, like in a sci-fi movie.

'What's wrong, baby?' He opened his eyes to see Niamh unrolling the condom over his softening member. 'Not in the mood?' She was trying to sound encouraging, but Fuad could see the irritation in her eyes. He reached out between her legs, but she pushed his hand away. 'No fingers. I don't need another infection.'

'No.' Fuad again closed his eyes, this time trying to focus on something that might make him hard. His brain settled on his go-to image of Gabriella on all fours, her skirt pushed up over her haunches as he pumped her from behind. He was faintly embarrassed to be fantasising about Obeid's girlfriend, but Gabriella was hot, and she invariably got the job done. He felt Niamh manoeuvre him inside her, shifting her weight as he began to thrust upwards. After a few moments, they began to establish a rhythm. Digging his fingernails into her buttocks, his thrusts began to quicken as she leaned forward, whispering encouragement in his ear.

Just as he started to come, there was an enormous crash, followed by the sound of male voices. Niamh fell off the bed and began to scream. Fuad opened his eyes to see two men standing in the doorway. Dressed in dark suits, with white shirts and matching ties, they looked like something out of a Tarantino movie. The *Reservoir Dogs* effect was completed by the handgun that one of them had pointed at Fuad's crotch.

'It looks like someone's going to die happy.' Jamal Alsukait smirked.

Fuad was too scared to try to cover himself. He glanced at Niamh, who was now whimpering on the carpet. 'Shut up.'

Niamh's only response was to resume screaming.

Jamal turned the gun on her and casually pulled the trigger.

Khaldoon Ghosn stepped into the room, the dismay obvious on his face. 'Was that really necessary?'

'The bitch wouldn't shut up,' Jamal reasoned.

'You don't even know who she was.'

There was a defiant gleam in Jamal's eye as he tried to brazen it out. 'Does it matter?'

'Not now,' Khaldoon Ghosn said grimly. This really was the final straw. He was going to do everything he could to get the idiot dropped from his team at the earliest opportunity. 'We need to get out of here before the cops turn up.' He turned to Fuad. 'Get dressed.'

They were not going to kill him, too. Not here, anyway. Adrenalin surged through Fuad's body and he had to fight the urge to laugh hysterically. Wiping himself with a sheet, he scrambled from the bed, shimmying into his boxers as he reached for his jeans.

'Do you know who I am?' the older man asked.

Fuad shook his head. It was half true: he didn't know the guy's name, but he had to be one of Prince Bader Goyalan's henchmen. Obeid had predicted they would come after them. But to have been found so quickly? That was a most unpleasant surprise.

'We want the material you stole from us.'

'I haven't stolen anything from anyone,' Fuad protested, pulling a T-shirt over his head.

'Boy, you are as bad a liar as you are a lover. Where is Obeid Idris?'

'Who?'

'Don't lie to us.' The younger guy waved his gun in front of Fuad's face.

'Jamal, calm down.' The older man picked up a down jacket from the floor and threw it at Fuad. 'Come. We need to move. Now.'

FOURTEEN

Walking down Cork Street, Carlyle found the Molby-Nicol Gallery closed. A small sticker in the bottom corner of the newly replaced front window advertised the services of a 24/7 glazing company, and a security grille had been installed on the inside of the glass. Across a poster advertising the Sigmund Kessling exhibition someone had written 'REOPENING SOON' in black marker pen. Pressing his nose against the glass, the commander peered inside. The gallery itself was dark but the door at the back was ajar and he could see a light coming from inside Dom's office. Pressing the doorbell for a couple of seconds he stood back and waited. His finger hovered over the bell a second time when Dom's head finally appeared round the office door. Recognising Carlyle, he gave a cheery wave and signalled that he would be there in a minute. The commander wasn't best pleased to be left waiting on the street but managed to offer a thumbs-up before Dom ducked back inside.

In the event, the best part of ten minutes had passed before Dom reappeared to unlock the door. 'You took your time.' Carlyle paused the game he had been playing on his phone.

'Sorry.' Dom stood aside to let his visitor in. 'I was talking to the insurance assessor.' Relocking the door, he led the way into the back.

'How's that going?'

'You know what it's like. Everything's a matter for negotiation. The buggers will always try to wriggle out of things. It's in their DNA. If it wasn't for the fact that I'm required to have cover to put on shows, I would self-insure.'

The commander looked around the empty walls. 'That would be rather expensive in this case, I should imagine.'

'I could afford it. Anyway, if you compare it to the premiums over ten or twenty years, I'd still come out ahead.'

'I see that you've revamped the security already.' Carlyle gestured over his shoulder at the new shutters.

'Everyone likes closing the stable door after the horse has bolted. Still, you can't afford to let something like this happen again.'

Moving into the office, Carlyle dropped into the chair facing Dom's desk. 'Still no word on who did it?'

'Investigations are, as they say, ongoing.' Dom didn't spell out just whose investigations he was referring to. It crossed Carlyle's mind that Dominic Silver might not be the best choice of art dealer to rob. Dom sat down behind his desk. 'Meantime, I'm going to further beef up security by installing a night-watchman.' He pointed at the ceiling. 'There's a small studio they can have upstairs, so if you know someone it could be quite a good deal.'

Carlyle immediately thought of Daniel Hunter. The ex-military policeman was homeless, broke and *very* credible. Heading for a military prison, however, he was unlikely to be available for some time.

'If I'm going to stay in business,' Dom went on, 'people have to know that this was a one-off. Anyway, it will help keep the insurance premiums down. From that point of view, it will more than pay for itself.'

'I'll let you know if I've got any ideas.'

'Thanks. We'll need to have someone in place by the time we reopen next month.' Opening a desk drawer, Dom pulled out a bottle of whisky and two shot glasses. Placing the glasses on the table, he offered the bottle to Carlyle. 'Have a look at this.'

Reaching across the desk, Carlyle took it and inspected the label. 'Svensk Rök?'

'"Swedish Smoke". I tell you what, it's not half bad.' Retrieving the bottle, Dom removed the seal, unscrewed the cap and poured out two generous measures. Handing one to Carlyle, he lifted the other in a toast. 'Onwards and upwards.'

'Onwards and upwards.' Taking a cautious mouthful, Carlyle let the whisky linger on his tongue before swallowing.

'Nice, eh?'

'Excellent.' If anything, it was a bit *too* nice. Carlyle told himself he should stick to just the one.

Dom showed no such restraint, knocking back a full measure and immediately refilling the glass. 'I've got a container load of Sigmund Kessling works being shipped over from Canada.'

Carlyle relaxed into the chair. 'I'm a bit surprised that Mr Kessling is happy to give you more of his work.'

'I don't suppose he is,' Dom savoured another taste of the Swedish Smoke, 'but that doesn't matter.'

Carlyle raised an eyebrow.

'When his agent told him about the robbery, Siggy had a massive heart attack, dropped down dead.' Dom snapped his fingers. 'Just like that.'

'Bloody hell.'

'People have been waiting for him to die for years. His selling price is expected to double. Ironically, the robbery will push prices up, too.'

'Good to know there's a silver lining to all of this.'

'Basic law of supply and demand,' Dom pointed out. 'In some ways, the art business is far more ruthless than the drugs game.'

'In some ways.'

'Although people tend not to shoot each other over a painting.'

'The very definition of civilised.'

'So much of life is just a matter of chance, unintended consequences. Look at what's happened here. Someone drives through my window, steals my stock, and suddenly I'm looking at a nice windfall profit. It's almost as if I planned it.'

Carlyle stiffened. 'You didn't—'

'Certainly not. Apart from anything else, the hassle's immense. Plus I had no idea there would be more Kessling paintings coming my way. Fortunately, he had a barn full of pictures that no one knew about. Otherwise we'd have been stuffed.'

'When will you reopen?'

'That depends on how quickly the bureaucracy gets dealt with. Right now, the family can't get the estate wrapped up fast enough. They want to get a deal done on death duties before the taxman realises what the haul may be worth and takes them to the cleaner's. Then they'll ship it all over to me and we'll have the first major retrospective of the final works of the late Sigmund Kessling.'

'Sounds like you've got it all sorted out.'

'I know it sounds a bit mercenary,' Dom conceded, 'but it's all the family's doing, it really is. From what the agent tells me, they all hated the old man.'

'But they can't wait to get their hands on his cash.'

'Makes it all the sweeter, I suppose.'

Carlyle finished his drink and, ignoring his own advice, helped himself to another. 'Whatever happened to the idea that everybody loves you when you're dead?'

'Looks like poor old Sigmund Kessling is going to be the exception to that particular rule.'

Three large ones later, Carlyle contemplated the half-empty whisky bottle with dismay. I'm drunk, he mused, not daring to try to get out of his seat. Helen's not going to be happy.

'I'm still going to catch the bastards who did this.'

'Huh?'

'I'm going to get them.'

Dom looked to be holding his booze better than the commander. Then again, Carlyle reflected, there was more of him to absorb it. 'You don't want to be getting all vigilante on me.'

Dom reached for the whisky. 'Another?'

'Nah.' Carlyle held up a hand. 'I've had enough. I'd better get home.'

Putting the cap back on the bottle, Dom returned it to the drawer. 'By the way, what did Bernie have to say for himself?'

You should have got down to business earlier, Carlyle thought, and admonished himself as he struggled to recall the details of his conversation with the journalist. Bernie Gilmore was the reason he'd come here in the first place.

'You did speak to him, didn't you?'

'Yes, yes, but we didn't discuss much of substance, other than his weight-loss programme.' Carlyle explained about the hack's gastric band.

'That doesn't bear thinking about.' Dom groaned. 'What did he say about Tuco?'

'Not a lot. We danced around the issues for a while. As I suspected, the bottom line is he's willing to trade.'

'He'd better be,' Dom muttered grimly, 'for his sake.'

Not catching his friend's eye, Carlyle hoped this was just the whisky talking.

'What about his source?' Dom asked.

'I was never going to get him to tell me that.'

'Well, it isn't Gideon. I went to see his aunt. He's still travelling. Last time she heard from him, which was about a month ago, he was in Cambodia.'

Carlyle pushed out his lips. 'They have phones in Cambodia. Email.'

'Yeah, but come on. Bernie would have to know about him,

find him and get him to talk. This is Gideon. The guy only ever opened his mouth if it was absolutely necessary. And even then, only when he was in the mood, which wasn't very often.'

All points well made, Carlyle had to acknowledge.

'And why would he stitch us up? Gideon was solid. He *is* solid. Totally solid.'

'So it's not Gideon.' Getting ready to take his leave, Carlyle sat forward in his chair. 'Whoever it is, they clearly don't have enough for Bernie to rush into print. He was happy to tell me he doesn't have much.'

'He has Tuco's name.'

'He has the name,' Carlyle conceded, 'and he knows about his son being arrested in London.'

'Alain Costello.' Dom stared into his glass. 'He must be the source. I'd hoped we'd seen the back of that little bastard.'

'There's no reason to assume that that's not the case.' Carlyle tried to sound convincing. 'All Bernie has to go on are the two names and the clippings on Tuco's death. It's like he's missing nine hundred and ninety-eight pieces of a thousand-piece jigsaw. He's not going to be writing anything about Tuco any time soon.' He explained about the proposed series of articles on police corruption. 'Bernie promised to let me know if he gets anything more.'

'And you believe him?'

'Yeah. Apart from anything else, he'll want a quote.'

'We'd need to move before then.'

It suddenly felt extremely hot in the room. 'Don't worry, it won't come to that. There's plenty of low-hanging fruit to pluck before he gets to us.' Carlyle mentioned a couple of the more salacious scandals that had hit the Met in the last couple of years. 'And his number-one priority is writing the definitive piece on Andy Wick.'

Mention of the errant chief inspector seemed to cheer Dom

somewhat. 'That would be more of a job for the Marquis de Sade than Bernie bloody Gilmore.'

'You know Wick?' Carlyle stifled a burp.

'Yeah, quite well. He was a good client of mine for ages – in my old job, obviously.'

'Obviously.'

'The drug hadn't been invented that Andy didn't like.' A dreamy look appeared on Dom's face as he headed down Memory Lane. 'And, once he got off his face, he could be very entertaining. There was this one time—'

'Sorry, but I've heard enough Andy Wick stories already.' Carlyle struggled out of his chair. 'I need to get going. I'll keep you posted on Bernie, but it looks like he's got his first victim in his sights and it's not us.'

'I wonder if he's got the story about the community support officer and the police Alsatian?' Dom ran his tongue along his lower lip. 'If Wick's finally going down, I'll happily give him a push if it helps get Bernie off our back.'

Trying not to gag, Carlyle stumbled towards the door.

'Hold on,' Dom called after him. 'I'll need to let you out.'

FIFTEEN

At last, some sun. Feeling more than a little pleased with himself, Obeid Idris scratched at his trunks and sipped his beer. Wet, grey London was a world away. Life was good.

Idris's gaze fell on the copy of the *Miami Herald* lying open by the side of his sun lounger. On the World News pages was a short profile of Prince Bader Goyalan. Under the headline *A New Power Broker Emerges in the Middle East*, a photograph showed the prince shaking hands with the President of the United States.

Somewhere overhead the not-so-distant sound of an airliner told Idris it was making its descent into Miami International. From behind his sunglasses, he watched as a lithe blonde completed a lazy lap of the swimming pool and pulled herself up the ladder on the near side. As the woman emerged from the water, he couldn't help but notice that she was wearing the smallest thong imaginable. Hovering on the lip of the pool, she cast around for an audience. Moving directly into his line of vision, she vigorously shook the water from her hair. Making a conscious effort to keep his tongue in his mouth, Idris hastily crossed his legs as he watched her saunter towards the poolside bar.

'Are you staring at that woman's ass?' Propped up on the neighbouring sun lounger, Gabriella arched an eyebrow.

Idris cleared his throat. 'Just watching the world go by.'

'You know what they say, sweetie. You can look but you can't touch.'

His attempt to come up with a witty reply was cut short by the harsh sound of Run the Jewels coming from his phone. Ignoring Gabriella's disapproving stare, Idris reached for the handset and squinted at the screen.

Fuad.

'How's it going, man?'

All he got by way of reply was a howl of pain.

'Fuad?' Jumping from the lounger, Idris moved out of earshot of his girlfriend. 'Speak to me, man.'

A cool voice said: 'We have him.'

'Who is this?' Idris walked past the blonde at the bar and made his way inside the hotel. Conscious of his accelerated heart rate, he looked around the lobby. By the lifts a couple of fat tourists were sharing a joke. Otherwise, the place was empty.

'You were surprisingly easy to find.'

'Who is this?'

'Who do you think?' the caller shot back. 'I'm one of the people you ripped off.' It was the voice of an older man. Idris strained to pick out any details that might help him recognise the location of the caller, but it was a futile exercise.

'What do you want?'

'Don't play games with me. You know what we want. You need to return everything you stole from us.' The man paused. 'Well, not everything. You can keep the money. We're not interested in that. We just want the pictures on the phone you stole. *All* the pictures. And any copies you might have made. I'm assuming you didn't take the phone on vacation, so I'm giving you three days to bring them to me in London.'

Idris looked over his shoulder, checking that Gabriella had stayed by the pool. 'And if I don't?'

'If you don't, your young associate here will die.' In the background there was another scream.

That wouldn't be the end of the world, Idris reflected. He liked Fuad – a lot – but, at the end of the day, their relationship was just a business partnership. And business partnerships were terminated all the time.

'And then,' the man continued, 'we will kill Gabriella. Finally, we will kill you.'

That would be more problematic, the last bit at least. Idris tracked the blonde from the pool as she walked through the lobby, a mojito in hand. 'If I die, you won't get anything back.'

'Maybe not, but your death will be a reasonable consolation prize.'

Idris caught the blonde's eye as she reached the elevators. 'Prince Bader Goyalan would still be facing a difficult dilemma. He wouldn't thank you for killing me if you haven't recovered the phone.'

'That's my problem. I'm not going to negotiate. You have three days. I will be in touch.'

Call over, Idris considered his options. Out by the pool, his beer would have gone warm. In the lobby, a ping signalled the arrival of the elevator. As the doors opened, the blonde shot him an enquiring glance as she stepped inside. Smiling, Idris jogged over before they closed behind her.

'So that's it?' Jamal Alsukait whined. 'We have to sit around here for the next three days, babysitting this idiot?' He aimed a kick at the cowering car-jacker.

Placing Fuad Samater's phone carefully in his jacket pocket, Khaldoon Ghosn looked at Mansour Hayek, as if to say, *See what I have to put up with?*

Not in the least bit interested in Ghosn's concerns, Prince

Bader Goyalan's special adviser smiled blandly. 'This Obeid Idris, who is he?'

'A professional criminal. A man with certain skills who likes to prey on easy targets.'

'And we were an *easy* target, Khaldoon, with you looking after us.'

'As you are aware, I had to operate under certain conditions. We used the same route we had taken many times before. I had advised that we needed to vary the arrangements.'

Hayek tapped impatiently at the stained concrete floor with the leather sole of his shoe. 'Will he come?'

'I believe so,' Ghosn said stiffly.

'All right.' Hayek turned to Jamal. 'You can shoot him.'

A strangled cry climbed out of Fuad's throat as he tried to struggle to his feet. Pulling his revolver from the waistband of his trousers, Jamal looked to Ghosn for confirmation of the order.

'That would be premature. We still need him.'

'I don't think so.' Hayek started towards the door. 'He has served his purpose. Or do you want to sit in this cellar for the next seventy-two hours in the hope that Idris will deliver?' Having said his piece, he disappeared into the corridor.

Licking his lips, Jamal flicked off the safety. Taking a step backwards, he pointed the gun at their captive's head.

Too weary to argue any further, Ghosn followed Hayek out of the room, not slowing his pace when he heard the muffled shot behind him.

Standing on the street, Hayek scratched the back of his neck. 'Is there a decent café nearby?'

'Sorry?'

'I want some tea.'

Ghosn laughed. 'Do you know where we are?'

Hayek contemplated the dilapidated neighbourhood. 'Not exactly.'

'This isn't Knightsbridge,' Ghosn pointed out.

'No, but still. I feel the need for a nice cup of tea and twenty minutes with the *Telegraph*'s Cryptic Crossword.'

'I would head back into town. We don't want to be too conspicuous around here.' Ghosn waved at the driver in the Range Rover parked twenty yards down the road. 'You enjoy your tea, we'll clean things up.'

'Very well.' Hayek sighed. 'I suppose I can start my crossword on the way.'

'You like your puzzles, don't you, Mansour?'

'I find it a way of refreshing the mind – it keeps me alert.' Hayek pointed towards the door from which they had just emerged. 'These youngsters, they spend all their time playing on their telephones. It's rewiring their brains and not in a good way.'

'I agree.' Ghosn didn't like digital technology any more than Hayek did: it made him feel old.

Hayek watched the Range Rover ease to a halt in front of them. 'They are either playing stupid games or they are photographing themselves doing disgusting things. Why do they do that?'

Without any children of his own, Ghosn felt unable to comment on the foibles of the younger generation.

'Some things should be kept behind closed doors.'

Yes, they should. 'The phone. What happens if we don't get it back?'

Hayek lifted his gaze to the grey sky. 'If the photos were to fall into the wrong hands the prince will have a very uncomfortable time. And we will all be out of work.' He turned to face Ghosn. 'Do you think he will deliver?'

'Idris? Why not? He won't want to spend the rest of his

135

days looking over his shoulder. He's already ahead on the deal. They cleared what, three hundred thousand in cash from the carjacking?'

'It was closer to double that,' Hayek corrected him.

'Then there's the money stolen outside the bank.'

'We have no reason to assume that was the same people. Anyway, the money doesn't matter. There's always leakage, but it can never be more than a drop in the ocean.'

'So, Idris can keep the money and we let him walk.' Ghosn scratched his chin. 'That sounds like a reasonable deal to me.'

'Let's hope you're right.' Hayek reached for the rear door handle. 'I suppose we'll know soon enough.'

'Good luck with your crossword.' Ghosn watched as Hayek clambered inside the Range Rover. As the vehicle drove down the road, he lingered at the kerb before reluctantly heading back inside.

Walking onto the deck, Obeid Idris dived into the pool, hoping that a couple of gentle laps would wash the smell of sex from his body. Emerging from the water, he held Gabriella's suspicious gaze.

'You've been gone a long time.'

'Work.'

'You're supposed to be on holiday,' Gabriella grumbled.

'You know how it is.' Burying his face in the towel, Idris tried to focus on an image of the athletic blonde on all fours in her hotel room. Instead, he came up with a mental picture of Fuad looking down the barrel of a gun. He had little doubt that the threat against his comrade's life was credible. For all he knew, Fuad might be dead already. After vigorously drying his hair, he let the towel fall at his feet. 'I might have to go back to London for a couple of days.'

Getting ready for an argument, Gabriella pushed herself up on her elbows. 'What?'

'Just for a couple of days,' he repeated.

'And what am I supposed to do, stuck here on my own?'

'Just chill and enjoy the rays. I'll be back before you know it.'

'Obeid—'

'I'll be as quick as possible.' Leaning forward, he kissed her gently on the lips. 'I'm sorry, but it has to be done.'

SIXTEEN

'Nice motor.' Pulling the door shut, Carlyle settled into the passenger seat and placed his paper cup on the dashboard. He had agreed to meet Alison Roche at the Tulchan Road mortuary, deliberately turning up twenty minutes late in the hope that the sergeant would have dealt with Chris Hallam, the pathologist, on her own. The commander had become less squeamish over the years, but he still had no desire to hang out with a bunch of corpses.

'Quite a collector's item by all accounts.' Ignoring his poor timekeeping, Roche mentioned a name, and some other automotive details that meant nothing to the commander, then invited him to move the cup. 'Make sure that doesn't leave a stain or Alex will go mental. It's almost like another child for him.'

Carlyle obediently recovered the offending object. 'I never had old Shaggy pegged as a petrol head.'

Roche glared at him. 'I thought you were going to stop calling him that.'

'Yes. Sorry.' It was more a ritual incantation than a genuine apology – Carlyle just couldn't help himself. Show a bit of interest, he admonished himself. 'How's he getting on?'

'Fine.' Roche seemed appeased by the minor show of contrition. 'He's working on the Andy Wick case.'

'Surely the Federation wouldn't want to go anywhere near that tosser,' Carlyle harrumphed.

'Everyone's innocent till proven guilty. Anyway, Wick's a member of the union – all his dues are paid up to date – so what can they do? They have to give him representation.'

'Alex and Andy. The A Team.' Carlyle sniggered.

'What are you saying?'

'Nothing, nothing.'

'The way you insist on taking the mickey out of my partner the whole time,' she reflected, 'people might think you were jealous.'

'Me?' Carlyle felt himself blush. 'Hardly.'

'You know what they say.' Roche's tone contained more than a little malice. 'There's no fool like an old fool.'

'I like to consider myself as more of a middle-aged fool, if you don't mind.' Carlyle laughed. The sergeant joined in, defusing the tension that had been building in the car.

'Anyway,' she said, once things had calmed down a bit, 'Alex isn't on his own. There's a team of seven lawyers looking after Wick's case.'

'They could have seventy lawyers on it but it wouldn't do the chief inspector any good. That guy is toast. And quite right too.'

'There but for the grace of God.' Roche gazed across the mortuary's car park.

'Whaddaya mean?'

Roche shot him a sideways glance.

'I'm nothing like Andy Wick.' Carlyle watched a small woman emerge from the mortuary building. Buttoning up her coat, she shuffled off in the direction of the nearby bus stop. 'Nothing like him at all,' he muttered, more for his own benefit than for Roche's.

'I wasn't saying you were.' Roche placed a hand on the steering wheel. 'I was just pointing out that we all have one or two skeletons that we'd rather keep buried.'

139

You can say that again. Carlyle took a deep breath. 'Speaking of skeletons, do you remember Alain Costello?'

Roche looked at him, her mouth forming a perfect O. A very attractive O. Carlyle hastily pushed that thought from his mind.

'Tuco Martinez's son,' he reminded her.

'I hadn't forgotten.' The colour ebbed from Roche's face as she sifted through a stack of unpleasant memories. 'What about him?'

'He's back in circulation. There was some kind of presidential amnesty and they let him out.'

'Some kind of *amnesty*?' Roche's face scrunched up in disbelief.

'Politics, budgets, all the usual crap. You know what the French are like.'

'You don't give people like him a free pass.'

'Whatever, he's out.' A call to the Police Attaché's Office at the French Embassy had confirmed that Costello had been free for almost six months. According to the Home Office, he wasn't on any watch list and was at complete liberty to enter the UK.

'And he's coming back to London?'

'There's a suggestion that Costello blames Dom Silver for the death of his father.'

'I should have known that muppet would be involved in this somehow,' Roche snorted.

'Tuco was shot in France, years ago now. The French authorities never arrested anyone for the crime.'

'I didn't mean Tuco.'

'It's not Dom's fault.' Carlyle focused on a crow dancing along the branch of a recently pruned tree. 'Looks like Costello's hired an investigative journalist to try to do a story that says the Met backed Dom in a turf war against Tuco.'

'By "the Met" you mean Commander John Carlyle,' said Roche icily.

140

The atmosphere inside the car was getting rather stale. Carlyle wound down his window a couple of inches and was rewarded with a blast of cold air. 'I was an inspector back then. It's all bollocks, but you can see how it could easily be moulded into a story about police corruption. Which brings us back to Chief Inspector Andy bloody Wick.'

'He's certainly not doing us any favours.'

'There are so many tales about Wick – it's easy copy.'

Roche agreed. 'Alex told me about Magnus Castledean.'

Carlyle made a face. 'Who?'

'A microscopic member of the royal family – something like seventy-fifth in line to the throne. A lotta people would have to die before he got his hands on the prize. Anyway, his party piece was to smear coke over his dick and have Wick suck it off.'

'Classy.' The commander wondered how much of the gossip was true and how much of it was just urban legend, doing the rounds because people wanted to believe it was true. Not that it mattered much, one way or the other. He made a mental note to feed that titbit back to Bernie. Every little helped.

'There's a video of it, apparently, complete with the money shot.' Roche shook her head in disbelief. 'And to think Wick was being talked about as a future commissioner.'

'Only by Wick.'

'He's gonna cause us a lot of grief.'

'He already has.'

'Anyway, what about Costello?' Roche asked.

'We'll just have to wait and see. I'll keep you posted.'

'Fine. But, remember, if the little shit were to get shot in the head while trying to evade arrest that would suit me just fine.'

Me, too. Carlyle glanced towards the mortuary. 'What's the verdict on Karen Jansen?'

'Don't you want to go inside?' Aware of Carlyle's visceral dislike of the slab, the sergeant gave him a sickly smile.

141

'Didn't you speak to Hallam already?'

'Chris is off today. But I spoke to one of his assistants. Poor old Karen was in great shape.'

'Apart from the bullet wounds,' Carlyle quipped.

'Quite. All things being equal, Hallam reckons she could've lived to a hundred.'

Could've.

'Her parents arrive tomorrow.'

'That's something for Inspector Thomson to deal with. How's her investigation going?'

'Slowly,' Roche admitted. 'There are some CCTV images of a van entering the building site where the body was located but the plates are fake and the vehicle itself hasn't been found. There was no night-watchman. The driver used a security fob and a key code to enter the site. The fob had been reported missing but not deactivated. We're looking into the site manager's background, but nothing yet.'

'Fair enough.'

'Thomson and I went through Jansen's flat,' Roche continued. 'A nice place in St John's Wood. Views of the cricket ground, but basically empty. The woman was no nest-builder.'

'And Vernon?'

Roche bit her lower lip. 'Thomson hasn't made the connection to Vernon Holder yet but it's only a matter of time.' She looked at Carlyle. 'We need to tell her.'

'First things first.' Carlyle invited her to start the car. 'Let's go and pay the old bastard a visit.'

SEVENTEEN

The departures board said Eurostar 9042 to Gare du Nord should be boarding in about twenty minutes. Roche's shift had been extended so she could babysit two French cops and their prisoner, Alain Costello. Waiting to take Costello back to Paris, Commissaire de Police Jean-Pierre Grumbach alternated between flirting with Roche and bitching with his partner, Lieutenant Ginette Vincendeau. Costello ignored the cops, playing a game on a PSP console despite his handcuffs.

'Why do you let him have that?' Roche asked.

'Keeps him quiet,' Vincendeau explained. 'Just like taking your kid on a trip.'

The sound of gunfire, rapid and precise, was followed by a moment of silence. Then the screaming started. People fled in all directions.

Raising her weapon, Roche began walking steadily towards the gunfire in search of a target. Vincendeau was down, her blood pooling on the concourse. Standing in the mess, apparently oblivious to the chaos, Costello was still hunched over his PSP. Looking beyond him, Roche identified the shooters. Two males, dressed in combat pants, sneakers and hoodies, wearing joke-shop masks.

Another volley of fire brought more screams. Knots of people cowered behind whatever cover they could find while others dashed for the exit. Over the PA system, a strangely seductive female voice: 'Can Mr Black please report to the station manager's office immediately? Mr Black to the station manager's office. Thank you.' The code for a level-one emergency incident.

Roche felt the acidic taste of vomit rising in her throat and swallowed hard. Where the hell was Grumbach? She answered her own question almost immediately as a clump of passengers scattered and she almost tripped over the commissaire's body. She regained her footing and screamed into her radio: 'We have two officers down.'

The gunmen were passing through the barriers, looking to make their escape through the guts of the station. It was too late to get a shot off. Costello, however, was barely five yards in front of her. 'Stop.' It was less of an order than a croak. Coughing up as much spit as her parched throat would allow, she tried again.

'Stop! Police!'

Still concentrating on his game, Costello walked slowly away.

Where the fucking hell was everybody? Roche wondered. In the distance, she could hear sirens. 'STOP!' she screamed, at the top of her lungs. 'POLICE. PUT YOUR HANDS IN THE AIR OR I WILL SHOOT.'

Costello broke into a casual jog.

'Fuck, fuck, fuck.' At this distance, a two-second burst from her MP5 would cut him in half. Suspect shot in the back while trying to escape: she could hear the jokes already. And what if she were to hit an innocent bystander? Fuck it. Closing her eyes, she squeezed the trigger.

Nothing happened.

Roche's brain felt like it was going into meltdown. The safety. The fucking safety. With trembling fingers, she flicked it off and took aim again. Costello was gone.

*

144

'What're you thinking about?'

'Huh?' Roche shook herself into the present. 'Nothing.' She didn't want to admit to having such a vivid flashback. Her disastrous stint in SO15 – Counter Terrorism Command – was best forgotten. Over the years, she had gone quite a way to convincing herself the whole thing had never happened, that it was just a false memory. 'I was just thinking about today's nursery pick-up.'

The commander glanced at his watch.

'Don't worry,' she reassured him. 'I've got plenty of time.'

'Right.' Carlyle started towards the door. 'Let's do this, shall we?'

Vernon Holder greeted the appearance of two police officers in his office with minimal fuss. Clearly, the businessman had been expecting such a visit for some time. Stepping into the room, Carlyle unbuttoned his jacket. The only illumination was a 60-watt light bulb hanging from the ceiling, and it took a moment for the commander's eyes to adjust to the twilight. 'Thank you for seeing us, Mr Holder. I am—'

'I know who you are.' Holder didn't offer a hand. 'So let's skip the preliminaries, shall we?' Although well into his sixties, Holder had the healthy glow of someone who was enjoying the benefits of regular exercise. The commander was reminded of Bernie Gilmore's similarly gaunt look. Everybody's on a bloody health kick. Pulling in his stomach, he vowed to take a trip to his local gym as a matter of some urgency, adding it to his mental to-do list, along with a reminder to check back in with the journalist about the progress of his Tuco Martinez story.

A secretary appeared in the doorway, seemingly poised to offer the visitors some tea, but Holder shooed her away, closing the door and retreating behind his desk.

145

'This is my colleague,' Carlyle continued evenly. 'Sergeant Roche.'

'The bag-carrier,' Holder scoffed.

Roche coloured slightly.

'Take a seat if you want.' Holder introduced the man sitting in the corner, balancing a cup and saucer on his knee: 'This is Ashley Cotterill, my lawyer.'

Cautiously lowering himself onto a shabby piece of office-surplus furniture, Carlyle gave the desiccated Saul Goodman-lookalike the most perfunctory of nods. 'You were expecting us, then?'

'Ashley just happened to be here,' Holder replied. 'He might as well sit in, to help ensure fair play.'

Carefully placing the cup and saucer on the carpet, the lawyer lifted himself from his seat and handed each officer a business card. Roche responded in kind.

'This is just a friendly visit,' Carlyle advised.

'There is no such thing as a friendly visit from you lot.' Holder's eyes narrowed, and his visage took on an altogether more lupine appearance. He looked from Carlyle to Roche and back again. 'How can I be of assistance to you, Inspector?'

'Commander,' Roche corrected him.

Holder offered Carlyle his congratulations. 'Our mutual acquaintance, Ronnie Score, always spoke very highly of you.' It was a very calculated wind-up. Ronnie Score was a bent cop, widely considered to be on Holder's payroll, until someone had shot him dead.

'Now that you've moved up in the world,' Holder continued, 'doesn't that make you rather too senior to be hassling the likes of me?'

'I like to keep my hand in.'

'That's always a good idea. Anyway, now that we're all up to speed with the latest developments, what brings you here?'

146

'Karen Jansen,' Roche announced.

'I read about that.' A reflective look passed across Holder's face. 'A very nasty business.'

Clearing his throat, Cotterill sat up in his chair. 'I am assuming that Mr Holder is not a person of interest in your investigation.'

You can assume what you like. Ignoring the lawyer, Carlyle addressed his host: 'Ms Jansen was an employee of yours.'

'She was.' Holder placed the palms of his hands on the table. 'And a very good employee at that.' He glanced at Cotterill. 'I was very sorry when she left us.'

'When was that?' Roche asked.

Cotterill didn't miss a beat. 'Last year, November the seventeenth.'

'He's good on the details,' Holder pointed out.

Cotterill took the plaudit as his due. 'Karen resigned in October and worked a notice period of one month.'

Irked at being spoon-fed irrelevant details, Carlyle inched the conversation forward. 'Why did she leave?'

'She didn't specify a particular reason.'

'And you were happy to let her go?' Roche asked.

'My business is like any other. People come and go. I don't take on indentured labour. Staff turnover is always an issue. Keeping good people is always a struggle. I made Karen a good offer to stay but she felt that it was time to do something new. There's nothing wrong with that. She was thinking about going home to Australia.'

'Never got there, though,' Roche put in.

'No. Very sad.'

'Any idea why someone would kill her?' the sergeant asked.

'None at all. Karen was a well-respected colleague. If I had to describe her in one word it would be "professional". I don't think she had any enemies. Certainly, no one that I was aware of.'

'She did your pimping for you,' Carlyle pointed out. 'I can

147

imagine that brought her into contact with a range of dubious characters.'

'Mr Holder runs a professional operation,' Cotterill interjected. 'It serves only HNWIs or UHNWIs, all of whom are properly vetted.'

Carlyle groaned. Now they were shoving bloody acronyms down his throat. 'And what are HNWIs?'

'High Net Worth Individuals,' Cotterill explained, 'and *Ultra* High Net Worth.'

'Rich people,' Roche translated.

'It doesn't matter who they are,' Carlyle snapped. 'They're still not above the law.'

Holder conceded the point. 'What makes you think that a former client was responsible for Karen's death?'

'It's just one possible line of enquiry,' Roche offered blandly.

'She does a lot of your talking for you,' Holder teased Carlyle. 'You're quite a team.'

Carlyle felt a stab of nostalgia for the old days in Charing Cross and wondered if it might be possible to get Roche transferred. He could do with a few allies in Paddington Green. 'So, what you're saying, Mr Holder, is that Karen Jansen's death was nothing to do with you?'

'Nothing at all, as far as I can see.'

'And you don't believe that a client could have been involved or that it could have been in any way business-related?'

'Well, I don't spend my time focused on the operational side of things, these days, but I wasn't aware of any particular issues. Karen never mentioned any specific concerns.'

'Who's doing Karen's job now?' Roche asked.

'I'm still looking for someone,' Holder answered. 'Why? Are you interested?'

Roche started to reply but Carlyle cut in: 'I don't imagine it's the kind of operation that runs itself.'

'We're getting by,' was all Holder was prepared to say.

'How's business?' the commander enquired.

'We're doing all right, not brilliant, not crap.' Holder kept his gaze on Roche. 'The clients are relatively recession-proof. In this business, it's more a question of the supply, rather than the demand. Getting the right staff and managing them properly is the main issue. That's why I paid Karen so well.' He mentioned a number that was a multiple of Carlyle's salary. 'She was worth every penny.'

Carlyle scratched his chin. 'You took over Harry Cummins' old business, didn't you?'

'Now there's a name from the past.' An amused look settled on Holder's face.

'It's not that long ago,' Carlyle suggested. 'Harry was one of your competitors – until someone shot him.'

'Shootings seem to be a recurrent theme of this conversation,' Roche chipped in.

'It's a dangerous old world,' Holder offered. 'What can I say? The thing about Harry, he was, first and foremost, a playboy. Me, I'm a businessman. And, no, I didn't take over his business. These days, it's run by his missus. Or, rather, she *owns* it. True, I run parts of it for her. But Victoria lives in the country, somewhere out by the Welsh borders.'

'We'll need an address,' Carlyle wondered if he could send Inspector Thomson off to the provinces to speak to the widow, 'and some contact details.'

'Ashley can sort that out for you.'

'And, while we're at it, we'll need to see your books.'

Cotterill started to protest but Holder cut him off: 'Be my guest. Everything is in order.'

'Finally,' Carlyle asked, 'where were you on the night that Karen was shot?'

'I need an alibi?'

'Everybody needs an alibi.'

'When was it?'

Roche gave him the date.

Thinking about it for a moment, Holder settled back in his chair. 'As it happens, I was playing in my regular poker game. I left at about two in the morning and went home to my dear wife. Won quite a few quid. It was a good night.'

EIGHTEEN

'That was a total waste of time,' Roche complained. 'The bastard told us nothing.'

'It's always good to see the whites of their eyes,' Carlyle suggested. 'And you did get a job offer out of it.'

'Very funny.'

'Good money, too.' The commander dodged a puddle on the greasy pavement.

'Crap prospects, though.' Roche recovered her sense of humour along with her car keys. 'Look what happened to the previous incumbent.'

'Hm.' Carlyle had to admit she had a point.

'I wouldn't want to end up face down in a building site.'

'No.'

'And, on a more mundane level, I don't suppose old Vernon would be too accommodating when it came to things like childcare and maternity leave.'

Carlyle watched her unlock the door on the driver's side. 'Are you and Sh– you and *Alex* going to have another, then?'

'None of your business,' Roche snapped. Reaching the car, she signalled for him to go round to the passenger side. 'I'll have to explain to Thomson what I've been up to this afternoon. What do you want me to tell her?'

'Just that you've interviewed Jansen's boss, her *recent* boss, and he's got an alibi.'

'And what about you?'

Carlyle's hand hovered over the door handle. 'What about me?'

Roche contemplated the decaying office block that housed Vernon Holder's HQ. 'How do I explain you coming up here?'

'Just leave me out of it for now. Let's see how things develop.'

'What's that supposed to mean?'

'It means that I know Holder is up to his neck in all of this. I just need a bit of time to *prove* it.'

Roche got inside the car. 'You seem to be forgetting this isn't your case.'

Settling in his seat, Carlyle fumbled with his seatbelt. 'Aren't I supposed to be the boss?'

'Yeah. Right.' Roche shoved the key into the ignition and the engine rumbled into life. 'Thomson will have a fit when she finds out what you've been up to – just like you would have done if Simpson had ever tried to do something like this to you.'

'My predecessor had a very different management style. I'm not so much of a meetings man.'

A solemn expression descended on Roche's face. 'It was a total bugger, what happened to her, wasn't it?'

'Yes,' Carlyle agreed sadly. 'Carole was dealt a shitty hand in many ways but that was definitely the worst of it.'

'Do you think she knew she had cancer? I mean when she resigned.'

'I can't see her having called it a day otherwise.'

'It must've been a hell of a shock.'

Carlyle didn't know what to say to that. 'It happens,' was all he could muster.

'I worry about that,' Roche admitted.

'About what?'

'About the possibility that we spend our whole lives working and keel over at the end of it, like some knackered donkey, you know?'

'Like some knackered donkey?' Carlyle laughed.

'You know what I mean.'

'Are you worried about your health?'

'No, not specifically. I mean I'm tired all the time, but who isn't? It's more than that. We run around on all these cases. Anyone could end up like Simpson – or like Karen Jansen for that matter. What's the point?'

'I'm not really the person to help with an existential crisis. It seems to me, you're sitting pretty – family, job, prospects and all that.'

'I suppose.' Roche sounded less than convinced.

'Plus,' he added, trying to inject some levity into the conversation, 'how many sergeants have got a commander at their beck and call, to help with their cases?'

'Truly I am blessed.'

'And, if I can help with your current investigation, what's wrong with that? I'm not going to steal your thunder. You and Thomson can have all the glory.'

With a snort of derision, Roche released the handbrake and eased away from the kerb.

A hundred yards down the road, stopped at a traffic light, Carlyle felt a headache building around his temples. He hadn't eaten for hours and he could feel his spirits plummeting, along with his sugar levels.

Peering through the window, he tried to locate a café. 'Fancy a coffee?'

'Don't have time. I'll have to drop you at the tube, I'm afraid.'

'Which station?'

'Whichever we come to next.'

That suited Carlyle well enough: wherever there was a station, there would be food of some sort.

The lights changed and Roche pulled away. 'Holder gave me the creeps. The way he looked at me . . .'

'Don't let him get to you,' Carlyle advised.

'Why've the Vice Squad never taken him down?'

'I think it basically comes down to something along the lines of better the devil you know. I'm sure that Ronnie Score wasn't the only cop he's paid off over the years and, as for the rest of them, well, the consensus was that we – "we" being the Met – could live with Vernon. The fear was that if he was taken down, he would only be replaced by someone worse.'

'God.' It wasn't clear whether Roche was groaning at the sentiment or at the driver of the grimy green Astra that shot out of a side road in front of them. As she stomped on the brakes, Carlyle nervously gripped the door handle.

'Whatever the reason, Vernon Holder has been a fixture of the London crime scene since before my time.'

Roche shot him a sideways look. 'Did you think he was untouchable?'

'I never had any reason to go after him.'

'That doesn't sound much like the John Carlyle I know.'

'You can't chase all the buggers.' Carlyle watched in dismay as they slipped past a nice-looking café. 'You've got to pick your battles.'

'What?' Roche scowled. 'Even after Umar was shot?'

'Umar Sligo was the architect of his own downfall.' Carlyle noticed that he had a broken thumbnail. He started nibbling at it.

'That's a bit harsh.'

'Not at all,' Carlyle muttered, from behind his hand. 'Our esteemed colleague had a good job, a wife and a young child. He threw the job away and abandoned his family. He ended up working for that posh scumbag Harry Cummins, which allowed him to indulge his taste for booze and pussy at every opportunity.' He grimaced at his infelicitous use of the P-word. It was not the kind of language Helen would let him get away with at home.

'So that justified someone shooting him, did it?' A tube sign appeared up ahead and Roche began looking for a spot where she could pull in. 'Is that why you didn't go on one of your personal crusades to find the killer?'

Personal crusades? 'As you will recall, Ronnie Score tried to frame me for the murder of Umar and his unfortunate girlfriend.'

'I remember that well.' Roche parked the car between a flower-delivery van and a minicab. 'After all, who was it who had to get you out of your prison cell?'

Releasing his seatbelt, Carlyle gave a small bow. 'I'm very grateful to you – and to Alex.' He felt pleased with himself for using the young man's proper name for once. 'But, as you can imagine, that was a bit of a distraction. I had other things to worry about at the time, rather than who killed Umar. Anyway, even though the case was never formally closed, it's a decent bet that Score was the shooter. So, to that extent, the problem solved itself.'

'So that's what you think? Score killed Umar and Holder killed Score?'

'Something like that. More or less. Umar must have been an obstacle – real or perceived – to Vernon muscling in on Cummins operation. Score just outlived his usefulness. By that stage, he had too much on Holder. He was a loose end.'

'And Holder can get away with murder?'

'At the time, I think he probably did.'

'Do you think we'll really get him now?'

'We'll certainly give it our best shot.' Carlyle saw a couple of boys walking along the nearside pavement in their school uniforms. He hoped he hadn't made Roche late for collecting her son. He reached for the door handle. 'It's always been a long game with Vernon. This revenge is going to be served cold indeed.'

Roche stared grimly at the traffic in front of her. 'Revenge?'

'Well, I don't see Vernon going to jail. Do you?' Pushing open the door, Carlyle swung his feet out onto the pavement.

Eyes front, Roche kept her expression neutral. 'Maybe,' she mumbled, 'you can get your mate to do him.'

Carlyle froze.

'Dominic Silver. I hear he's good at that kind of thing.'

'That's just an urban myth,' the commander insisted.

Roche was about to say something when her phone, sitting in a cradle on the dashboard, started to ring. Squinting at the screen, the sergeant cursed as she stabbed at the receive button.

'Where are you?' a staccato female voice demanded.

Roche looked at Carlyle and mouthed, 'Thomson.' She spoke into the phone: 'I've just been interviewing Karen Jansen's boss or, rather, her ex-boss.'

'Well, I need you to get over here.' The inspector recited an address on Kingsway. 'We've got another.'

Glancing at her watch, Roche looked like she was on the brink of tears. Tears of frustration. 'Another?'

'Another body.'

NINETEEN

The orange and white banner fluttering in the breeze proclaimed that he was in Midtown. Until recently, the neighbourhood around Holborn tube station had survived perfectly well without a name. Now the crass rebranding operation extended to bowler-hat-wearing 'assistants' on the lookout for lost tourists to redirect towards the British Museum up the road. Worst of all, the area that the commander had long considered home was now attracting a steady stream of hipsters, on the lookout for a new part of the city to colonise as rents in east London continued to rocket. A dark mood settled on Carlyle as he walked past a newly opened club that was part of a chain originating in Shoreditch. If I wanted to live in bloody Hoxton, he fumed, I'd've moved there.

The address Thomson had given Roche was flagged by a uniform standing at the front door. The officer was posing for a selfie with a young Chinese tourist. As he approached, Carlyle recognised the gangly figure of PC Paul Dombey, an amiable figure from the Charing Cross station.

'Dombey.'

'Inspector – sorry, I mean Commander.' Disentangling himself, the constable attempted a salute while the girl took a few additional shots with her camera.

'No need for that,' Carlyle said. 'How're things?'

For a moment, the youngster seemed flummoxed by the

question. The girl gave him a wave as she headed down the street. 'In general?' he stammered. 'Or upstairs?'

'Either. Both.'

'In general, things are good. Upstairs, things are a mess.' Dombey shook his head. 'It had been really quiet for months and now we've got two at once – both shootings, as well.'

The commander looked along the street. 'Not had any journalists?'

'We had one TV crew earlier, but they didn't stay long. Not a lot to see, really, is there?'

'No.' Carlyle pointed at the glass door leading to a small lobby area and a set of lifts. 'Where is it?'

'Top floor. I was first on the scene, with Granger.'

'How is Granger?' Carlyle had a lot of time for Wendy Granger. She was one of those reliable, no-nonsense cops who would always be undervalued by the Met. 'Is she still into her fishing?'

'Big-time.'

'Good.'

'It's nice to have something that helps you relax,' Dombey said. 'You need something to take your mind off the job.'

'Yes,' Carlyle agreed, despite never having had a hobby in his life, unless you counted supporting Fulham. That was about as far from relaxing as you could get. Having done with the small-talk, he reached for the door. 'Is Granger still here?'

'She went back to the station about twenty minutes ago.' Dombey turned and punched a code into a keypad by the door. The lock released and Carlyle stepped inside.

'Inspector Thomson's in charge,' Dombey called after him. 'She's in a foul mood.'

On the eighth floor, Thomson looked suitably surprised by his arrival. 'What are you doing here?'

'I wanted to take a look.' Carlyle vowed not to let the inspector push him about. After all, he was the boss, was he not? He stepped over to the window. They were at the back of the building. Outside there was a small terrace and a view of Lincoln's Inn Fields. Carlyle recalled the time when some workmen had dug up a body in the square. That case had turned into a murder mystery going all the way back to the Second World War. Hopefully this would prove a lot more straightforward. 'We don't like people getting shot on our patch. This is a serious business.'

Thomson could only agree.

'Sergeant Roche gave me a call.' Carlyle recited the fib he had agreed with Roche earlier. 'She wondered if there might be any connection with the Jansen shooting.'

'There's nothing to suggest that, so far at least.' Thomson was just about managing to keep her irritation under control. 'Although I'm sure that when *my* sergeant turns up, we'll be able to pursue all avenues of enquiry.'

'She had to go and pick up her son.'

'I don't have enough manpower on this,' Thomson huffed. 'Do you know how many outstanding murder cases there are in London right now?'

'I'll get you some more bodies,' Carlyle promised.

One of the crime-scene technicians appeared at the door, nodding at Carlyle before addressing Thomson. 'We're ready to take her away.'

'Let the commander have a look first,' Thomson replied casually. 'After all, he knows her.'

'Sorry?' Carlyle looked at the inspector in astonishment.

'What are the odds? Two women shot to death in separate incidents and you're connected to both of them. If you didn't have an alibi, you'd be my prime suspect.' Thomson arched an eyebrow. 'You do have an alibi, don't you?'

Not wanting to get caught up in an argument between his superiors, the tech disappeared back down the hallway.

'Who was she?' Carlyle was not in the mood to be toyed with.

'Niamh Grieg.' Suddenly Thomson seemed to be enjoying herself.

Carlyle took several seconds trying to place the name before admitting defeat. 'And I know her?'

'Grieg was her married name. Before that, she was Niamh *Sligo*.'

'Sligo? As in Umar Sligo?'

'That's right.' Thomson started towards the door, beckoning him to follow. 'Someone popped your ex-partner's sister.'

TWENTY

The owner of the Erythraean café, a grumpy exile called Kateb, was not one for wasting money on heating. Shivering inside his coat, Carlyle contemplated a less than discreet neon sign for the International Bank of the Red Sea through the rain-splattered window.

'I didn't know that eggs, beans and toast was a speciality of Mediterranean cuisine.' Taking a sip of her peppermint tea, Roche watched the traffic struggling along the Edgware Road.

'I suppose you'd call it fusion food.' Carlyle shovelled the last of the meal into his mouth and washed it down with a mouthful of sharp coffee, as black as tar and almost as thick. He lifted his gaze inward, towards the counter. However, the rush hour was in full swing and the Lebanese café was doing a brisk business trade. Deciding it would be too much of a palaver to order another coffee, he remained in his chair.

Roche looked disdainfully at his empty plate. 'The last I heard, you were supposed to be on a diet.'

'What Helen doesn't know won't hurt her.'

'Oh, yes? And what else do you keep from your wife?'

'Nothing of any import.' Carlyle went on the offensive: 'Anyway, you should be more concerned with what Shaggy keeps from *you*.'

'*Alex* doesn't keep anything from me,' Roche snarled. 'He knows that if he did, I'd have his balls.'

'Happy families,' Carlyle quipped.

'Speaking of which, I never knew Umar had a sister.'

'He was always very coy about his family in Manchester and the reasons for his coming to London. I just think he was embarrassed about it all. He felt trapped and had to run away.'

'Sounds like Umar,' Roche mused. 'He was always good at running away from things.'

'I met the sister once. Umar and I were in a café just off Shaftesbury Avenue.' Carlyle was surprised by the vividness of the memory. 'She walked in and started having a go at him about a girlfriend in Manchester he'd dumped. The family had expected Umar to get married and she was trying to pressure him into going back up there. He was well on the way to marrying Christina by that stage.'

Roche rolled her eyes. The marriage of Christina O'Brien and Umar Sligo had crashed and burned with depressing predictability.

'She seemed a bit of a cow,' was Carlyle's final comment on the encounter.

'That's no way to speak of the dead,' Roche chided him.

Never one to sugar-coat his opinions, Carlyle offered an unsympathetic grunt. 'Speaking of which, what kind of mood is Inspector Thomson in today?'

'She's gone off to speak to Niamh's parents, thank God. They live somewhere in Cheshire. At least it means I can catch up with my paperwork in peace.'

Maybe we should swap jobs, Carlyle thought. You could have the meetings and the regular hours, and I could go back to being a cop. 'Why has she schlepped up there? Couldn't the parents come down here?'

'They're in poor health apparently.'

'So, get some plod up there to speak to them. After all, what're they going to say? "Oh, yes, Inspector, we know exactly who put a gun to our daughter's head and blew her brains out. And, while you're at it, here's the address you'll find them at."' He emitted a dismissive snort. 'Not very likely, is it?'

'Keep your voice down.' Roche glanced nervously at the diners occupying the nearby tables.

'Don't worry about it. Half the people in here are cops, and the rest don't speak English. Come to think of it, those two groups are not mutually exclusive.' He chortled at his own gag.

Roche looked around the café. 'Is this your new regular haunt?'

The commander gave the question some serious consideration. 'Not sure. It's got potential.'

'Finally,' Roche suggested, 'a replacement for Il Buffone.'

They both took a moment to remember the long-lost Italian café that had once stood opposite the Carlyle family home in Covent Garden.

'Do you ever hear from Marcello, these days?' Roche asked, referring to Il Buffone's owner.

'Not for a long while. Hopefully he's still enjoying his retirement in north London.'

'Hm.' Roche finished her tea, signalling that it was time to get down to business. 'Thomson seemed happy enough to go up to Manchester. She likes to give the impression of being busy.'

All too aware of the type, Carlyle looked suitably dismayed.

'Meantime,' Roche continued, 'we're waiting for the final ballistics report but, as things stand, there's no reason to suppose the two killings are connected. It looks coincidental.'

'If it is, it's a hell of a coincidence.' Carlyle recalled the wise words of Auric Goldfinger: *'Once is happenstance. Twice is coincidence. The third time it's enemy action.'* The commander

163

had the clear sense that there would be more bodies. The question was, who was the enemy? There was Vernon Holder, for a start. But who else? It was not a question he was going to answer sitting around amid the hookah pipes. He pushed back his chair. 'I need to get to the station.'

'Important meeting?' Roche smirked.

'Bound to be.' Getting to his feet, Carlyle recognised a couple of familiar faces. The two men from the Project Scimitar meeting had just walked in, accompanied by a third, younger, man. 'Bollocks.'

'Eh?'

'Nothing.' One of the men – the bank guy – caught his eye. Muttering something to his colleagues, he stepped over to the table.

'Commander.' Groomed to within an inch of his life, in a suit that looked like it must have cost thousands, Gregory Cosneau might have stepped from the pages of *GQ*. He cast an appraising eye over Roche.

'This is a colleague,' was all Carlyle offered.

'Excuse me, but I have to go.' Roche nodded at her boss. 'Thanks for lunch. I'll see you later.' Not waiting for a response, she fled.

'Good timing,' Carlyle suggested, keen to follow her. 'We've freed up somewhere for you to sit.'

'I was speaking with Michelle last night.' Cosneau took the chair Roche had recently vacated.

Pillow talk? Carlyle reluctantly sat back down.

'She says she's still waiting for your update on Project Scimitar.'

'I was aware of that.' Carlyle gritted his teeth. What the hell was DAC Michelle Mara playing at? Letting her boyfriend think he could use police resources to run his own private investigation. He seriously wondered about the deputy assistant commissioner's judgement. If this carried on for much longer, he'd have to think about making a formal complaint of some sort.

Cosneau seemed unaware that he was stepping over a line. Perhaps he just didn't care. He had the air of a man who considered himself a natural leader in a world where everyone else had been created simply to do his bidding. 'How are your enquiries going?'

'Things are coming along. As you might appreciate, there's quite a lot happening right now.'

'Ah, yes, the shootings. I read about them in the paper.' Cosneau glanced at his colleagues, who were still waiting at the counter for their order. 'Not good for your PR, is it?'

'I'm sorry?'

'Well,' Cosneau waved a hand in the direction of the street beyond the café window, 'crime out of control doesn't look good, does it? Bad for business, bad for tourism, bad for investment.'

Was the guy trying to wind him up? 'Crime isn't out of control,' Carlyle shot back. 'Two very unfortunate incidents in quick succession, it's just a coincidence, nothing more. London has more than eight million people. Thankfully, incidents like these are rare. It is a very safe city.' He just managed to stop himself saying 'unlike yours'. Apart from anything else, he didn't know precisely where the annoying git was from.

Seeing he had hit a nerve, Cosneau pushed further. 'These things are disconcerting, at least for members of the public. Ordinary people don't like to see a pattern emerging.'

'There is no pattern,' the commander snapped.

'I was thinking about a pattern in terms of a rise in gun crime, rather than about a connection between the two killings.' A flicker of something indecipherable flashed across Cosneau's face. 'I'm sure, like you say, they're not connected.'

'And *I'*m sure we'll catch the people responsible.'

Cosneau's amusement seemed to be rising by the minute. 'You sound very confident about that.'

'Why wouldn't I be? We have very high clean-up rates when it comes to murder.'

Carrying a tray of drinks and pastries, the younger man picked his way carefully between the other tables. Following him, Khaldoon Ghosn offered Carlyle a nod of recognition and sat down.

'The commander is investigating the shootings of those two poor women,' Cosneau explained. 'A most nasty business.'

Ghosn remained silent. The younger man placed the tray on the table and found himself a seat. Neither Cosneau nor Ghosn felt moved to make an introduction.

'We got you a coffee.' Ghosn handed Carlyle a small cup.

The commander graciously accepted.

Taking that as his cue, the third man grabbed a pastry. Ghosn glared at him before gesturing at the tray. 'Would you like something to eat, Commander?'

'I'm good.' Carlyle held up a hand, pleased by his self-restraint.

Ghosn handed Cosneau a drink, then reached for the sugar bowl sitting in the middle of the table. Retrieving two lumps of brown sugar, he dropped them into his own cup. Lifting his teaspoon, he began stirring mechanically. 'Did you find out anything about the two gentlemen we discussed previously?'

Carlyle downed his coffee in two swift gulps. 'Sorry?'

'Fuad Samater and Obeid Idris.' Ghosn lifted the cup to his lips and took a noncommittal sip.

Cosneau muttered something in a language that Carlyle presumed to be Arabic.

Mara had told him to check out the names. Carlyle made a mental note to get on with it. 'Not so far. These things can take a bit of time.'

'I think it's safe to say that these two gentlemen are no longer of such concern.' Cosneau kept his gaze on Ghosn as he spoke.

'We don't think they're operating in London, and we don't want to waste your precious time.'

'I appreciate you letting me know.' Getting to his feet, Carlyle shook hands with Cosneau and Ghosn. He ignored the younger man, who was still shoving cake into his mouth.

'Are you going to leave any for us?' Ghosn asked, irritated, as he watched the policeman head out onto the street.

'I'm hungry.' Jamal Alsukait wiped a large crumb from his mouth. 'That was the cop?'

'Yes,' Ghosn confirmed, 'that was the cop.'

'He doesn't seem much.'

'Michelle says he's a nobody who's been over-promoted.'

Jamal eyed another pastry. 'Who's Michelle?'

'Deputy Assistant Commissioner Michelle Mara – that guy's boss.'

'Gregory's girlfriend,' Ghosn sneered.

'One of many.' Cosneau patted his colleague on the shoulder. 'That's why I'm such a happy man.'

'White women are whores,' Jamal remarked casually.

'How would you know?' Ghosn gave the youngster a not-so-friendly clip round the ear. 'Don't be such an idiot. If I ever need your opinion on anything, I'll ask for it.'

Cursing under his breath, Jamal reached for another cake.

'And leave those alone.' Ghosn smacked his hand away. The youth really was insufferable. He would need to have another conversation with Mansour Hayek about having him replaced. Turning to Cosneau, he said, 'Idris is on a flight that is due to arrive at Heathrow in the next hour. We'll give him a couple of hours to sort himself out. If he hasn't been in contact by then, I'll have him picked up.'

'And if he doesn't have what we want?'

'If he doesn't bring us the phone,' Ghosn scowled, 'he will regret it.'

'What's so important about those damn photos anyway?' Jamal asked. 'For all you know, he could have posted them on some faggot website already.'

Cosneau sighed. 'There's no sign of that. I have two companies monitoring the web twenty-four/seven. They haven't come up with anything, so far. Anyway, think about it: if Idris put the images online he would destroy their potential value to him. They wouldn't be worth anything, would they?'

Jamal's eyes grew wide. 'He's a blackmailer?'

'Obeid is an *entrepreneur*,' Ghosn corrected him. 'If he has something of value, he will trade it. He didn't attack the convoy for the phone. He was after cash and the bearer bonds. The pictures were a bonus – a bonus on top of winning the lottery. He might just dump the phone. Or he might sell it back to the prince. Or, there are plenty of other people who would pay – and pay handsomely – for the photos.'

'Prince Bader Goyalan has a position to protect,' Cosneau observed. 'It goes without saying that those pictures could be very damaging.'

'He took it up the ass.' Jamal giggled. 'So what? This is the twenty-first century, is it not?'

This from the boy who had just described white women as whores. Ghosn couldn't get his head round it. 'Technically, sodomy is still punishable by death.'

'At home.'

'Where do you think the prince's political ambitions lie?' Ghosn scowled.

'The king is ninety-three now,' Cosneau explained. 'He's been in poor health for years. A month ago, he was admitted to hospital with pneumonia. The power struggle is already well under way.'

'Goyalan's uncle, Crown Prince Ziyad Alarab, is seen as next in line,' Ghosn added, 'but he has cancer and may not live long enough to take the throne.'

'That,' Cosneau predicted, 'will leave Goyalan fighting it out with his two cousins. One is famous for losing twenty million dollars in a single night at a roulette table in Nice, then taking the casino to court to try to get his money back. The other has rather unfortunate links to al-Qaeda.'

'The transition to the next generation of princes does not look particularly appealing,' Ghosn said, 'but Goyalan is in the driving seat – if he can avoid any scandal.'

'And if he can't?' Jamal scratched his chin. 'What happens then?'

'If the prince goes down, we all suffer,' Cosneau told him. 'Remember the kind of people we'll be dealing with. Idiots who declare fatwas against snowmen. They burn newspapers no one has ever heard of because they don't like the cartoons. Even if they didn't detach the prince's head from his shoulders, or sentence him to death by stoning, punishment will be harsh. Only the other day, a man was sentenced to three years in jail and four hundred and fifty lashes after he was caught using Twitter to arrange dates with other men. They found him guilty of promoting "the vice and practice of homosexuality". He was arrested following a honey trap by the Commission for the Promotion of Virtue and Prevention of Vice.'

'The prince should have left his phone at home,' Jamal suggested.

'The prince has so many phones,' Cosneu observed, 'he can't keep track.'

'He has doubtless forgotten the night in question,' Ghosn added, 'even if we haven't.'

'What does Hayek think?' Jamal asked.

'Hayek is like us,' Ghosn advised. 'He's a pragmatist. He sees this as a problem we have to resolve as quickly and quietly as possible.'

'His future depends on it as well,' Cosneau added. 'We're all in this together.'

Jamal picked at the crumbs on the plate in front of him. 'I guess that means the guy coming into Heathrow's gonna be one more body to dispose of.' He looked up at Ghosn.

'We'll see,' Ghosn replied, 'but I definitely wouldn't rule it out.'

Fuad Samater. Obeid Idris. Vernon Holder. Karen Jansen. Niamh Grieg, née Sligo. 'That's a fairly random list.' Pushing the sheet of paper away from his stomach, Carlyle reached for the only splash of colour in front of him. The postcard had arrived in his office that morning. Someone had dropped it into one of the reusable Manila envelopes used for internal mail. From the date on which it had been posted, it looked as if the missive had spent weeks, if not months, making its way around the building. The picture on the front showed an impossibly deep sunset over Ibiza. On the back, an excited scribble simply said, *Congratulations! When are you coming to visit? xx*

Carlyle spent a few moments remembering Susan Phillips, a glamorous ex-colleague who had retired to the Mediterranean to run a designer guesthouse. 'At least someone made it out of here alive,' he muttered to himself. What were his chances of persuading Helen that they should pay her a visit? Ibiza would make a welcome change from Brighton, their default holiday destination. His wife wasn't a great fan of sunshine – or of his ex-colleagues – but there was at least a chance that he would be able to talk her round.

Using two fingers, he started to type 'Fuad Samater' into the PND. Ten minutes later, he had established that the name was not to be found on the Police National Database. Grumbling to himself, he tried the second name that Khaloon Ghosn had given him. Carefully typing 'Obeid Idris' into the National Database, he hit send.

After 7.24 seconds the system brought up precisely . . .

nothing. The fixed-line telephone next to the PC started to ring. Ignoring it, Carlyle switched to the Europol Information System, typing in the name and hitting send. The phone fell silent. After approximately five seconds, Linda appeared in the doorway. The expression on her face reminded Carlyle of Mrs Gilloway, his fifth-form teacher, when he was trying to feed her some nonsense about why he hadn't done his maths homework.

'You're not answering your phone.'

'Huh?'

'DAC Mara's on the phone. She wants to speak to you.' Before Carlyle could start to protest, Linda added, 'She knows you're in.'

I wonder how. Carlyle liked Linda well enough, but her unwillingness to lie on his behalf was a shortcoming he would have to address, assuming he stayed in the job for any length of time.

'And she sounds a bit hacked off.'

'Put her through.' Linda retreated behind her desk. The phone chirruped and he lifted it to his ear, just as the computer screen suddenly flooded with data. 'Bloody hell.'

'Commander?'

'Yes, I'm here.' He quickly tried to digest the information in front of him while listening to his boss.

'You are a very hard man to track down.'

That was what Carole Simpson used to say. Carlyle grunted something noncommittal.

'And I heard that you missed a budgetary meeting yesterday.'

Quite possibly. 'I've been chasing up this Project Scimitar thing,' he offered.

'And?'

'And it looks like Obeid Idris, who your boyf–' he affected a minor coughing fit in an attempt to cover up his gaffe '– that the,

171

er, gentlemen from the Red Sea bank are interested in, is quite a character.'

'How so?' Mara asked coolly.

Carlyle picked out a few highlights from the list that had just appeared in front of him. 'It would appear he's ex-army, wanted for questioning in four different countries in connection with spectacular well-organised robberies targeting, erm,' – what had Vernon Holder's lawyer called them – 'ultra-high-net-worth individuals.'

'A military man?'

'Yes.' Given Daniel Hunter's stint with the Military Police, the commander wondered if Hunter might know Idris or, at least, have heard of him. Unlikely, he decided.

'Do you fancy Idris for the bank robbery?'

'No.' Unencumbered by any knowledge, Carlyle answered instantly. 'That seemed more a crime of opportunity. Or, at least, a quick smash-and-grab based on a tip-off. Maybe an inside job.' He paused to let Mara reflect on that for a moment. 'It seems too random for a guy like Obeid Idris. The whole thing was too risky – doing a job in central London, there are too many variables, too many things that can go wrong. Idris is a cool customer. His MO is for highly planned, military-style operations where as many of the variables as possible have been eliminated.'

'What about the other guy?' Mara asked.

'There's nothing on any of the databases about Fuad Samater.'

'Fine. At last you've made some progress. Keep digging.'

'Will do.' Did Mara know that her squeeze didn't seem interested in the two raiders any longer? Carlyle decided not to mention his conversation with Cosneau and Ghosn in the Erythraean café.

'And I still need a report. As soon as you like.'

TWENTY-ONE

A cat appeared at the empty window, jumped down and slowly made its way across the concrete floor. Tufts of fur were missing from the emaciated animal's back and it walked with a discernible limp. A pair of green eyes considered the two men in the derelict room with wary detachment. Having seen enough, the animal slipped through a narrow door in the far corner, heading deeper into the wrecked building.

'Let's get on with this, shall we?' Obeid Idris shivered in the chill air. Wishing that he was still in Miami, he took a final drag on his cigarette before flicking the stub in the direction of the door.

'I'm sorry we had to interrupt your vacation.' Khaloon Ghosn's face offered a vague facsimile of apology. 'But under the circumstances . . .'

Idris waved away his words. 'It's nothing.' Gabriella had stopped complaining when he had promised to take her to Disneyland on his return. Pulling a phone from his pocket, he tossed it to Ghosn. 'That's what you wanted, isn't it?'

'This is the one you took from us?' Tapping the screen, Ghosn flicked through a series of images, grumbling to himself as he did so.

'Why would I switch it? Those things cost more than fifty grand – if you can get your hands on one.'

'How can something that is so expensive be so ugly?'

Weighing the phone in his hand, Ghosn shook his head in disgust. 'A platinum phone encrusted with diamonds.'

'It looks more like a child's toy than anything else.' Idris remembered Fuad begging to be allowed to keep it. If he'd let him have the ridiculous phone, maybe the kid would still be alive. That, however, was a matter of pure speculation. And Idris wasn't the kind of man who wasted his time on speculation, pure or otherwise.

'At the last count, Prince Bader Goyalan had eight of the damn things.' Ghosn seemed genuinely upset by the fact. 'What a waste of money.'

'It's not your money, though, is it?'

'No, I suppose not.' Ghosn dropped the phone into his jacket pocket and took a step towards the door.

Idris felt his heart rate rising. 'My apologies for taking it in the first place. I was only after the cash. And the bearer bonds. I don't steal phones. And I'm not a blackmailer. I did not mean to cause His Highness any unnecessary stress over this.' He paused. 'No *additional* stress, anyway.'

'The prince is not aware that the phone was taken. As far as he is concerned, you only made away with the cash and cash equivalents. He has more important things to worry about.'

'Remind me to rob him more often.' Idris chuckled.

'Your people were pretty professional. It was a shame about the casualties, but I know that wasn't your fault.' A look of mutual respect passed between the two men. 'Sadly, some of my team can be a little trigger-happy.' Ghosn glanced in the direction of Jamal Alsukait, skulking in the shadows. The gun in the boy's hand unnerved them both. 'It was most unfortunate.'

'It can be hard to get good people.'

'Don't I know it. However, if you were ever looking for a new challenge . . .'

'I only ever work for myself.'

'I understand.' Ghosn's disappointment seemed genuine.

Idris moved on. 'I apologise for the deaths. I wish they could have been avoided.'

'We cleaned it up. There will be no follow-up from the local authorities. As far as they were concerned, it never happened. And the families will be compensated.'

'And the prince?'

'His Highness has the attention span of a goldfish. To the extent that it registered in his consciousness, he had forgotten about it by the time we reached the airport. Three hours later, he was partying. Hard. I don't think there will be any psychological damage.'

'Good.' Idris meant it. People who didn't care always made the best targets.

'That doesn't mean you can rob him again.'

Idris tried to look offended at the suggestion. 'Rest assured that I will not be coming after the prince again. That would be unfair. I like to quit while I'm ahead. I'm not greedy.'

'So, we have an understanding?'

'We have an understanding.' Idris pointed towards Ghosn's pocket. 'And you have evidence of my goodwill. When I realised what was on that phone, I was happy to return it.'

'We are done.'

'Yes,' Idris cleared his throat, 'but there was no need to kill Fuad.'

Stepping from the darkness, Jamal finally spoke. 'We didn't kill him.'

A look of profound irritation crossed Ghosn's face as he waved away the blatant lie. 'Everyone has made mistakes in this.'

'Yes,' Idris agreed.

'It is my turn to apologise to you.'

'Apology accepted.'

Ghosn patted the phone in his pocket. 'You've seen the pictures?'

Idris nodded. 'Not very imaginative.'

'But potentially very damaging. Why do you think he did that?'

'Men are simple creatures, however much money they have.' Idris recalled the quote from Oscar Wilde – *Everything in the world is about sex, except sex. Sex is about power.*

'The acts themselves, well, that is a matter of personal taste. But the need to photograph them? That I struggle to understand.'

'It is what young people do.' Idris shot another glance at the kid with the gun.

'The prince is not that young,' Ghosn pointed out. 'He should know better.'

'For sure he will need to be much more discreet if he is to succeed his grandfather.'

Ghosn raised an eyebrow. 'You know about that?'

'It's been in the newspapers – a curiosity for the Western media.'

'Did you copy any of the pictures?'

'Only the good ones.'

'That wasn't the deal,' Jamal Alsukait hissed.

'There are three sets of the best – or worst – images sitting on memory sticks,' Idris explained calmly, 'in different parts of the world. If anything happens to me, my associates will post them on a selection of carefully chosen websites. They should cause quite a stir.'

'He's bluffing. I should kill him.'

'Be calm, Jamal.' Ghosn groaned. 'We have a deal.'

Can the older man control his protégé? Idris rocked onto the balls of his feet. 'We do, indeed. I came across the pictures by accident. What consenting adults get up to is not my concern. As I said, I'm no blackmailer. It is just a prudent insurance policy on my part.'

'Indeed,' Ghosn agreed.

'He's bluffing,' Jamal repeated.

'Are we done?' Idris asked.

'No.' Stepping forward, Jamal raised the gun. 'I should kill him – like I did his little bitch.'

'Jamal.' Ghosn reached for the gun but the kid held it out of reach, his eyes shining.

Idris had seen enough. Skipping forward, he delivered a vicious kick to the boy's crotch.

'Ouuufff.' Jamal sagged but did not go down. A punch to the head saw him drop his weapon and a second kick left him on the floor, gasping for air. As Ghosn looked on, Idris picked up the gun. It was a simple semi-automatic, probably manufactured somewhere in Eastern Europe. Checking that there was a round in the chamber, he stepped over the body and shot a single round into the top of the skull. A hundred and forty decibels bounced around the room before escaping through the various exits.

'He must have been hard work.'

Ghosn waited for the ringing in his ears to die away. 'He was.'

'We still have a deal?'

'We do.'

'Just to be on the safe side . . .' This time, Idris used two bullets. Ghosn went down with a minimum of fuss. 'That was for Fuad.' Careful not to step in the blood seeping across the concrete, Idris squatted next to Ghosn. Slipping a hand into the dead man's pocket, he recovered the gaudy phone before heading for the door. There was still plenty of time to make his return flight to MIA.

TWENTY-TWO

Alain Costello looked up from the game running on his hand-held console. 'Your story hasn't appeared yet. Why is that?'

'Well . . .' Bernie Gilmore glanced nervously round the hotel room.

Costello wasn't interested in explanations. 'How hard can it be to write a couple of thousand words, eh, Ivan?'

Ivan, a heavy who looked like he would have difficulty writing his own name, grunted.

'I was aiming for more like six thousand,' Bernie pointed out.

'Very good.' The Frenchman looked like he was wasting away – a thin layer of skin stretched tightly over his skeleton – but his eyes were full of malevolent mischief. 'And how many have you actually written?'

'At the present time?'

Costello nodded.

'A few, probably. I'd have to check the precise number.' Bernie glanced at his watch. To add insult to impending injury, he was supposed to have a date. How long would Miranda, thirty-four, a history teacher from Finchley, wait for him to turn up? Half an hour, max, was his considered guess. Another dismal episode in his internet dating history loomed large. He was beginning to wonder whether the agency membership fee was £39.99 a month well spent.

'I'm sorry.' Costello's voice dripped with sarcasm. 'Am I keeping you?'

'I was actually on my way to meet another source,' Bernie lied, 'when your, erm, employee brought me here.'

'He was stuffing condoms into his wallet,' the oaf chortled.

'Yes, well . . .' Another £11.99 wasted. 'That was in relation to a subsequent engagement planned for later in the evening.'

Ivan laughed harder as he offered a brutal but fair critique of Bernie's chances of getting laid.

'I explained what I wanted.' Costello tossed the console onto an overstuffed sofa. 'You were paid to write about the cop.'

Bloody John Carlyle. That man had always been more trouble than he was worth. 'I am writing about the cop. But I have to do it properly. I have to get my facts right.'

'I gave you the facts,' Costello snapped.

'Yes, but I have to *verify* them.' A wave of self-pity swept over Bernie. He had hoped to be getting his knob polished. Instead he was having to offer up a lesson in Journalism 101. 'We only get one shot at this. My piece needs to be watertight. If it doesn't stand up, the guy will get away with it.'

Cursing, Costello ran a hand through his thinning hair. It would have been a lot easier to walk up to the cop and put a bullet in his brain. But his father had vetoed such simplicity. Anticipating his own death, the ever-paranoid Tuco had pointed the finger at Dominic Silver and his sidekick, the dirty cop, Carlyle and prescribed their punishment. *'If I go,'* he told his son, *'you can be sure that those two are the guilty men. And you, my boy, must be judge, jury and executioner. Kill them, but make them suffer. Do the cop first. If I die, I want to die with a smile on my face, knowing how much pain you will inflict on the bastards. That will be my revenge. Revenge from beyond the grave.'*

Yes, Father.

179

Sitting in his cell in La Santé, Alain Costello had worked out a plan that, he hoped, complied with his father's wishes. He had found Bernie Gilmore through a mutual acquaintance, a journalist on *Le Monde* who was deep in debt to Costello, thanks to the unfortunate combination of a bad cocaine habit and very poor judgement when it came to choosing winners at Enghien. A deal had been struck with the British journalist just as Alain was walking free with his presidential pardon.

'I've been paying you for almost a year now.'

'Proper *in-depth* investigations take time.' Bernie contemplated a stain on the front of his Smashing Pumpkins T-shirt. Post gastric-band surgery, it covered him like a tent. He really should update his wardrobe. 'You need to follow a careful process. I have consulted with many sources and I am now engaging with the principals.'

'*Quoi?*' The look on Costello's face suggested he was in no mood for Bernie's hack bullshit.

'I have to give Carlyle and Mr Silver the chance to respond to the allegations before my editor will agree to publish.'

'And what would your editor think if he knew I had paid you more than twenty thousand euros to write this long-awaited story?'

'It's a woman.' Bernie felt his face flush with shame. There was no way round it: his much-prized 'journalistic integrity' was shot to hell. At least the money – used for his stomach-reducing surgery – had been spent on something worthwhile. And once the medical bills had been settled there had been just enough for a week's much-needed R-and-R by a pool on Kalamata.

'What would *she* think?'

It was obvious what Francesca Culverhouse would think. If the Investigation Unit's founder ever caught wind of the fact that Bernie had been taking backhanders, she would have him out on his arse faster than you could say, well, faster than you could say, '*You're out on your arse.*' His reputation as a lion of fearless reporting would be instantly destroyed. His journalistic career would be over. The best-case scenario after that was that he would see out his working days as a shabby PR lickspittle for some obscure consultancy, a fate worse than death.

'I want to see something published by the end of the week, six thousand words.' Retrieving his console, Costello signalled that the meeting was over. 'Or there will be consequences. Serious consequences.'

Knowing better than to enquire as to what those might be, Bernie retreated towards the door. If he was to have the remotest chance of meeting Costello's deadline, he was going to have to get his finger out. First things first, though: if he could grab a cab, he might just be able to catch Miranda before she headed back to Finchley.

Alison Roche groaned. There were delays of one sort or another on just about every tube line. It looked like she was going to be late at the nursery again. As the sergeant grabbed her bag, her phone started buzzing. Her first inclination was to leave it. However, somehow, her free hand automatically reached into the bag, pulled out the handset and hit Receive.

'Yes?'

From the other end of the line came the sound of traffic.

'Who is this?' Hoisting the bag onto her shoulder, Roche headed for the lifts.

Silence.

'Hello?'

'Karen Jansen.'

The sergeant froze. 'What about her?'

'I know why she was killed.'

The male voice seemed familiar, but Roche couldn't quite

place it. She hesitated for a moment before turning and heading back to her desk. 'Why?'

Another pause.

'I can't tell you over the phone.'

Why the hell not? Roche felt profoundly irritated. 'Who is this?'

'Meet me in an hour. Where she was killed.'

The line went dead.

'Fuck.' Roche checked the screen, but the caller's number was unknown.

'Fuck, fuck, fuck.' She pulled up Carlyle's number. It took a few moments for the call to connect. Almost immediately, the commander's voicemail kicked in. Useless bastard. 'Call me as soon as you get this.' The next call was to Alex.

Happily, her rather-more-reliable partner picked up immediately. 'How's it going?' he asked cheerily.

'Look, babe, sorry to do this to you, but could you collect David for me?'

'Awwwwww. Come on. You were going to do that.'

'I know, but something's come up, something important. Sorry.'

'Bloody hell, Ali, I've got a meeting with Andy Wick in an hour. We're supposed to be finalising his defence today.'

Good luck with that. Roche never ceased to be amazed by the brass neck of the errant chief inspector. 'What defence?' She snorted. 'Temporary insanity?'

'Looks like we're going down the entrapment line,' Alex offered sulkily.

'I'm sure you can give it a miss. The Federation's put loads of people on the Wick team.'

'And I don't matter, huh?'

Taking a deep breath, Roche tried to get the conversation back on an even keel. 'Look, I'm sorry, but this is *really* important. I've got a lead on Karen Jansen that I need to follow up.'

'Get Thomson to do it.'

God give me strength. 'Thomson went up to Manchester on something else.' The inspector might have made it back by now, but there was no way Roche was going to hand this over. 'I wouldn't ask if it wasn't important.'

'Hm.'

'We could ask your mother.'

'There isn't time. I'll have to get going right now.'

Roche brightened as he conceded defeat. 'You'll do it?'

'I don't suppose I really have much choice, do I?'

'I'll make it up to you, promise.'

'How?'

'Well,' Roche chuckled, 'we'll have to think about that.'

It was business as usual at the building site where Karen Jansen had been slain. Lorries came and went, backing up the traffic, while the cranes overhead went steadily about their work. Standing by the entrance, Roche watched a four-man team pouring concrete onto the approximate spot where the body had been found. The foundations were being laid and the skeleton of the building would soon start rising out of the ground. In the end, the construction work had been delayed for less than twenty-four hours.

The site manager was talking to a couple of builders working a cement mixer. Looking up, he caught Roche's eye, before looking away. If he recognised the policewoman, he didn't let on. Unsure as to where to go, the sergeant gazed at the computer-generated images advertising the development that had been plastered to the wooden fencing surrounding the site. It looked exactly like a hundred others that were being thrown up all over London, with the usual eye-watering prices.

Studios from only £1.85m. Sales office now open. Talk to our on-site financial advisers.

£1.85 million for a space not big enough to swing a cat. The sergeant tried grumpily to calculate how long it would take her to come up with a deposit. Four lifetimes, at the very least. She was shaken from thoughts of poverty by the phone in her hand starting to vibrate.

A message from Alex.

Picked up David. All good. What would you like for supper? x

God bless the boy. Out of the background traffic noise burst the sound of a car horn. Roche looked up from her screen to see a black cab pull up at the kerb. The call light was off, but the back seat was empty. As the taxi came to a halt, the driver wound down his window and invited her to get in. It took a couple of seconds for Roche to put a name to the shabby features of Ashley Cotterill, Vernon Holder's lawyer. Shoving the phone into her pocket, she pulled open the door and slid into the back seat.

The door lock clicked shut and Cotterill pulled out into the traffic. Wondering if this was such a good idea, the sergeant pressed the switch for the intercom. 'What's with the cab?' she asked. 'Are you moonlighting?'

Cotterill glanced at her in the rear-view mirror. 'This is my pride and joy. An LTI FX4. My third taxi. Lots of people have them. Celebrities, too, like that Stephen Fry bloke. Kate Moss. And that useless fellow from the Happy Mondays who waves a tambourine about.'

'Interesting.' Roche somehow doubted that the useless bloke from the Happy Mondays qualified as a celebrity.

'It's all legal, as long as we don't tout for fares. Best cars ever built – the last of the line as well. The firm that makes them is owned by the Chinese now.' He scratched his ear. 'Most of the new ones are built in Shanghai.'

Probably for the best, Roche mused, given the dependability of your average British worker.

'I'm the president of the North London Black Cab Appreciation Society.'

'Everyone should have a hobby.' The cab rolled to a halt at a red traffic light. Roche watched a pair of women emerging from an underwear shop, laden down with heavily branded shopping bags. 'Where are we going?'

'Wherever you like.' Cotterill seemed eager to please.

Nowhere sprang to mind. 'What did you want to talk about?'

Sliding open the glass partition, Cotterill offered up a thin green file. *CLIENT CONFIDENTIAL* had been stamped across the cover in red ink. Underneath was the logo of a firm called Cotterill, Smith & Hurd. 'It's all in there. Everything you need to get Vernon.' A shrill blast from the horn of the car behind signalled that the lights had changed. Releasing the handbrake, Cotterill waited for a man in a suit to skip across the road before setting off again. 'Put him away for a good long time.'

Opening the file, Roche began flicking through a sheaf of papers maybe half an inch thick.

'Where to?'

Sitting back in her seat, Roche mumbled the name of a tube station, from where she could easily get home.

'No problem.' Cotterill signalled left. 'And would you mind putting your seatbelt on? It's the law, I'm afraid. They've got rules for everything, these days.'

Ignoring the request, Roche stared at a page of figures on her lap. 'What is all this stuff?'

'Everything you need to know about Vernon's business over the last few years: accounts, details of meetings, a copy of his contract with Vicky Cummins.' He corrected himself. 'Victoria *Dalby*-Cummins. Harry Cummins' widow.'

Roche looked up from the file. 'They have a contract?'

'Vernon's a great believer in the rule of law,' Cotterill stated.

'He has a framed copy of the Magna Carta on the wall of his home office. He likes things written down. Nothing left to chance.'

Good for him. Roche wondered if she might not like some salmon for dinner. She was pretty sure there was some in the fridge. Pulling out her phone, she texted Alex, asking him to put it in the oven. The fish would go nicely with a bottle of wine – she'd pick one up on the way home.

'Which means,' Cotterill continued, 'that there's a paper trail for just about everything.'

Roche tapped the papers with an index finger. 'What does all this tell me?'

'You've got the highlights of the last ten years or so.'

'The highlights.' Nothing was jumping off the pages at her. 'Talk me through them.'

Cotterill kept his eyes on the road. 'Well, for a start, Ronnie Score was paid almost sixty grand in the year before he was killed.'

'We knew Ronnie was bent,' Roche mumbled.

'No one stopped him, though, did they? Thirty K of that was for whacking Harry Cummins and his people.'

Roche raised an eyebrow. 'You know that for a fact?'

Cotterill nodded. 'It was a favour for Cummins's wife. Vicky agreed to go into partnership with Vernon if he got rid of Harry and his girlfriend.'

'His girlfriend?'

'Zoë Connors. She was a nice girl. A bit scatty – I never had much time for all that new-age malarkey, my body is a temple, organic this, organic that, stuff – but Zoë was a nice person, you know? I don't know why Vicky took against her particularly. It wasn't like she was Harry's only bit on the side.'

Roche flinched at the everyday sexism. For a lawyer, Cotterill made a pretty good cabbie. 'Maybe she was just the straw that broke the camel's back.'

'That's one way of looking at it. Harry was a real skirt-chaser,'

Cotterill continued, oblivious to the sergeant's dismay at his antediluvian language. 'After all, you get a lot of opportunity in the nightclub business.'

'Do you get a lot of opportunity, Ashley?' The guy was handing her – potentially at least – a monster collar but she still couldn't resist the urge to needle him just a little.

'Me? No.' Cotterill blushed. 'I mean, look at me. Come on. And, anyway, my wife wouldn't let me.'

'Being married didn't stop Harry Cummins.'

'Harry was quite a lad.'

'He was a pimp.'

'Yes, well . . .' Cotterill shifted uneasily in his seat. On the kerb, a man in a sheepskin coat tried unsuccessfully to wave him down.

'Just like Vernon Holder.'

'I'm well aware of all that,' Cotterill snapped. 'All I'm trying to do here is help you out. I'm not trying to airbrush anything.'

'So, Score killed Cummins and his girlfriend.'

'Not forgetting your mate, Umar Sligo, the ex-cop.'

'He wasn't my mate.'

'Didn't you two work together?'

'He was before my time,' Roche lied.

'Lucky for you. If ever there was a man who couldn't keep it in his trousers, it was Umar. He was even worse than Harry – tried it on with just about everybody, by all accounts. Karen Jansen turned him down flat. I think Zoë was just too nice to say no. Once she realised that Harry wasn't serious, she kind of fell into a revenge relationship with Umar. Unlucky for him, the poor bugger ended up as collateral damage in Vicky's clean-up operation.'

'And Karen Jansen?'

'What about her?'

'Where does she fit into all of this?'

'Karen tried to keep her distance. Vernon always described

her as semi-detached. But he knew she was smart – we all did. It was no surprise when we found out she'd been keeping records of her own.'

'What do you mean?'

'She had her own file,' Cotterill explained. 'She was doing a Vernon on Vernon.'

'Where's Karen's file now?'

'Destroyed.'

'Hm.'

'I don't think she was going to do anything with it, you know. It was just for insurance purposes. But Vernon didn't like that, especially if she was going home to Australia.'

'So, he had her killed?'

Cotterill nodded. 'A guy from Belgium did it. He was in and out of the country in a day. Completely untraceable.'

We'll see about that. 'What was his name?'

Cotterill stared at the car in front. 'Dunno.'

Convenient. Roche moved on. 'Why shoot her at the building site?'

'Synergy.'

'Synergy?' As they moved away from the centre, the traffic eased. Closing the file, Roche stared out of the window. 'I don't understand.'

'Vernon's negotiating to buy five or six flats in that development. He used the bad publicity and the threat of delays to the timetable to ask for an extra two per cent discount. That might not sound like much, but it adds up to a lot of cash.'

'How very practical.'

'"Killing two birds with one stone" was how he put it.'

'And did he get it?'

'The discount? Dunno.'

'Vernon doesn't take any prisoners. Aren't you worried you'll be next?'

'Why do you think I'm talking to you now?' Cotterill laughed nervously. 'I'm not stupid. I need to get out. All I want to do is retire and run about in my cab. You'll get my full cooperation in exchange for a free pass. Vernon goes down for good. I don't want to be his next victim.'

'No.' Roche considered offering the lawyer police protection but there wasn't the manpower available to make good on such a promise. She shoved the file into her bag. 'I'll need to take a careful look at what's in here.'

'There's plenty more where that came from.' Cotterill pulled up outside the tube station, as Roche had requested. 'Here we are.'

'Bloody hell, that was quick.' Roche reached for the door handle. 'You'd make a hell of a taxi driver.'

'You reckon?' Cotterill seemed genuinely pleased at the compliment.

'A new career beckons.' Pushing open the door, Roche slid off the seat and stepped out onto the pavement. 'Just let me get this stuff properly analysed and I'll be in touch.'

'One final thing,' Cotterill shouted after her. 'Vernon and Vicky have a quarterly business meeting, usually in London. The next one should be coming up soon.'

'Good to know.' Roche slammed the door and headed for the ticket barriers.

TWENTY-THREE

The salmon had been overcooked but was still edible. Pushing away her plate, Roche took a mouthful of Sauvignon Blanc as she glanced at the mercifully silent baby monitor. David had been asleep when she had returned home; she wondered if she might have the chance of a decent night's kip.

'What d'you think?'

Sitting across the table, Alex scratched his head. In his Nirvana T-shirt, he looked more like a student than a thirty-something lawyer.

You need a haircut. Roche immediately started remonstrating with herself. Leave him alone. You'll be calling him Shaggy next.

Bloody Carlyle. The man just couldn't resist putting people down. Since he had started using the vaguely insulting nickname for Alex, Roche had been unable to get it out of her mind. Maya Angelou sprang to mind: *People will forget what you said, people will forget what you did, but people will never forget how you made them feel.* No wonder her boss had made so many enemies. Carlyle wasn't a stupid man – certainly not by the standards of the Met – but, as far as he was concerned, empathy was too much of an optional extra. That, in her opinion, was why he would never be a top-top-drawer cop.

'There's a lot of stuff here.' Alex began placing the papers in front of him in an orderly pile. 'It's difficult to come up with a

190

clear picture of what they're telling us. There seems to be plenty of detail about Vernon Holder's business affairs, but whether there is indication of criminal behaviour is anyone's guess.' He shoved the papers back into the file. 'Maybe he's been fiddling his taxes.'

'I'm sure he has. Vernon Holder's not going to be the kind of guy to hand over any money to HMRC willingly.'

'Maybe that's the best way into this,' Alex suggested. 'Get the Revenue to nail him. That's how they got Al Capone.'

Roche looked at him blankly.

'Capone got eleven years for income-tax evasion in 1931,' Alex explained. 'By the time he was released, his health was shot – he had syphilis – and he was unable to resume the gangster life. He died just after the Second World War.'

'Thank you, Mr Wikipedia.'

'Follow the money.' Alex lifted his empty glass in mock toast. 'What you really need is a forensic accountant. I'm not really in much of a position to comment.'

Right now, however, Roche could have done with a slightly better steer than 'Follow the money.' Reaching for the bottle, she refilled his glass. 'Ashley Cotterill says there's plenty more where that came from, but I want to get a better handle on what I'm looking for, you know?'

'And you trust him?'

'Trust him? No. But I think his desire to escape from the clutches of Vernon Holder is genuine. The guy was scared. He wants out.'

'If Cotterill's worked for Holder for so long, he must be up to his neck in all of this.' Alex took a sip of his wine, before closing the file and sliding it back across the table. 'You want to give him a free pass?'

'Not my call,' Roche sniffed, 'but if he helps us get Holder, I'd probably be cool with that.'

191

'And what does Nayla Thomson think?'

'She doesn't know yet.'

Alex raised an eyebrow.

'She's been up north.'

'I see that Inspector Carlyle's bad habits are rubbing off on you.'

'*Commander* Carlyle.'

Alex shook his head. 'Unbelievable. How that guy ever got promoted is beyond me. No wonder the Met's in the mess it's in.'

'He's a good cop.'

'He's *so* not a team player,' Alex countered. 'You've got to be careful. Now that he's gone to Paddington you should do more to keep your distance. Get pigeonholed as his bag-carrier and you'll get a bad reputation.'

'I'm not anybody's bag-carrier.' Roche bridled.

'We're all somebody's bag-carrier.' Alex rested his elbows on the table, an earnest expression on his face. 'Commander or not, the guy has plenty of enemies. Andy Wick certainly doesn't like him.'

'I didn't think they were particularly acquainted.'

'He still doesn't like him.'

'Your client is a busted flush. He'd try to drag anyone – up to and including the Queen – into the shit, to try to save his hide.'

Alex laughed. 'Did you hear the story about when Wick was at Sandringham?'

'I've heard enough stories.' Roche groaned. 'Compared to Andy Wick, John Carlyle is an angel. An absolute saint.'

Alex looked doubtful. 'There are some nasty rumours about him.'

'Yeah. I know all about Carlyle and his relationship with Dominic Silver. The things they got up to down the years, all the way back to doing speed on picket-lines duty during the miners' strike. It's the stuff of legend.'

'It's the stuff of corruption trials.'

'Carlyle's not bent,' Roche asserted.

'Some of the stories might suggest otherwise.'

'I've heard them. We all operate in grey areas. That's the nature of the job.'

'Some areas are greyer than others.'

'No doubt. But I prefer to make my own judgement. I've worked with Carlyle for years now and he's definitely one of the good guys.'

'Says you.'

'Yeah,' Roche said defiantly. 'Says me.'

The look on Helen's face told him that Ibiza was a complete non-starter. 'I can't really see why you'd want to go there,' she mused. 'It's for teenage clubbers, isn't it?' When Carlyle started to demur, his wife offered the *coup de grâce*. 'Anyway, we can't afford it. And Alice won't want to go, not with her exams on the horizon. Which reminds me, are you still all right for the Imperial open day?'

Damn. Carlyle realised he'd forgotten all about that. Reaching for his phone, to check his diary, he saw he had four missed calls. Having long since given up trying to understand how these things happened, he scrolled down the call log. Both Alison Roche and Dom Silver had tried to speak to him; neither had left a message.

'John.' Helen gave him a gentle prod with a stockinged foot. 'Can't you leave work alone for a moment?'

'Sorry.' Switching to the calendar, he was relieved to find that the time had been blocked out for his university visit with Alice. 'Thursday at four.'

'You can't be late. Alice has a series of meetings booked with different professors and things. It's important. And, remember, she wants *you* to go with her.'

'I know. Don't worry, I won't mess it up.'

'Good.' Reaching for the evening paper, Helen turned to the crossword puzzle. Finding the right page, she stuck out a hand. 'You couldn't get me a pen, could you?'

Trooping off into the kitchen, Carlyle tried Roche and Silver in quick succession. With no one picking up, he found a biro and helped himself to a bottle of beer from the fridge before returning to join his wife.

Helen relieved him of the Bic and the beer, taking a swig from the latter before handing it back. 'Very nice.'

Carlyle gave a mock bow. 'Glad to be of service, ma'am.' He flopped onto the sofa and reached for the TV remote. Before he could switch on the TV, however, his phone flashed into life.

'Carlyle.'

'This is Michelle Mara.' The deputy assistant commissioner sounded slightly inebriated. The noise in the background suggested she was in a particularly loud restaurant. 'Where are you?'

'At home.'

'You live in Covent Garden, don't you?'

'Yeah.' Carlyle's heart sank. The last thing he needed was his boss turning up drunk on his doorstep.

There was a pause, followed by a muffled conversation.

'Do you know Man-Machine?'

'Sorry?'

'Man-Machine,' she repeated. 'It's a new restaurant on Shaftesbury Avenue. Doesn't live up to the hype, if you ask me, but still . . .'

'What about it?' Carlyle snapped.

'Get over here, now.'

Gregory Cosneau wasn't looking his best. The ICBRS security chief was blind drunk, slumped in a back booth of the restaurant bar. Glassy-eyed, his clothes dishevelled, he looked like he belonged on the other side of the glass, out on the pavement with the West End's resident collection of winos, rather than in an establishment where a small beer cost more than twelve pounds.

Mara was trying to persuade him to drink some black coffee. She didn't look up as Carlyle approached their table.

'Khaldoon Ghosn's missing,' was the DAC's opening gambit.

How's that my problem? Carlyle was irritated at having been dragged from the bosom of his loving family. On the other hand, he was curious to see how this little situation would develop. He took a seat a safe distance from *GQ* Man, just in case he decided to puke. 'What about the other one?'

'Who?' Mara managed to get Cosneau to hold the cup. Taking a cautious sip, Cosneau's eyes seemed to refocus slightly. Lifting his head, he contemplated Carlyle without any sign of recognition.

'The kid. Ghosn's sidekick.'

'Jamal.' Cosneau downed more coffee and pushed himself up in his chair. 'Jamal Alsukait. He's gone missing too. They're dead. I know it.'

'Keep your voice down,' Mara hissed. She looked nervously around the bar, but it was largely empty. Dinner service was in full swing and almost all of the patrons had decamped to the restaurant. 'We don't know that.'

'I think we do.' Grabbing a paper napkin, Cosneau blew his nose. 'Obeid Idris. The bastard's killed them.'

'You said he'd left the country.' Carlyle ignored Mara's quizzical stare.

'He came back.'

Mara glared at her lover. 'When did this happen?'

'Yesterday.' Balling up the used napkin, Cosneau tossed it onto the table.

Mara wrinkled her nose in disgust. 'And you didn't think to mention this to me?'

Don't let me get in the way of your little domestic. Carlyle kept his mouth shut.

'There was a gentlemen's agreement.' Finishing his coffee, Cosneau signalled to a passing waitress that he would like a refill. 'The matter had been dealt with. We were just tidying up loose ends.'

'Have you filed a missing-person report?' Carlyle asked.

'John,' Mara snapped, 'if Greg had filed a report, would I have called you over here?'

A waitress appeared with a pot of coffee and some fresh cups, saving Carlyle from having to reply. Better steer clear of that, he decided, or I'll never get to sleep tonight. Instead, he ordered a double Jameson's. The drink would be insanely expensive, but it was Mara's tab. 'Straight, no ice.' As the waitress skipped off to fulfil his order, Carlyle considered the pair in front of him: a drunk and a woman who was trying her best to commit career suicide. To his surprise, he felt a pang of sympathy for his boss. He had no interest in bringing Mara down. And, if a killer was on the loose, that should demand his full and immediate attention.

'So,' he asked finally, 'what do we actually know?'

TWENTY-FOUR

Francesca Culverhouse groped for the spectacles on the top of her head. Grabbing them at the second attempt, the founder of the Investigation Unit waved the frames in the general direction of Bernie Gilmore's face. 'I'm not publishing this crap,' she fulminated, her anger revealing the slightest hint of an otherwise long-lost Flemish accent. 'It's not been properly put together. You haven't done your homework. Just – not – good – enough.' She tapped out the words on a desk using the spectacles. 'The Investigation Unit is committed to the highest standards of research and editorial rigour.'

Here we go. Bernie had heard the proprietor's spiel so many times that he could recite it. *If we are to provide a public benefit, etc., etc.*

'If we are to provide a public benefit,' Culverhouse continued to play with her glasses as if she was conducting an invisible orchestra, 'we have to live up to the standards by which we would hold others to account. Proper reporting requires in-depth research into the people who hold power in today's world.' She shot him an exasperated look. 'We cannot just make this stuff up.'

'I haven't made anything up,' the reporter protested.

'And where are your sources?'

The hack coughed nervously. 'They cannot be named.'

'I'm not asking you to name them publicly, Bernard,' the

proprietor scolded. 'You know that. But *I* need to have a better idea of who they are if *I* am to publish this piece of work.'

'I have to protect my sources.' He wasn't going to tell Culverhouse about Alain Costello. A French hoodlum from a notorious crime family was hardly a credible source.

'Well,' Culverhouse declared, 'we've reached an impasse.'

'Yes.' Bernie watched Conrad Stockhausen, the Unit's lawyer, emerge from his office and head towards them.

Slipping on her glasses, Culverhouse's expression softened. 'Your story just needs a bit more work. If we're going to accuse one of London's top cops of being in the pay of a drug dealer it needs to be completely watertight. We're not in any rush here.'

You might not be, but I certainly am. Apart from anything else, the Costello fiasco was doing nothing to help get his love life back on track. Miranda, the history teacher from Finchley, had given him the elbow after Bernie had missed their date. The lonely hack now had his eye on Natasha, thirty-eight, a marine biologist working at London Zoo, who professed an interest in Blur and European movies. Personally, he had no interest in either Britpop or arthouse cinema but, in both cases, he was confident he could fake it. That, however, was contingent on not being turned into fish food by Costello and his thug.

The smirking lawyer joined their little cabal. Stockhausen, a stooping giant, was seventy-five, if he was a day. A republican, vegan socialist, he had made his name in the early 1980s as in-house lawyer for a short-lived socialist Sunday paper called the *Bugle*, which had had six of its journalists jailed for contempt of court after refusing to reveal their sources for a story about an IRA cell operating in London. A drinking buddy of Culverhouse's husband, IT tycoon Edmund Thornton, Stockhausen had been brought out of retirement for one last hurrah with the Unit.

'Conrad agrees with me. Don't you, Conrad?'

'I always agree with you, Francesca.' Dressed in a white shirt and black suit, the lawyer towered over both of his colleagues like a baddie from a Bela Lugosi film. 'What are we talking about in this particular instance?'

Culverhouse lifted her gaze to the stratosphere. 'I was just talking to Bernie about his piece.'

'Ah, yes. The co-rr-upt po-lice-man. A staple of British journalism over the last century or so.' The lawyer clasped his hands together as if in supplication. Whether he was praying to be spared bent cops or rubbish journalism – or, indeed, both – was not clear. For a moment, it seemed as if he had stopped breathing. Culverhouse and Bernie were waiting anxiously for signs of life when he finally added: 'It has the potential to be an explosive story, truly ex-plo-sive. But, in the wake of the Merriman debacle, there is simply no way in which we can countenance running it in its current form. It would be grossly irresponsible for me to allow that. The potential risks – financial as well as reputational – are simply too great.'

'Merriman was Kelvin's fault,' Bernie whined. 'Absolutely nothing to do with me.' He cursed Kelvin Porter, the self-styled 'king of investigative journalism', who had published a series of unverified and probably unverifiable allegations on the Unit's website about Augustus Merriman, a veteran member of the House of Lords, and boys from a care home in Kent. Merriman's lawyers had had the story removed from the Unit's website in less than two hours. Following a 'comprehensive and detailed internal investigation', Porter was sacked the next day. After some pushing from the trustees, the Unit's editor-in-chief had also resigned. Culverhouse had had to pay an undisclosed sum – reported to be somewhere in the region of £150,000 – out of her own pocket to a charity for abandoned Spanish donkeys, his lordship's choice, as part of an out-of-court settlement.

'Merriman provides the rather unfortunate context in which we are having this particular conversation.' Stockhausen considered the grubby journalist with practised dismay. Mr Gilmore had been considerably larger when he had last seen him. The man seemed to have gone on a crash diet. Either that or he was seriously ill. Perhaps there was something going on behind the scenes that was impeding the man's judgement about the merits of his story. 'Everything we publish at the present time,' he opined, 'has to be beyond reproach. Not open to challenge from any angle whatsoever.'

'That,' Culverhouse chipped in, '*always* has to be the case.' She glanced at her watch. 'I've got to go. It's the Women in Journalism Awards tonight. That glass ceiling isn't going to smash itself.' Declaring the conversation at an end, she gave Bernie a consoling pat on the arm. 'Don't worry, we'll get there in the end. This guy Cassidy seems like a right crook.'

'Carlyle,' Bernie corrected her.

'Yes, right. A most nasty piece of work – even worse than that terrible man . . .'

'Andy Wick,' Bernie reminded her.

'That's it. At least Mr Wick has some amusement value.'

'He certainly provides more colour,' Bernie agreed.

'Just make sure you do a proper job.' With a nod to Stockhausen, Culverhouse drifted towards the door. 'Give it a bit more time. Keep Conrad in the loop.'

Watching the boss float out of the newsroom, Stockhausen suggested, 'Let's see where we are next week.'

Most likely without any kneecaps, Bernie thought morosely. 'I'll get you a new draft as soon as,' he promised, without enthusiasm.

The lawyer headed back to his office. 'I look forward to it.'

Sitting on the cheap sofa that stood against one wall, Daniel

Hunter looked up from a copy of the *Guardian*. 'It says here that there are nearly two thousand cases of alleged police corruption that haven't been properly investigated.'

'As few as that?' Hanging his coat on the back of the door, Carlyle looked at the smear of paint above the former military policeman's head. Linda had found a tester pot of Cool Grey Silk and had tried it out for his consideration. On first inspection, the commander wasn't sure if he was as taken with it in his office as he had been when he saw it adorning the cell walls at Charing Cross. In fact, it looked rather depressing.

Hunter began reading from the story: 'A report by Her Majesty's Inspectorate of Constabulary has found that no action was taken in two-thirds of the investigations into alleged police corruption last year. Drug-related offences, bribery, theft, sexual misconduct and other serious cases have all gone without investigation.' Closing the paper, he carefully placed it on the torn arm of the sofa.

The last thing Carlyle wanted to do right now was discuss drug-related corruption with a man who should have been behind bars. He slid behind his desk. 'By the way, what the hell are you doing here?'

'I was waiting for you.' Hunter pointed towards an empty mug sitting by his feet on the floor. 'Linda's looked after me very nicely.'

'Glad to hear it.' Settling into his chair, Carlyle offered a wan smile. 'You're not on the run again, are you?'

'Not at all. I'm a free man.' Hunter held his arms open wide. 'Free as a bird.'

'The army let you off?' Carlyle scowled. Did no one want to put this deserter-cum-killer in jail?

'Dishonourable discharge.' Hunter tapped the breast pocket of his coat. 'I've got my papers in here.'

'Unbelievable.'

'The army wasn't any more interested in incarcerating me than you were.'

'I think you're confusing me with my colleagues in the provinces.' Carlyle silently cursed the hopeless Colchester plod, DI Tommy Plant.

'And you would have handled it differently?'

Carlyle mumbled something suitably vague.

'Pragmatism.' Hunter seemed energised by his unexpected freedom.

'That's one way of looking at it.'

'My ex-colleagues took one look at the facts of my situation and decided it was in everyone's interest to have the whole thing swept under the carpet. Apart from anything else, Peterborough is currently at 115 per cent capacity.' Peterborough was the only military prison in England. 'They had nowhere to put me.'

'I'm sure they could've found somewhere,' Carlyle muttered.

'Plus there is the small matter of the one million plus it would have cost to keep me in prison for six or seven years. What's the point? After speaking to my ex-CO, the Military Police decided they didn't want to pursue it. Case closed.'

It all sounded plausible enough. Justice everywhere was subject to budgetary constraints. Anyway, why should he resent Daniel Hunter's good fortune at the hands of the system? Hunter had been a dedicated and determined cop, just like Carlyle. He had paid an enormous price for that dedication, losing his wife, his children. His entire life had been destroyed. Who should sit in judgement of such a man? 'Let sleeping dogs lie.'

'Something like that.'

Carlyle stared at his desk in search of something that might indicate what he should be doing right now. 'So, what brings you back here?'

Getting to his feet, Hunter stood in front of the desk. 'I need to find a job. I might not be in prison, but my pension's gone out the window.' Sticking his hand into his pocket, he pulled out a small selection of coins. 'I've got precisely . . . sixty-seven pence to my name. Totally skint, in other words. You mentioned that when I got out you might be able to help me with something.'

Yeah, like in ten years or so. However, the commander recalled Dominic Silver and his need for a security guard at his Cork Street gallery. 'Let me see if I can make a call.' Hoping that the vacancy was still open, he reached for the phone and pulled up Dom's number.

Miraculously, God's gift to the art world answered on the third ring.

'Where the hell have you been?' Dom enquired cheerily. 'I've been trying to get hold of you for ages.'

'I'm a busy manager. You know how it is.'

'We're all busy,' Dom countered. 'That doesn't mean we don't know how to use a phone. Impossible though it may seem, I think you're getting worse at answering yours.'

'That's quite possible.' After decades of unsolicited comments about his inability to use a phone properly, the commander was completely immune to any criticism in that regard.

'It's probably something to do with the onset of pre-senile dementia,' Dom speculated.

'Probably.' Carlyle glanced at Hunter. 'Anyway, quick question, have you got a new head of security yet?'

'Ha. The job agency sent over a couple of people this morning.' There was a grunt that suggested Dom had been less than impressed with the candidates. 'Where do they find these clowns?'

Carlyle raised an eyebrow. 'Not suitable?'

'They could hardly speak.'

'So, you're still looking?'

'At the current rate of progress, I'll be looking for the next year.'

'Are you at the gallery now?' Carlyle asked Dom.

'Nah, slow start to the day.'

'Meet me there in an hour. I've got someone for you who can definitely do the job.'

'This isn't some old lag you feel sorry for, is it? I need someone reliable and presentable, with common sense and social skills. And no criminal record – that would completely bugger my insurance cover, which, as expected, has gone through the bloody roof.'

'This guy is better than you could ever hope for. And he's got a clean record.'

'Bring him over and I'll take a look.' Dom still sounded doubtful. 'Who is it?'

'I'll explain when we get there. See you in an hour.' Ending the call, Carlyle gave Hunter a thumbs-up. 'We're on.'

TWENTY-FIVE

'But you've got an ESPL meeting,' Linda objected, as she realised that her unreliable charge was immediately heading back out of the building.

'Can't you send anyone else?' Carlyle wasn't entirely sure what ESPL might be but he had very little interest in finding out.

'It's the Executive Committee,' Linda explained. 'It's really quite important.'

'I have an urgent matter to attend to. Send my apologies.' Seeing the disappointment on her face, Carlyle added, 'There must be someone who can stand in at short notice.'

'I could perhaps see if Chief Superintendent Nathan would be free.'

'That's a *very* good idea.' Carlyle beamed. Paul Nathan was the perfect choice: a man who did all his fighting from behind the safety of a desk. There was nothing that the chief super liked more than a diary full of meetings – it saved him having to do any work or, worse, having to leave the sanctuary of the police station. Nathan treated the job as an endless exercise in office politics. The man doubtless had ambitions on Carlyle's job – and his office – but the way the commander was feeling, the chief super was more than welcome to it. 'See if he can do it. Tell him that I'll be suitably grateful. And remind him to make sure he has a full report on my desk by the end of the day.'

'I'll speak to his PA.'

'Perfect.'

'It won't help your reputation, though.'

Carlyle let out a nervous laugh. 'Surely it's rather too late for me to worry about that.'

'It's not a joke,' Linda scolded him. 'You're already bottom of the senior management performance tables.'

'Eh?' Carlyle scowled. What performance tables?

'For meeting attendance.'

'Oh, that.'

'Not just in the bottom quartile but absolutely the bottom.' Linda highlighted the harsh reality of his failings as a bureaucrat with a certain relish.

Someone's got to be, I suppose, all things being relative. The commander hopped from foot to foot, trying not to let his irritation show. He didn't appreciate getting a dressing down in front of Hunter.

Linda was on a roll now. 'You're failing on your other personal KPIs as well,' she pointed out.

Carlyle was vaguely aware of the Key Performance Indicators, but he knew better than to ask for the details.

Linda issued the final blow: 'DAC Mara is currently compiling the latest set of quarterly stats and yours are not going to make good reading.'

Surely the deputy assistant commissioner had more important things to worry about. He made a mental note to give Mara a call later in the day, if for no other reason than to put her on the spot about her boyfriend. It dawned on him that if his boss were to cut up rough over his meeting-attendance record, he could easily fight back by threatening to expose her unprofessional relationship with Gregory Cosneau.

'Couldn't you just fiddle the figures?' Hunter smirked. 'That's what we'd do in the army.'

'No, I could not.' Linda shot him a look that could only be described as outraged. 'That would be cheating.'

'We never fiddle the figures around here,' Carlyle deadpanned. 'Nathan'll be keen to boost his own KPIs so, really, I'm doing him a favour. I'm sure he'll be delighted to take the meeting.'

Linda muttered something he didn't catch.

'Oh, and one other thing.' Carlyle was pushing his luck, but he didn't much care. 'The Cool Grey Silk.' He pointed to his office. 'I don't think I like it in there.'

'You think you don't like it, or you know you don't like it?'

'I don't like it. Maybe we could try for something, I dunno, warmer.'

'I'll see what I can do.' Linda stalked off.

'By the way,' Hunter asked, 'did you ever find out anything about that shell casing I found near Biggin Hill?'

'Er, no.' Carlyle glanced at the desk drawer where the offending item had been left.'

Hunter looked mildly irritated by the admission. 'Weren't you going to check it out?'

'I've got other priorities right now. Like finding you a job.'

'I was just interested.'

'If there had been a gun battle in deepest, darkest Kent we'd have heard about it by now, don't you think?'

'Maybe I should give Mike Stoner a call,' Hunter mused. 'See if he's come across anything else.'

Who the hell was Mike Stoner?

From the other side of the door, Linda finished her call to Paul Nathan's office. 'The chief superintendent will do the ESPL Executive Committee,' she called out, 'so you're in the clear.'

'Jolly good.' Carlyle led Hunter out of his office. 'Seeing as we're on a roll, why don't you find out if you can do anything to improve my performance stats, like Mr Hunter suggested. Just a little bit, maybe?'

Linda remained implacable as he sashayed past her desk. 'I said "no" and I meant it.'

'Only joking,' Carlyle fibbed. 'I won't be too long.'

A poster in the window of the Molby-Nicol Gallery showed a black-and-white close-up of an old guy who bore a striking resemblance to Samuel Beckett, albeit Beckett after a week-long bender and a kip in a ditch. Beneath the poster was the legend: *Sigmund Kessling – The Final Years.*

The wheels of commerce never stop, Carlyle reflected, pressing the bell. After a few moments, Dom appeared from the back. 'Come on in. My apologies for the state of the place – we're in a bit of a mess, I'm afraid.' Dressed in jeans and a pink V-neck sweater over a blue shirt, open at the neck, he remained – despite his recent travails – the epitome of bourgeois bonhomie.

Carlyle felt a twinge of jealousy at his friend's healthy glow. After introducing Hunter, he asked, 'Been away?'

'Eva and I had a long weekend in Seville.' Dom locked the door behind them. 'We stayed at the Hotel Alfonso the Thirteenth. Great spa. You should check it out.'

Yeah, right. Carlyle would never stay at the Alfonso XIII or go to Seville. The realisation left him feeling vaguely frustrated.

'I could've happily stayed there for a month, but this place won't sort itself out.' Dom contemplated the empty walls. 'We're a while off reopening. The family's still arguing over the estate – Kessling had six children by four different women, so it's rather messy.'

Where did he find the time? Carlyle wondered. And the energy? 'These things always bring out the best in people,' he noted sardonically.

'Sorting things out could take months. Sigmund's prices are going up, though, which is the main thing. I'm hoping they'll release the paintings so that I can get on with showing them. All the revenues will go into the pot and then – in terms of who gets what – I couldn't care less. As long as I get my commission and the gallery gets the kudos of organising the first Kessling retrospective anywhere in the world, they can burn their cash for all I care. We'll sell the lot on the opening night, I'm fairly sure of that. You'll have to come, John. It'll be quite the circus.'

Waiting patiently to be drawn into the conversation, Hunter stepped over to the receptionist's desk and picked up a catalogue. Resting his backside against the edge of the desk he flicked through the heavy pages.

'What about the paintings that were stolen?' Carlyle asked.

'Still in the wind.' Dom sighed. 'They could be anywhere. I don't think we'll ever see them again.' He turned to Hunter. 'Would you mind if I just had a moment with the commander? I need to ask him about a couple of things.'

Hunter looked up from the catalogue. 'Sure.'

Dom led Carlyle into his office at the back of the gallery space. 'What's the latest on Bernie Gilmore?'

'Nothing to report on that front.' Carlyle dropped into the battered leather chair in front of Dom's desk. 'But I wouldn't read anything into it. These things take time. Months, at least. And this story isn't going anywhere. Bernie hasn't got anything he can use. He's like a guy trying to complete a jigsaw with most of the pieces missing.'

Perched on the corner of his desk, an uncomfortable look passed across Dom's face. 'So, we're saying it's a case of publish and be damned?'

'More a case of wait and see. If Bernie ever does get close to publishing anything, we'll head him off with the offer of something better. In the meantime, I'll keep him sweet with some titbits on Andy Wick.'

Dom wasn't interested in Wick. 'I don't like "wait and see".'

Exasperated, Carlyle spread his arms wide. 'For God's sake.

Think of all the scrapes you've been in over the years. This is nothing by comparison.'

'Scrapes – that's one way of putting it.'

'I appreciate that's perhaps a bit of an understatement when it comes to Tuco Martinez, but come on.'

'Bloody hell.' Dom shook his head. 'You've changed your tune. I remember after we sorted Tuco out, your head had gone. You couldn't handle it.'

'And if I hadn't been able to handle it, what would you have done about that?'

Dom ignored the question. 'I knew you'd get your head right, in the end.'

'My head's right on Bernie, too. We just need to sit tight and be cool. It would be a mistake if we were to jump in now and overreact. A big mistake.'

'And what about Alain Costello? What're we going to do if he comes after us?'

'Let's cross that bridge if we get to it. From what I recall, the guy was a total fuck-up who spent all his time playing computer games.'

'People change.'

'We'll deal with him in due course,' Carlyle said. 'If we have to.'

Leaning forward, Dom placed a hand on his shoulder. 'All right, Commander, you're the boss.'

'We'll be fine.'

'I know we will.' Dom moved behind the desk. 'So, tell me about Mr Hunter.' Sinking into his chair, he pulled the last of the Swedish whisky from the drawer. 'Another blast from the past.' He waved the bottle at his guest.

'No, thanks,' Carlyle said. 'Too early.'

'You're right,' Dom agreed. 'A bad habit to be getting into.' Putting the booze away, he slammed the drawer and pointed towards the gallery. 'This guy Hunter, he's the Redcap, right?'

'Yeah, he was a military policeman. How did you know that?'

'You told me.'

'I did?' Carlyle failed to recall that conversation.

'Your memory's going.'

'True enough,' Carlyle admitted.

'*I*, on the other hand, am as sharp as a tack. Anyway, it's not the kind of story you forget – bloke smokes gangster who killed his family. Your pal makes us look like amateurs. I doff my cap to him, and I'd like to help, but I can't hire him.'

'Why not?'

'Because of the insurance thing. I told you. I can't hire anyone with a criminal record – certainly not someone who has just walked out of prison having done time for murder.'

'He hasn't been to prison.'

'He's on the run?' Dom shifted uneasily in his seat. 'You're not seriously expecting me to harbour a fugitive from justice? That would completely invalidate my insurance cover.'

'Hunter's a free man. No criminal record. No outstanding warrants for his arrest. Simply a bloke who needs a job, an ex-serviceman looking to make his way in this cruel, cruel world. It would be good karma to help him out.'

'I've helped out many former service professionals,' Dom mused.

'At least this one will be working within the law,' Carlyle pointed out.

'And his pay packet will be suitably anaemic.'

'Funny you should mention that. The guy has precisely sixty-seven pence to his name. He could do with a small advance on his salary.'

'First things first.' Dom scratched his head. 'We're getting ahead of ourselves. The guy committed murder. Whatever the circumstances, you'd normally expect to go to jail for that. What happened?'

'According to the official record, a guy called Kurt something or other,' Carlyle struggled to recall the name, 'Kurt ... Zerlkderik, something like that, was responsible for shooting Andrew Carson.'

'Carson was the guy who killed Hunter's wife and kids.'

'Right.'

'What did he have to do with the other guy?'

'Kurt Zerlkderik? Nothing, as far as I know. He was a tramp and a drifter who stumbled over Carson's body. The cops found him at the scene after Hunter had legged it. It was an open-and-shut case.'

'With the wrong man.'

'No one really cared to dig deeper. Zerlkderik had a screw loose. He didn't have a proper defence. Then he conveniently topped himself in prison. As far as the cops involved are concerned, the case is closed, and it's staying closed. Not the most edifying story, but we are where we are. Daniel Hunter didn't engineer any of this. He didn't even know about it until a few days ago.'

'Life is stranger than fiction every time.'

'You couldn't make it up,' Carlyle agreed. 'Hunter appeared at Paddington Green to turn himself in. When it became clear that the police investigation wouldn't be reopened he turned himself in to the army as a deserter. They didn't want to know either. They didn't have the cell space for him.'

'And he just walks?'

'If anyone deserves a break, Danny Hunter does, don't you think?'

Dom didn't seem all that convinced. 'If he hasn't been in jail, what's he been doing for the last few years?'

'He joined the Foreign Legion.'

'The Foreign Legion?' Dom laughed. 'You're kidding me – Beau Geste and all that?'

'Hunter did very well.' Carlyle glanced at his watch. He didn't have infinite time to sit and talk. 'And I'm sure that his French is excellent,' he quipped, 'if you need some help with your Monte Carlo-based clients.'

'My French is perfectly serviceable,' Dom informed him.

'Look, this is a total win-win. He needs a job and, frankly, you're lucky to get him. He's going to be a million times more reliable than any muppet you'll get from the job agency. Plus you don't have to pay me a finder's fee. So just bloody get on with it.'

Dom stared at him, unblinking.

'What more do you want? A written reference?'

'All right, all right.' Dom jumped up from his chair. 'I'll give him a go.'

'Good.' Carlyle followed him to the door, keen to be on his way. 'I'll leave you two to bond. I need to get back to the never-ending fight against crime.'

Placing a friendly hand on his shoulder, Dom murmured, 'Just make sure you keep me posted on Bernie. If there are any developments, I want to know straight away.'

As they approached, Hunter looked up from the catalogue. 'I'd never heard of this Kessling guy before but he's really quite interesting.'

'Hm.' The commander couldn't care less when it came to dead Canadian painters.

'The academic who wrote the notes sexed it up a bit,' Dom pointed out. 'He fancied he was auditioning for a BBC4 gig.'

'But still,' Hunter countered, 'all that stuff in New York. No wonder he ended up in jail.'

'That kind of thing was just par for the course back then. It was a fairly normal part of what, these days, you might call building your brand.'

Hunter pushed out his lower lip. 'Yeah, but the stuff with the circus performers,' he tossed the catalogue on to the desk, 'that was just weird.'

Circus performers? Carlyle hovered by the door.

'Personally,' Dom vigorously scratched his chest, 'I think he was just faking it.'

'Well, I'm not faking it,' Carlyle put in. 'I'm heading off.'

Hunter shot him an enquiring look. 'I've got the job?'

'Yeah. I'll leave Dom to show you the ropes.'

'Thanks.' The ex-soldier seemed genuinely grateful.

'Don't thank me, thank Dom,' Carlyle advised. 'By the way, I mentioned that you're a bit skint, so he's going to bung you a few quid as an advance on your salary.'

Muttering to himself, Dom unlocked the door.

Carlyle tipped him an imaginary hat. 'I'll pop round later to see how you're getting on with the new recruit.'

'You just worry about the other stuff,' Dom instructed, waving him off.

TWENTY-SIX

Inspector Nayla Thomson contemplated the folder on Roche's desk as if it could blow up in her face. 'How much is a forensic accountant going to cost?'

Alison Roche didn't have a clue. 'Not too much,' the sergeant ventured.

'We simply don't have a budget for this,' Thomson complained. 'As it is, I'm going to have to fight to get my rail fare to Manchester reimbursed.'

Roche wondered about the arrangement that allowed on-duty officers to travel for free. 'Didn't you use the rail-travel concession?'

'I left my warrant card at home and some jobsworth guard on the train gave me a penalty fare.' She shook her head in dismay. 'Two hundred and seventy-eight quid and a whole day wasted so that Umar Sligo's parents could tell me what a great guy their shagger son was.'

'They weren't very helpful, then?'

'Three hours, four cups of tea, three chocolate digestives.' Thomson patted her belly. 'They even wanted me to stay for dinner. And all so I could get the fantasy version of their son. The Sergeant Umar Sligo none of us ever knew – quiet, shy and unassuming. Punctual, respectful of authority, polite and deferential when it came to women.'

'They didn't mention the willy photographs, then?' Roche chuckled.

'They didn't have a clue,' Thomson confirmed. 'He obviously never told them why he left the Force.'

'I can understand that,' Roche reflected. 'I mean, "Hey, Mum, I had this thing where I liked to photograph my knob and send it to girls at work I wanted to impress." That's not a conversation you want to have over Sunday lunch, is it?'

A question filtered through Thomson's brain before slipping from her mouth. 'Did he ever send you one?'

Roche wasn't going to go there. She said, 'He knew I wouldn't stand for that kind of nonsense. He only sent them to young girls who wouldn't complain.'

'Well, he got that wrong, didn't he?'

Not wanting to extend the discussion of Umar's member, Roche asked, 'What did the parents say about him leaving the police?'

'They gave me a line about him setting up as a private-sector consultant. There was nothing about him working for a pimp. It was clear they knew absolutely nothing about what was going on.'

'What did they have to say about the sister?'

'Niamh? Not too much.'

'It must be hard to lose two adult children like that,' Roche mused.

'Yeah.' Thomson's expression suggested that she hadn't given the matter much consideration. 'At least they've got a second son.'

As if that made much difference. You're a cold fish, Roche decided, channelling the fervour of one who had recently become a parent.

'He's an accountant,' Thomson continued, 'thirty-two. Still lives at home. I met him. Quiet. Don't think he's ever had a girlfriend. His mother still makes him a packed lunch to take to work every day. Doesn't drink alcohol, has a bad Diet Pepsi habit. In short, not at all like his brother.'

'That's no bad thing.'

'He didn't have much to say, either. Apparently, though, the parents hadn't been very happy about the daughter's impending divorce. They liked the husband – a dentist in some posh part of Cheshire. The local police spoke to him – says he hadn't seen his wife for more than a month before she was killed.'

'Happy families.'

Thomson didn't express a view. 'I didn't meet the husband – just the brother and the parents. None of them knew anything about Niamh having any enemies – or any current boyfriends.'

'She was certainly active on that score.' Roche pointed at a document on her computer screen. 'The pathologist found evidence of recent sexual activity. Although that's hardly surprising, seeing as she was shot in the act.'

Thomson winced at the crude description of Niamh Grieg's demise. 'We don't know that.'

'It's a reasonable assumption,' Roche countered. 'The poor sod certainly didn't bow out with any dignity.'

The inspector muttered something under her breath. 'Funnily enough, I didn't mention that to her mum and dad.'

'No point speaking ill of the dead.'

'Not really. Not unless it helps us get to the truth. And we're not going to do that through the family. The brother is living in his own little world and the parents seem to have chosen a path of selective amnesia when it comes to their kids. It's almost like they're living in a different universe.'

'At least you've crossed them off the list.' Roche tapped the folder that Cotterill had handed over. 'Now we need to focus on Ashley Cotterill.'

'I don't trust him.' Thomson pouted. 'You don't work for

someone like Vernon Holder for so long without learning a few tricks. He could still be selling us a pup.'

'Alex had a quick look at this last night and—'

Thomson adopted a pained expression. 'You showed this to your boyfriend?'

'My partner,' Roche corrected her. 'He's a lawyer with the Police Federation.'

'He's still a civilian. He shouldn't be looking at evidence. That could end up compromising us in court.'

'We're a long way from getting Holder anywhere near a court.' Roche was annoyed at being put on the spot.

'Procedures have to be followed. Everything has to be done properly or we'll trip ourselves up.'

Roche had taken enough of Thomson's head-girl schtick. 'If we're going to work together you've got to let me get on and do my damn job.' Thomson started to reply, but the sergeant continued talking over her. 'What kind of cop do you want to be? The kind who ticks boxes and writes nice reports or the kind who solves cases? You can't be both, not in this universe – maybe in the parallel one occupied by Umar's parents, but not here. There are times when you need to follow the path of least resistance. In the Karen Jansen case, that means going through Cotterill to get to Vernon Holder.'

Thomson refused to acknowledge the point, but Roche could see a flicker of acceptance in the inspector's eyes.

'And what about the Niamh Grieg case? What's the path of least resistance on that one?'

No bloody idea. 'One thing at a time,' was Roche's lame response. 'Jansen is moving forwards more quickly and we have to run with it. If Cotterill helps us break the case open, great. If not, we'll look at something else. In terms of his dossier, I took an initial informal opinion from an independent source and they suggested that we have the materials properly reviewed by a qualified forensic accountant.'

'Which we can't afford,' Thomson repeated.

'Well, Inspector, you'd better see about squeezing some extra cash from the budget because I've hired one.'

'What?'

'And here he is.' Roche pointed to a callow youth in a cheap-looking suit who had just emerged from the lift on the far side of the room. She waved him over.

'Chris?'

The young man gave a nervous nod. He had a mop of unruly blond hair and an angry zit on his chin. His tie was at half-mast and there was what looked suspiciously like a ketchup stain on the lapel of his jacket. He carried a cheap briefcase in one hand, an empty sandwich packet in the other. The overall impression was of someone on day release from a young-offenders institution.

'Chris Dalston. I'm from PEM. They sent me over to look at some files.'

Thomson's frown deepened. PEM was one of London's largest accountancy firms, a gigantic global outfit, with hourly rates to match.

'Just the one file.' Roche lifted the article in question before dropping it back on her desk. 'I'm Sergeant Roche and this is Inspector Thomson.'

No one offered to shake hands.

'No problem.' Placing the sandwich packet on Roche's desk, Dalston fumbled in his pocket. After several moments' searching, he came up with a couple of business cards, handing one to each of the police officers.

Thomson turned the card in her hand. 'You have an MSc in forensic accounting?'

Dalston confirmed that was the case. 'From Portsmouth University.'

This failed to impress the inspector. 'How long ago was that?'

'Last year,' Dalston admitted.

'And have you done this kind of thing before? For real, I mean.'

To his credit, Dalston didn't seem particularly put out by the question. 'I've been a qualified accountant for more than six years. Since going to Portsmouth and moving into forensic accounting, I have been responsible for more than twenty million pounds' worth of assets being recovered by law-enforcement agencies in England and Wales, including the recent Sonnering-Wakefield case.'

A look of non-recognition passed between the two cops.

'We helped the local authority recover more than four million pounds from a group of cyber-criminals operating out of Hartlepool.'

'What we're after here isn't primarily about asset recovery,' Roche said.

'Oh.' Dalston bit his lower lip. 'What kind of investigation is it, then?'

The sergeant gestured at the dossier. 'What I need is an analysis of the data in there. You tell me what's in here and then we can think about where we go with it.'

'Sounds a bit vague.'

'Just see what you can find.' Getting to her feet, Roche ignored the smirk on Thomson's face as she switched off her computer. 'You can work at my desk. I'll be out for the rest of the day. Let's review what you've discovered tomorrow morning. The loos are one floor down and there's a coffee machine in the kitchen, by the lift. I'm sure if you need anything else, the inspector'll be happy to help you out.'

'Got it.' Sliding into Roche's chair, Dalston placed his case on the floor and quickly got down to work.

Roche started for the stairs.

'Where're you going?' Thomson called after her.

'I've got a follow-up meeting with Ashley Cotterill,' Roche

replied, not breaking her stride. 'He's going to take me for another ride in his taxi.'

Approaching a red light, Ashley Cotterill brought the taxi to a halt behind a battered milk float, a rarity on the streets of London, these days. The traffic had been terrible all the way into town and he was on the cusp of being late for his rendezvous with the female cop. On the back of the float was an advert for cheese straws. Cotterill recalled his wife putting them into the kids' packed lunches, back when the boys were in junior school. He often found himself in trouble for nicking the odd packet from the kitchen cupboard and scoffing them as a late-night snack.

'They're not for you,' Sarah would cheerily scold him, before coming up with extra supplies from the supposedly secret stash she kept by the freezer in the garage.

The traffic lights were now on green, but a bus was blocking the junction. A few drivers leaned on their horns in a desultory manner. As the lights turned to orange and back to red, Cotterill took his phone from its mount and typed in 'Cheese Straws'. His search was interrupted by someone rapping their knuckles on the window of the driver's door. Without looking up, Cotterill pointed towards the light on the front of the cab, which was not illuminated. 'Sorry, mate, I'm not for hire.'

Another knock on the window, this one more insistent.

Cotterill finally looked away from his screen to face a very large Asian bloke in an ill-fitting suit.

'I'm trying to find Correction Street.'

'Where?'

'Correction Street.' The guy wore the angst-ridden expression of a middle-manager who was running behind schedule. His boss – or maybe a client – would be waiting for him, pissed off at his poor timekeeping.

'It's supposed to be somewhere off Golden Square.'

'You're in the wrong place,' Cotterill offered unhelpfully, in the spirit of his taxi-driver persona.

'Are you sure?' With a gloved hand, the man pushed down his tie, which had taken flight on a gust of wind. 'It's definitely somewhere around here.'

Irritated, Cotterill stared out of the windscreen. Up ahead the bus was still blocking the traffic. Losing patience, someone in front of the milk float gave an extended blast on his horn. He was going to be at least fifteen minutes late picking up the cop. Maybe he should send her a text. Then again, he didn't want to leave any unnecessary traces of his dealings with the police. He wasn't convinced that Vernon could trace his phone, but he couldn't rule it out either.

'It *is* somewhere round here.' The businessman placed a phone up against the window.

Sighing, Cotterill glanced at the street map on the screen. 'Let me have a look.' Pressing a button in the door, he listened to the buzz of the electric window as it slid down.

Leaning into the cab, the man handed Cotterill the phone with one hand and reached forward with the other. Cotterill didn't see the blade but he felt it tear the skin as it was pulled across his throat. 'Vernon says, "See you in hell."'

With the knife still embedded in his neck, Cotterill watched as the milk float finally resumed its forward movement. From behind him came the sound of angry horns. He paid them no heed. His eyes began to lose their focus and he felt a chill eating at his guts. From somewhere in his brain came peals of hysterical laughter. His final thought was about cheese straws.

TWENTY-SEVEN

'What do we do now?' Thomson sounded like a sullen teenager. It was almost as if the inspector was taking a perverse pleasure in the fact that their best lead had just had his throat cut.

'We still have Cotterill's file.' Roche glanced at her watch. Thank God Alex had the day off. Otherwise she'd have been embroiled in another argument over nursery pick-up duty. Maybe she could convert him into a house-husband. One thing was for sure, they couldn't go on like this: something had to give. Roche hated feeling torn in two directions at once, never quite in control of her life. 'Better to do one thing well,' her father had often pontificated, 'than two things badly.' All too often, it felt like she was doing ten things terribly.

'You'd better hope that kid comes up with something,' the inspector groused. 'You how much he costs? Sixteen hundred quid a day, plus VAT.'

Roche watched Ashley Cotterill's taxi being lifted onto a low loader. 'Where are they taking it?'

'Mile End.'

'Handy.'

'It's the nearest garage with any space.' Thomson hoisted a small leather bag onto her shoulder. 'Right, let's go. It's time to pay Mr Holder a visit.'

Roche stood rooted to the spot. 'I'd hold off on that. He'll have a decent alibi, for sure. We're not going to get a confession. But does he know we have the file?'

'He must do,' Thomson reasoned. 'Why else would he take out his long-time associate in such a ruthless manner?'

'All the more reason to think there's something worth knowing in there. Let's see what Chris Dalston comes up with. Holder can wait until tomorrow. In the meantime, we can go and see the widow.'

Thomson groaned. 'I've had more than enough of happy families, having to deal with Umar Sligo's lot.'

'Fair enough,' Roche conceded. 'Leave Mrs Cotterill to me. You get the initial report under way and I'll let you know when I've spoken to her.'

'All right.' Thomson clearly wasn't happy with being handed the paperwork, but it was better than the alternative. 'Let me know how you get on. I'll see you back at the station.' Not waiting for a reply, she turned on her heel and stalked off.

'Dad! The phone.'

'Eh?' Carlyle stuck his head out of the shower in time to see the bathroom door open. Alice's hand appeared in the crack, just above floor level, and slid his phone across the tiled floor.

'It's Ali Roche,' his daughter explained, already beating a hasty retreat.

The commander grabbed a towel and gave himself a less than adequate rub-down before picking up the handset.

'Hello?'

'Sorry, did I interrupt you?' The sergeant didn't seem that bothered by the prospect.

'I was in the shower.'

'Lucky for me that Alice picked up my call,' Roche mused. 'It's good to see she hasn't acquired your phobia about answering the phone.'

'I don't have a phobia,' Carlyle protested. Clamping the phone with his shoulder, he resumed drying himself off.

'She's a very polite young lady,' Roche teased. 'For a moment, I thought I'd dialled a wrong number.'

'She can put on a good front when she wants to,' Carlyle conceded grudgingly.

'You should be pleased.'

'Hm.'

'You hardly sound the proud parent.'

'Just you wait.' Carlyle made a mental note to tell his daughter to leave his phone alone. 'Anyway, shouldn't you be doing David's bath or something?'

'Alex is on bath duty tonight,' Roche explained, sounding cheerier by the minute.

'Good for Sh—' Carlyle corrected himself at the last moment. 'Good for him.' Wrapping the towel around his waist, he padded into the bedroom.

'The reason I was ringing,' Roche continued, 'is that there have been developments in the Karen Jansen case.'

'Oh?' Carlyle dropped the towel and grabbed a pair of pants from a drawer.

'Vernon Holder's lawyer, Ashley Cotterill, had his throat slashed. He bled out in his car in the middle of a traffic jam.'

'Nasty.'

'The crime scene was a hell of a mess,' Roche recalled. 'And Thomson isn't happy.'

'I don't think the inspector has ever known happiness,' Carlyle reflected, as he looked for his jeans.

'Vernon Holder's running scared.'

'I'd not be so sure about that.' Carlyle finally spotted one leg sticking out from under the bed. 'Vernon has never run scared from anything in his life. In his mind, it's probably just a bit of housekeeping.' He dropped to one knee. 'Are you off to see him?'

'Nah. I'm off to see the lawyer's widow first. I was wondering if you wanted to come with me.'

'Sure,' Carlyle replied. 'Just let me get my trousers on.'

A small television screen attached to the side of a cupboard, its sound muted, flickered with news of another lone-wolf terrorist attack on the continent. This one was in Belgium. Two policemen had been shot, another stabbed.

There are nutters everywhere. And cops the world over don't get proper protection. Picking up the remote, Carlyle hit the off button before taking a seat at the kitchen table with Roche and the freshly minted widow. Dressed in a grey cashmere cardigan over a simple white blouse, Sarah Cotterill came across as a rather elegant woman, not at all what he had been expecting. On first impression, it looked as if the dead lawyer had been punching considerably above his weight in the marriage stakes.

'Would you like a cheese straw?' Mrs Cotterill cautiously pushed a rectangular foil packet towards the commander. When Carlyle declined the offer, she left the snacks in the middle of the table. 'If you change your mind . . .'

'Thank you.' Carlyle felt a sudden urge to hold her hand. It was surprisingly strong, but he resisted.

'Mrs Cotterill,' Roche intoned solemnly, 'we are very sorry for your loss.'

'I saw them in the supermarket this morning.' The words were coherent, but the woman's brain was on automatic pilot. 'First time for years. I thought they'd stopped making them ages ago.'

Eh? It took Carlyle a moment to realise that she was still talking about the cheese straws.

'I always used to get them for the boys, for their school lunches. Ashley would regularly snaffle a packet, so I always made sure there were a few spare, just in case.'

'Hm.' Carlyle began to wish he had stayed at home.

'They tasted horrible, but the boys loved them. So did their dad.'

'Your sons,' Roche enquired gently. 'Do you want us to contact them?'

Mrs Cotterill shook her head. 'Kevin is in America, on business. Charlie's in Glasgow. He lives up there – he married a local girl.'

'Scottish.' A second-generation Scot himself, Carlyle tried to remember the last time he'd visited the mother country. It had to have been five years ago, at least.

'Polish.' Mrs Cotterill sniffed.

'I've already spoken to Charlie. He'll be here tomorrow. I'm still trying to get hold of Kevin. His PA at work says they'll get him to call me as soon as possible. She was very nice about it.'

'You shouldn't be alone tonight,' Roche suggested.

'My sister will come over.'

'Good.'

'She should be here soon. She's only in Ealing.'

Not wishing to be stuck in the kitchen any longer than was absolutely necessary, Carlyle breathed a sigh of relief.

'There'll be things to do.' Mrs Cotterill looked at Roche. 'I suppose you'll want me to come and identify the body.'

Jesus, no. Not until they manage to stitch the head back on at least. 'That can wait.' The commander looked at Roche. 'I'm afraid things might get delayed a bit by the investigation.'

'It might take some time,' the sergeant agreed.

'I understand.'

Roche placed a business card next to the packet of cheese straws. 'You can contact me at any time.'

Mrs Cotterill stared at it. 'How long do you think it will take, the investigation?'

'That's hard to say,' Roche replied. 'But we have a lot of

people working on this. As soon as it's possible to begin making arrangements we'll let you know.'

If the sergeant's words were in any way reassuring, Mrs Cotterill didn't let it show. 'What can you tell me about the actual attack?'

'Well,' Roche looked at Carlyle, who indicated for her to proceed with caution, 'your husband was attacked while driving his cab by a man we have yet to identify.'

'Was it quick? Did he suffer?'

It was a brutal assault. He would have died in considerable pain. Carlyle told his brain to shut up. 'Yes, it was quick. No, he didn't suffer.'

Roche moved swiftly on. 'There are several CCTV recordings of the incident, which should assist our enquiries considerably. We have also collected a large number of witness statements. We haven't got the person who did this in custody yet, but we will.'

'It was Vernon Holder, wasn't it?'

'From what we've seen, Mr Holder was not the man who attacked your husband.' Roche held the widow's gaze. 'It was someone younger.'

'Vernon didn't do the deed,' the widow pressed, the first hint of irritation creeping into her voice, 'but he was behind it, wasn't he?'

'What makes you say that?' Carlyle asked.

'I'm not a fool. I wouldn't have a Metropolitan Police commander sitting at my kitchen table if this was a routine mugging gone wrong, would I?'

'What you say falls into the category of what I would call "reasonable assumption",' Carlyle agreed. 'We have reason to believe that what happened to your husband was related to his work. Mr Holder is a person of interest. It's fair to say that we've been investigating him for some time.'

'For about forty years, and no one's ever laid a finger on him. Vernon's a sly dog.'

'That he is,' the commander confirmed.

Mrs Cotterill looked at each of the cops in turn. 'In some ways, it's a bit of a relief. We've known for a long time that this day would come. We talked about it a lot. Ashley was well prepared. Everything's in order. Right down to the funeral arrangements. He was always a very orderly man. The idea that he wasn't leaving any loose ends gave him a certain amount of comfort, pleasure even.'

Sounds like a bad case of OCD, Carlyle mused.

'Not that he wanted to die.'

'No,' the two cops murmured in unison.

'It was so stressful, looking over your shoulder the whole time. The anticipation was driving poor Ashley round the bend.' Mrs Cotterill looked at Roche. 'He told me he was going to give you that file. He was worried you'd turn out to be crooked – like the other guy – but he had to take the risk. It was his last chance to escape Vernon's clutches.'

'I'm sorry.' Bowing her head, the sergeant stared at the table.

'Which other guy?' Carlyle asked.

'Inspector Ronald Augustus Score.' Mrs Cotterill spat out the words as if they were sour milk. 'What a silly name. What a wretched little man.'

Carlyle was not going to disagree. 'I knew Ronnie . . . I didn't know his middle name, though.'

'When Vernon got rid of him, I worried Ashley was going to have a stroke. He was convinced that it was the start of a total clear-out of the operation. "The night of the long knives" was what he called it. But Vernon wasn't really like that. He doesn't go in for grand gestures. He likes to deal with troublesome employees one at a time, so one day Mr Score is dealt with. Everyone's on edge for a few days and then things go back to something approaching normal. Until the next one.'

'You know for a fact that Vernon was behind the killing of Ronnie Score?'

'As much as you do.' Mrs Cotterill looked him straight in the eye. 'If I had any *proof*, Commander, he'd be behind bars and Ashley would still be alive.'

Fair point, Carlyle reflected.

'Vernon is a sick man, paranoid, ruthless, completely lacking in empathy. That said, his track record is exemplary. He simply doesn't get caught. I don't think he's spent a night behind bars in his entire life.'

Roche finally looked up. 'How long had your husband been working for him?'

'It was a gradual thing. Ashley and I had been married for a few years when he first did some work for Vernon. I can't remember what it was, something completely innocuous, the transfer of a lease or something.' Mrs Cotterill fiddled with a button on her cardigan. 'Anyway, Ashley did a good job – he was always very low key, efficient. He liked to get on with things.'

OCD, Carlyle's brain repeated.

'Vernon kept coming back. At that time, we had no idea who he was. We were just grateful for the work. I was pregnant with Kevin. Money was tight – you know what it's like. Vernon paid well and, just as importantly, paid on time. He had a steady stream of work. Over the course of a year or so, he basically became Ashley's only client. By then Ashley knew what he was getting into – so did I, for that matter. We weren't stupid and we weren't naive. I remember one night when he came home and told me about a guy called Muirhead. Vernon was doing some business with him. Ashley sat down at the kitchen table – we were living in Walthamstow back then – and just said, "They're crooks, love, proper crooks, and I'm right in the middle of it."' She shivered at the memory. 'I'll never forget that conversation.'

'I knew Angus Muirhead.' Carlyle scratched his head. 'He was a well-known face in Soho. Died a couple of years ago. Cancer. He was a gangster, right enough, but he could be quite engaging. Old school – made a distinction between what he called "players" and civilians. He had a clear, if sometimes rather warped, sense of right and wrong. I had a working relationship, of sorts, with him. He wasn't like Vernon at all.'

'You don't do business with Vernon,' Mrs Cotterill said. 'You do what you're told. Once we were caught in his web, it was too late. We just didn't have an exit strategy.' A single tear rolled down her cheek. 'That's what Ashley used to call it, our "exit strategy". "We need to develop a foolproof exit strategy," he'd say.' She shot Carlyle a pained look. 'Well, he never did, did he?'

Roche leaned forward in her chair. 'What did he tell you about the file?'

'Not very much. Ashley tried to spare me the details as far as possible. He knew he was up to his neck in it, but he hoped that if he could help put Vernon away, he might be able to retire. We've got a place in France – near Nice – and we were going to move there.'

The tears came freely now, silent sobs that left Carlyle squirming in his seat. This was the worst part of the job. If the victims were past care, past help, their families were another matter entirely. He knew he would never get used to it, however long he managed to eke out a career as a copper.

Getting to her feet, Roche placed a comforting hand on Sarah Cotterill's shoulder. 'Would you like some tea?'

The widow wiped away her tears with the back of her hand. 'That would be nice.'

While Roche busied herself with the kettle, Carlyle asked, 'Did your husband ever mention a guy named Umar Sligo?'

'The sex addict?'

'Is that what he called him?' Dropping a teabag into a mug, Roche bit her lower lip.

The commander shook his head. Right now, he could have done with something stronger than tea. He looked around the kitchen in the hope of spying a bottle of Scotch but there was no alcohol to be seen.

'Among other things. Ashley thought the man was an idiot. There was something wrong with the wiring in his brain. It was like he was on heat the whole time.'

'It's quite possible,' Carlyle admitted.

'No offence.' Mrs Cotterill sniffed. 'I mean, I know he'd been a policeman.'

'He left the force to go and work for a guy named Harry Cummins.'

Mrs Cotterill nodded. 'The pimp.'

For someone who knew nothing, Carlyle mused, you seem to be very familiar with all the main characters.

Roche appeared at her shoulder and carefully placed a mug of steaming tea on a coaster on the table. 'Here you go.'

'Thank you.' Mrs Cotterill reached for the cup. 'Vernon regretted killing Harry.'

Carlyle glanced at Roche. 'Why do you say that?'

Mrs Cotterill took a sip of her tea and gave an appreciative nod. 'Because he could deal with Harry bloody Cummins with his eyes closed but he more than met his match in the wife.'

TWENTY-EIGHT

After they'd taken their leave of Sarah Cotterill, Carlyle luxuri-
ated in the cool night air and tried to order his thoughts. He had
imagined that his promotion would make it easier to rise above
the white noise of individual cases. If anything, however, the
reverse seemed to be true. He was dogged by an uneasy feeling
that had characterised his entire police career: the sense that he
just wasn't doing things right.

Roche looked out across the orange glow of the north London
night. 'Quite a woman.'

'Sarah Cotterill?'

'I was thinking of Vicky Dalby-Cummins.'

'Her reputation is certainly starting to go before her,' Carlyle
agreed.

'Have you ever met her?'

'I don't think so. At least, not as far as I know. I certainly
never saw her with Harry. By all accounts, they led separate
lives. She didn't like London – more the horse-riding type.'

'She runs stables and a large organic farm near the Welsh
borders,' Roche said. 'Comes from the west Herefordshire
Dalbys – they can trace their family tree all the way back to the
Domesday Book, apparently.'

Carlyle raised an eyebrow.

Roche waved her phone. 'I did a quick bit of research. The

233

family made a pile in the armaments industry during the First World War and have basically sat on it since.'

'Nice.'

'Want to go and see her?'

'Not really.' Carlyle had no intention of schlepping out to the middle of nowhere. Anything beyond Zone One of the tube map – Zone Two at a push – was a sea of mediocrity and despair in which he had no desire to swim. 'I don't have time. Neither do you.' He kicked a stone in the direction of the gutter. 'Maybe we can get Thomson to do it.'

Roche looked at him doubtfully. 'I don't know about that. I think she's getting pretty fed up with everything.'

'What d'you make of her?'

'She's on the management fast track. She'll spend a few years flitting from station to station, never staying anywhere long enough to learn much, and then she'll get placed behind a desk on Victoria Embankment where she'll go to lots of meetings and write lots of memos. Not much of a career, if you ask me.'

'No.'

'Speaking of the Embankment, have you been there yet?'

'The new Scotland Yard?' Carlyle made a face. 'It's just another office building. You walk in and it could be the HQ of an insurance company, or a bank – except there isn't any decent art on the walls.'

'I bet Thomson can't get in there quick enough – she doesn't like it out on the street.'

'No.'

'She's no mug, though. She's going to twig sooner rather than later.'

Carlyle tried to look innocent. 'Twig what?

'That you're – *we*'re – running a parallel investigation in the Karen Jansen case.'

'Hardly.' Carlyle pushed back. 'I'm just helping you out.'

'I'm not sure she'll see it like that. Anyway, Thomson's not going to make another trip up north just because it suits you. Plus, Jansen's parents are due to arrive from Australia tomorrow and I'm perfectly happy to leave the inspector to deal with them.'

'In that case,' Carlyle decided, 'Harry's missus'll have to wait – we've *all* got too much on our plates as it is.'

'There's no reason to think she's going anywhere,' Roche agreed.

'How're you getting on with Ashley's secret file?'

'We've got a guy looking through it. A forensic accountant. We'll see what he has to say tomorrow.'

'Jolly good.' Carlyle spied a pub up ahead. 'Fancy a drink?'

'I've gotta get home.'

'Sure.' Carlyle tried to keep the disappointment from his voice. 'Isn't Sh– Alex on domestic duty tonight?'

'He is, but you can't take the piss.'

Why not? 'No.'

'He's been a real star. I don't want to push my luck.' Reaching into her bag, Roche recovered the key to the battered Fiat standing by the kerb. 'I'll drop you back somewhere near the centre of town.'

'Still no story, huh?'

Bernie Gilmore looked at his trainers. The hapless hack enjoyed the novelty of being able to see his feet, but his stomach-reduction surgery was increasingly looking like a luxury he couldn't afford.

'Well?' Alain Costello demanded.

'I submitted the story,' Bernie mumbled. 'It's in the pipeline. They're checking a few facts.'

'Look at me.'

Bernie slowly lifted his head. Costello was dressed in a pin-stripe jacket over a white T-shirt and a pair of jeans. His greying hair was held in place with a purple Alice band, which served to make him look faintly ridiculous. It was the first time Bernie had ever seen the Frenchman without a games console in his hand. Beside him stood a new henchman. *What happened to Ivan?* Bernie wondered.

'Tell me, what facts are they checking?'

All of them. 'My boss just wants to make sure she's not going to end up getting sued. She's had a bit of a bad run in that regard recently.'

Costello waved away the explanation. 'I gave you the facts. *All* the facts.'

'They want verification. They normally insist on two separate credible sources. Sometimes three.'

Costello was implacable. 'When is the story going to appear?'

'I don't know,' Bernie admitted. He knew that lying would only drag this thing out longer. If he was going to take a beating, better to get it over with. Apart from anything else, he had another date lined up for tomorrow night – Natasha, the marine biologist from London Zoo, had blown him out, so he had turned his attention to a PA/conceptual artist from Hoxton called Marlene – and he wanted any marks on his face to be fading by the time he walked into the Ethiopian jazz café she'd picked for their rendezvous.

'Maybe in the next few weeks.'

'That's not good enough,' Costello snapped. 'Is it, Solomon?'

The new goon concurred with a grunt.

Solomon – what kind of name is that? Unable to help himself, Bernie stifled a titter.

'What's so funny?' Costello screamed. Flicking out a hand, he aimed a slap at Bernie's cheek.

Ducking out of the way, the journalist felt the blow fly harmlessly past his shoulder. *Enough of this nonsense*, he told himself. *Let's get it over with.* 'Look,' he held up both hands in submission, 'I don't know when the story is going to run. I'm doing more digging but there are so many holes in it that the lawyers might not let it run at all. They're being very conservative right now. Even if the cop, Carlyle, didn't sue us, it's a racing certainty that Dominic Silver's lawyers would be all over it. I'm trying my best, but that's it. There are no guarantees, in this game.'

Costello's eyes narrowed. 'That's not what you said when you took my money.'

'No,' Bernie returned his gaze to his shoes, 'well . . .'

'And the money?' Costello demanded. 'Where is it?'

'I spent the money.' Bernie sucked in his remaining stomach. 'It's gone.'

'That's not so good, is it?'

'Look, I understand your unhappiness about the situation.' He shot Solomon a nervous glance. 'If you want your man to give me a beating, that's fine. Go ahead. But we are where we are.'

A look passed between Costello and Solomon.

'We are where we are,' Bernie repeated.

'You misunderstand me,' Costello insisted. 'I'm not going to beat you up.'

'No?' Bernie relaxed slightly. Maybe things were looking good for his date with Marlene after all.

'No.' Costello smiled. 'Why would I want to do that?'

TWENTY-NINE

It had been a rough night. David wouldn't settle and Roche had enjoyed next to no sleep by the time she made it back to Charing Cross. Arriving at the station, the sergeant felt almost eviscerated by tiredness. 'Welcome to a new day,' she muttered to herself, as she exited the lift on the third floor. Sitting at her desk, Chris Dalston looked like he hadn't been home at all.

'What have we got?'

The young forensic accountant held up an A3 sheet of paper covered with scribbles and arrows. It reminded Roche of a pirate's treasure map. 'The data shows a flow of funds that links thirteen different companies, which are—'

Roche held up a hand, her brain beginning to melt. 'Before we get started, I think I need some coffee. Want some?'

Dalston nodded eagerly. 'I'll have a latte, please.'

'Good.' Dropping her bag on the desk, Roche reached inside for her purse. 'I'll be back in a minute.'

Downstairs, the sergeant was dismayed to see a lengthy breakfast queue. Calculating that it would take at least fifteen minutes to get served, she turned on her heel, heading for the Pret on the Strand, when she realised that Nayla Thomson was sitting at a table in the corner. The inspector had her head buried in a pile of papers. On the table was a large glass of green juice with a straw sticking out of the top.

Roche approached cautiously. 'What's that?' she asked, pointing at the glass.

'Kale juice,' Thomson explained. 'Full of good stuff.'

'Hm.' Roche pulled up a seat and sat down.

The inspector placed her reading on the table. 'Want to try some?'

Roche politely declined the offer. Everyone else seemed to be buying bacon rolls. 'When did we start doing kale juice?'

'It's a trial.' Thomson pointed at a row of juices lined up on the counter. 'I don't think it's going too well.'

'People here think that being healthy means passing on a second portion of chips for breakfast.'

'The Met has an obesity crisis the same as everyone else,' Thomson intoned, with all the emotion of a Speak Your Weight machine. 'Almost half of new recruits are overweight before they even start. Almost as bad, no one monitors the fitness of officers as they go through the ranks.' The inspector sucked a mouthful of the smoothie through the straw. 'Everyone's got to look after themselves, basically.' She placed her glass carefully back on the table. 'And this stuff is much better for you than coffee.'

'I might give it a go.' Roche failed to suppress a yawn.

A smug look descended on Thomson's face. 'Tough night?'

'Not really.'

The inspector let the matter drop. 'How's the accountant getting on?'

Roche looked at the queue, which was moving slowly. 'I'm just getting him a coffee and then I'll see what he's come up with.'

'He'd better've come up with *something*,' Thomson muttered.

'Want to come and see?'

Glancing at her watch, Thomson shook her head. 'I have to get going. Karen Jansen's parents should be landing in ninety minutes. I promised the Australian ambassador I'd go and meet them personally.'

'The ambassador?'

'Yeah. For some reason, this got kicked all the way to the top. It seems like the murder's caused quite a stir over there. The embassy's been calling just about every day for an update.'

'Don't worry, I'll deal with Dalston.'

'If he's not getting anywhere, don't flog a dead horse. We can afford two days of his time, max.'

'Understood.' Roche felt an almost irresistible urge to lay her head on the table for a quick nap.

'Meantime, have you seen the CCTV?'

Roche looked at her boss blankly.

'The man who killed Ashley Cotterill – it looks like we've got a lead.'

Carlyle had barely sat down at his desk when there was a knock at the door. He looked up to see Michelle Mara stroll into the middle of the room. Make-up absent, her hair pulled back across her skull, the deputy assistant commissioner was clearly in Warrior Princess mode. She eyed him with an all-too-familiar mixture of dismay and irritation. 'Project Scimitar.'

'Yes?'

'No need to worry about it now.' Mara folded her arms, as if challenging him to dispute the assertion. 'It's been closed down.'

On balance, Carlyle reflected, that wasn't much of a surprise.

'No need to write any further reports either.' The DAC tried to offer a conciliatory tone. 'I'll deal with the outstanding paperwork.'

'Thanks.' Carlyle wondered about her boyfriend, but he knew better than to push it. Instead he asked, 'The guys who went missing—'

'No one has been reported missing,' Mara interjected. 'As far as I know, they just left the country.'

240

'Ah. And what about the three million that was stolen outside the Edgware Road branch of the Red Sea Bank?'

'The Diplomatic Protection Group is still looking into that. But, from *our* point of view, there are no loose ends.'

'No.' The commander knew better than to ask any further questions.

'One final thing.' Mara turned towards the door. 'I'm moving on.'

Trying not to look too pleased, Carlyle picked a pencil from the desk. 'Oh?'

She paused in the doorway. 'I've been offered the chance to act as chief UK liaison for the Gender Balance in Global Law Enforcement Initiative.'

Carlyle had never heard of it. 'Sounds interesting,' he lied. 'Who'll be taking over from you here?'

'I don't know if they've appointed anyone yet.' Mara's expression said *I couldn't care less*. 'I'm sure they'll let you know in due course.'

'Yes.' Feeling a sudden stab of embarrassment, Carlyle began doodling over a report from the commissioner. 'Well, good luck.'

'You too, Commander. A word to the wise, though. If I were you, I'd see about improving my meeting-attendance record. My successor might not be as forgiving as me on those sorts of things.'

'It's top of my to-do list.' Carlyle gave his soon-to-be ex-boss a small wave. 'I hope you enjoy the new job.'

'I'm sure I will.'

As Mara took her leave, Carlyle wondered if he would ever see her again. Either way, he cared not a jot. Tossing the pencil onto his desk, he looked in dismay at the scribble he'd made on the commissioner's wise words. 'Damn.' Pulling open a drawer, he looked for a rubber to clean up the mess. All he came up with, however, was the shell casing Daniel Hunter had given him. 'I can't keep collecting all this junk,' he muttered to himself, tossing it into the bin, then padding into the outer office.

'Shame about DAC Mara leaving,' Linda offered, looking up from her computer.

'I'll get over it,' Carlyle muttered. 'In fact, I already have.'

Linda shot him a disapproving look.

'Any idea of who's going to replace her?' he asked.

'Why? Do you fancy the job?'

'Hardly.' Carlyle laughed. 'I think I've gone too far, too fast as it is.'

Linda didn't contest his analysis. Instead she mentioned the names of a couple of possible successors to the DAC, both of whom were currently employed by forces outside London. Not having an opinion on either of them, the commander moved swiftly on.

'What have I got this morning?'

Clicking her mouse, Linda looked at the screen. 'Do you really want to know?'

'Thrill me.'

'Well, there's the resources committee, which is starting in five minutes. That's due to run for an hour and a half. And then you've got a promotions board and after lunch—'

Carlyle held up a hand. 'I don't suppose CS Nathan is around, is he?'

Linda shook her head. 'The chief superintendent is on a course this week.'

'Of course he is,' Carlyle groused.

'A retreat in the New Forest – some kind of team-building exercise.'

'He must be in his element.' Carlyle observed. 'Maybe you could try to find someone else to fill in for me.'

'Commander,' she admonished him, 'you really are going to get the most terrible reputation.'

'I already have a terrible reputation.'

'You will when the performance tables come out, that's for sure.'

'Aren't you trying to, erm, *massage* the data for me?'

'I spent a whole day trying to *fiddle the figures*,' Linda told him, 'and you still ended up second from bottom across the whole of London.'

'Second from bottom?' Carlyle felt slightly miffed at losing his *lanterne rouge* status. How in the name of God can there be someone worse than me when it comes to attending meetings? he wondered.

'And that's only because poor old Commander Fry has been off sick for the last two months.' Benjamin Fry had been shopping in Westfield when someone had tried to mug his wife. Giving chase to the robber, the poor bloke had suffered a minor heart attack. It had made the local TV news. The anchor had rounded off the report with a gag about policemen and doughnuts. Ironically, Fry wasn't fat.

'How is Benny?'

'Doing well,' Linda assured him. 'He's due back at the start of next month, apparently.'

'At which point,' Carlyle rejoined, 'I should be able to reclaim my rightful place at the top of the meeting *non*-attendance league.'

Linda tapped a few keys on her keyboard. 'Are you going to these meetings this morning?'

'What do you think?' Waltzing towards the door, Carlyle gave her a mock salute. 'I'll see you later.'

THIRTY

At the gallery, Carlyle found Daniel Hunter deep in conversation with an elegant blonde. Noticing his arrival, Eva Hollander – a.k.a. Mrs Dominic Silver – came over and gave him a quick peck on each cheek. 'John, nice to see you. It's been so long. How are you?'

'I'm good,' Carlyle mumbled, feeling every inch the crumpled, middle-aged man that he was. For her part, Eva was clearly reaping the benefits of a rigorous yoga regime and regular holidays in the sun. She looked sensational in a pearl blouse and expensive jeans. A pair of red leather cowboy boots rounded off the ensemble to great effect.

'And how are Helen and Alice?'

'They're good.' Eva and Dom had far more kids than he could easily namecheck, so Carlyle simply asked, 'How about your lot?'

'They're all fine – increasingly scattered to the four winds.' There was more than a hint of regret in Eva's voice as she nodded in the direction of the back office. 'Basically, I only have the one big kid to look after now.'

'I'm sure that's a full-time job.'

Eva agreed that it was before mentioning that her upcoming lunch with Helen would need to be rescheduled. 'Tell her I'll call.'

'Will do.'

'How old is Alice now?'

'Too old.' Now it was Carlyle's turn to sound wistful. He clicked his fingers. 'The time goes like that.'

'Don't I know it.'

'It'll be university soon.' Carlyle couldn't help but sound proud. 'Alice is looking at different places. We're off to visit Imperial College.'

'Imperial?' Eva nodded approvingly. 'What's she thinking of studying?'

'Not entirely sure,' Carlyle admitted.

'Well, I'm sure she'll have a wonderful time,' Eva declared. 'And in the meantime, what brings you over here?'

'Just checking in.' Carlyle gestured towards Hunter, who was hovering in the background. 'Seeing how your new hire is getting on.'

'Daniel's great. Where did you find him?'

'It's a long story.'

'Well, we're grateful to you for pointing him in our direction.' Eva reached forward and gave his arm a gentle squeeze. 'I know Dom was tearing his hair out over the security here. The kind of people he was being sent,' she shook her head, 'you wouldn't put them in charge of anything.'

'Hopefully it will work out well all round.'

'I'm sure. I hope Dom is giving you a finder's fee.'

'Don't be daft.'

'Seriously, you should. This is a big deal. Finding someone to stay onsite was a condition of getting the insurance renewed. Sigmund Kessling's final paintings are due to ship next week and they wouldn't be allowed to leave Canada if we didn't have proper cover.'

Carlyle scanned the blank spaces on the walls. 'The family have sorted themselves out, then?'

'Looks like it. Or, at least, they've decided to sell what they can so they can then argue over the money.'

'Which won't be your problem.' Carlyle recalled his earlier conversation with Dom. Right on cue, the door to the office opened. The great man stuck out his head, invited Carlyle to join him and disappeared back inside.

'Looks like you've been summoned.' Eva laughed.

'Yep.'

Heading for the office, Carlyle nodded at Hunter. 'How're things?'

'So far, so good.' The former military policeman looked a bit sheepish. 'Not a lot to do, to be honest.'

'Those are the best kind of jobs,' Carlyle told him. 'Let me go and have a word with the boss and then maybe we can grab a coffee.'

'Sure.'

Carlyle's phone buzzed in his pocket. Pulling it out, he checked the screen. A text from Roche. Opening it, he gasped audibly.

Bernie Gilmore murdered.

Standing outside Dom's office, his first inclination was to call the sergeant for more details. Deciding that could wait, he snatched open the door and stalked inside.

Sitting behind his desk, Dom was talking on the phone. 'I've got to go,' he muttered into the mouthpiece, registering the look of fury on Carlyle's face. 'Speak later.' Not waiting for a response, he dropped the receiver onto its cradle.

'What have you done?' Taking a kick at the desk, Carlyle grimaced as his foot collided with the heavy mahogany.

'Eh? And what the hell are you doing?' The surprise on Dom's face looked genuine enough. On the other hand, Carlyle knew that his friend was a more than competent actor.

'I promised I'd take care of Bernie Gilmore. I told you to sit tight.'

'I haven't done anything to that fat slob. What are you talking about?'

Fat slob? Carlyle eyed his pal suspiciously. 'He's not so big now. He had weight-loss surgery.'

'Good for him. If he wants to have some more, I'll happily pay for it – as long as he drops that damn story.' Dom chuckled. 'It's probably tax deductible anyway.'

As the tension evaporated from the room, Carlyle slumped into the chair in front of Dom's desk. 'Bernie won't be needing any further surgery.'

'These fatsos are terrible backsliders,' Dom opined. 'He'll probably put all the weight back on in a month or two.'

'Bernie won't be putting the weight back on, seeing as he's dead.'

'Dead?' After a moment's silence, Dom started to laugh. 'Excellent.'

'He was murdered.' Carlyle waved his phone at Dom. 'Which is not so excellent.'

Dom still looked chuffed at the news. 'As long as the story dies with him, it's a result I can live with.'

'Not if it comes back to us.'

'Well,' Dom sat back in his chair, 'I didn't kill him. And I know you didn't.'

'How do you know *I* didn't do it?' Carlyle asked, conscious of how quickly the tables had been turned.

'You haven't got the balls.'

'Thanks a lot.'

'Some people – most people – would take that as a compliment,' Dom said. 'But we're getting away from the point.'

'Which is?'

'Which is, if *I* didn't kill Bernie and *you* didn't kill Bernie, who did?'

THIRTY-ONE

'Urgh. Jesus.' Carlyle took a gulp of his tea. 'It must have been a hell of a mess.'

'I'm glad I wasn't first on the scene,' Roche admitted.

Sitting opposite the commander, Daniel Hunter stared into his mug of coffee, pretending not to eavesdrop on his phone conversation.

'It's not Thomson's case,' Carlyle asked, 'is it?'

The sergeant confirmed in the negative. 'It's been handed to Chief Inspector Younge.'

'Simone Younge?' Carlyle made a face. 'Didn't she take early retirement?'

'She's winding down. That's why she had the capacity to take this one on. She's not happy about it, but what can you do? She should have retired to her place in Kent already but there's a delay with her pension deal, apparently.'

'Shame,' Carlyle mumbled.

'It is for Younge. She hasn't done any proper work for years.'

This, Carlyle decided, was a decent result. The superannuated chief inspector would have little interest in digging too deeply into the stories that Bernie Gilmore had been working on, which was just as the commander wanted it.

'HR's trying to move the goalposts,' Roche complained. 'There's a rumour that they want to push back the earliest age anyone can leave. Looks like the chief inspector's going to have to work for another three years. Younge is threatening to take them to court. She's brought in the Federation, but Alex says they're having to deal with hundreds of pension dispute claims. It's going to take years for them to get sorted out. In the meantime, the people affected have to keep working.'

'Bummer.' Carlyle found it hard to feel sorry for people like Younge, who had spent their entire careers thinking about little other than early retirement on fat guaranteed pensions funded by the taxpayer. Obviously, this wasn't a particularly popular view among his fellow police officers. To the commander's way of thinking, however, the numbers just didn't add up. 'Just as well you and I will be pounding the streets till we're well into our seventies,' he observed wryly, 'if not longer. We won't have to worry about pensions.'

'Speak for yourself.' Roche's tone was surprisingly vehement.

'Come on, what else would you do? Marry Shaggy and become a housewife?'

'What?'

'Er . . .' After an awkward silence, the commander tried to steer the conversation towards safer ground. 'Does Younge have any leads on Bernie Gilmore's killer?'

'Not that I've heard. The crime scene was badly contaminated. The body was found in a derelict property in east London. There was evidence that it had been disturbed by dogs, maybe a fox.'

'Poor old Bernie, he didn't deserve that.' Despite everything, Carlyle felt a smattering of affection for the deceased hack. If nothing else, the guy had been a bit of a character. God knew there were few of them around these days. And his stories were interesting, most of the time.

'The media'll certainly make a meal of it. In terms of column inches, one dead journalist has got to be worth at least a thousand dead members of the general public.'

'Younge will have to deal with that.'

'From what I hear, she's struggling to cope. When she first arrived at the crime scene, she almost threw up over the body. It's not every day that you see a man strangled with his own gastric band.'

'Bloody hell.' Carlyle winced. 'Really?'

'According to the pathologist, Gilmore was dead by the time that happened. They reckon they can recycle it.'

'Sorry?'

'The gastric band. Apparently, they can use it on someone else.'

'Too much information.' Carlyle almost spilled his tea. 'I don't want to know.'

From the other side of the table, Hunter gave him an amused look.

'I suppose these things are expensive,' Roche ventured.

'How can they be expensive? It's just a rubber band. Surely it's the actual operation that costs the money.'

'From what I heard, Bernie had a donor card. His band is being donated to a charity that organises operations for poor people.'

'I'm sure you can't reuse something like that.' Carlyle could feel himself going green. The idea of some poor sod getting Bernie Gilmore's second-hand gastric band was making him feel really quite sick. He took another mouthful of tea, then put the mug on the table. 'Anyway, why would some fat chav want Bernie's hand-me-down when they can get a new one free on the NHS?'

'You're *so* prejudiced,' Roche scolded him. 'You know you're not supposed to use the C-word.'

'At least I'm an equal-opportunity bigot,' Carlyle pointed out. 'I dislike all social groups equally.'

'Never heard that one before.' Roche almost chuckled.

'I'm consistent, too.'

'Consistent but boring. It's a miracle that someone hasn't strangled *you* by now.'

'I don't have a gastric band.'

'I know plenty of people who would happily throttle you with their bare hands.'

Water off a duck's back, Carlyle thought happily. 'Returning to the man of the moment, Bernie must have *really* pissed someone off this time.'

'This time?'

'He was an investigative reporter. Pissing people off was core to the job description.'

'I wonder if everybody's favourite bent cop Andy Wick has got an alibi.'

'Ha. Good point. You might see if Younge's checked that one out.'

'I think I'll leave it to her.'

'Fair enough.' Carlyle was happy to declare the Bernie Gilmore fiasco closed. Looking out of the café window, he contemplated the art gallery on the other side of the road. Once he'd finished with Roche, he'd go and give Dom an update.

It looked like they were in the clear.

'Meantime, I think we've got a lead on Ashley Cotterill's killer.'

'Oh, yes?'

'After checking different security-camera feeds, we've been able to trace the man who attacked him all the way back to City Airport.'

'About time CCTV came in useful,' Carlyle said. London was supposed to have more cameras than any other city in the world, but he couldn't remember the last time they'd helped him solve a crime.

251

'And we've got a name. Emmanuel Bole.'

'Manny Bole?' Carlyle's face hardened. 'The psycho giant who tried to kill me with a frying pan?'

'I don't think he *tried* to kill you,' Roche teased. 'Otherwise you'd be dead. And it wasn't a frying pan, it was a—'

'I want that bastard,' Carlyle growled. 'He's been in the wind too long.' Bole, a former Indian Special Forces commando turned thug for hire, had been in the process of drowning a restaurateur in a pot of stew in the victim's kitchen when Carlyle had blundered onto the scene. The inspector, as he then was, had taken a battering before Bole made good his escape.

'Don't make it personal,' Roche counselled.

'Easy for you to say. It wasn't your skull he tried to smash in.'

'I know but, still, you have to move on.'

Realising he wasn't going to get any sympathy, Carlyle did as he was told. 'What's Manny got to do with Ashley Cotterill?'

'We don't know,' Roche said. 'What we *do* know is that Bole was there when Cotterill was killed. Then he travelled to City airport and took a flight to Brussels three hours later. We're requesting help from our Belgian colleagues in trying to determine his current whereabouts. I'll keep you posted.'

'Good. Where's Thomson?'

'She's meeting with Karen Jansen's parents.'

'And what about the Niamh Sligo case?'

'There's been no progress on that at all,' Roche told him. 'Not that it's my problem any longer. The case has been handed to someone at the Holborn station. Thomson wasn't happy, but we simply couldn't run both investigations at once.' There was the sound of voices in the background. 'Look, I've got to go. But that's where we are. I thought you'd want to know. I'll give you a call later.'

After Roche hung up, Carlyle placed his phone on the table.

'Sounds like there's a lot happening,' Hunter suggested.

'A lot of running around in circles,' Carlyle responded, finishing his tea. 'Anyway, how about you?'

'I'm good. Dom and Eva are both very nice and the job's a doddle. I'm very grateful for your help. It gives me a chance to get my life back on track. And there might be more that I can do.'

Carlyle raised an eyebrow. 'Oh?'

'I've been doing a bit of digging. I think there could be some leads in terms of the guys who robbed the gallery. I know one or two people—'

'I bet you know lots of people,' Carlyle interrupted, 'but do me a favour. Leave it alone. The insurance will deal with it. And Dom will make far more money from his new exhibition anyway, so what's the point?'

Hunter looked dismayed by the commander's response. 'I might be able to help. And it would do me good to keep my hand in.'

'I'd leave it.'

'Okay.' Hunter stared at his empty cup. 'Separately, I spoke to Mike Stoner, nothing to do with the gallery. He's the farmer who saw the gunfight out in Kent.'

'The *alleged* gunfight.' Carlyle recalled the shell casing that Hunter had given him. Maybe he shouldn't have thrown it into the bin.

'Mike spoke to a neighbour who heard gunshots, too.'

'Has he found any more physical evidence?'

'No.'

Good. Carlyle fumbled for his wallet. 'I think we'll just have to keep that one on the back burner. Like you said, there's a lot going on right now.'

THIRTY-TWO

'I can't get a bloody signal.' Standing in what looked suspiciously like decomposing animal shit, Vernon Holder scowled at the outsized green wellingtons that had been loaned to him for the occasion. It had taken more than six hours to make the journey from London by car and an uncomfortable night in one of Sinkwith Farm's less than salubrious holiday cottages had done nothing to lighten his mood. Breakfast had been minimal, and now he couldn't even use his phone. The sooner he was back on the M54, heading south, the better.

Victoria Dalby-Cummins gave him a playful pat on the arm as she marched past, full of vim and vigour. 'There's no phone coverage for more than ten miles. And, before you ask, no, we don't have any Wi-Fi.'

'Everywhere has Wi-Fi, these days,' Holder grumbled.

'Not Sinkwith Farm. That's part of our appeal. When people want to get away from it all, they come here.'

'You can say that again.' In the far distance, Holder watched a jet making its way serenely across the blue sky. Wherever it was going, the old gangster wished he was on it. Barely twenty-four hours ago, he'd been standing at the departures gate at Gatwick, seeing off his wife, Val. By now, she'd be tucked up in bed at their holiday villa in Barbados. He would join her in a few days. One day, soon now, they would go to the Caribbean and not come back. First, however, he needed to sort out his business interests. And that meant sorting out Vicky.

'The idea is that you enjoy the peace and quiet.'

'Huh?'

'Switch off a bit. This is where the Cheshire smart set come for a complete digital detox – people can go for up to a week without checking their email or their Twitter.' Dalby-Cummins made it sound like some kind of modern miracle. She pointed towards a small group of cottages set back from the road, clustered around a courtyard. 'The holiday lets have been a great success. We've got plans to build another seven or eight over the next couple of years.'

Further down the road they came to a seven-bar gate, which closed off a large field. On the other side, a flock of sheep went casually about their business. Placing a boot on the bottom bar, Dalby-Cummins pushed a strand of implausibly black hair away from her face. 'This business is going to take off. I can feel it.' She paused for effect. 'You can still come in as an investor, if you want.'

Holder had no interest in becoming a farmer. Instead, he had a proposition of his own. 'If I buy out your share of the London operation, you'll have plenty to invest in this place.'

Dalby-Cummins let out a girlish laugh. 'Come on, Vernon. Do you think I'm daft? London is my cash cow. I hand that over to you, what am I supposed to do longer-term? Anyway, now would be a terrible time to sell up. You'd take me to the cleaner's.'

'I'd offer a very fair price.'

'If you become an investor in Sinkwith it would add another strand to our partnership. Cement the relationship.'

Holder scowled at the sheep. 'Rule number one. Don't invest in something you don't understand.'

'Ah,' Dalby-Cummins chuckled, 'so you're a conventional businessman, now?'

'I like to think I understand my limits. What do I know about the countryside?'

'That's where I come in.'

'Hm.' The place seemed deserted. 'Where are the punters?' Other than Dalby-Cummins, Holder hadn't seen another soul since his arrival the night before.

'It's a bit early in the season.'

'It's too far away,' he objected. 'I couldn't be running up here every time heads needed knocking together.'

'I'm perfectly capable of doing that.'

'I'm sure you are.' As he contemplated the line of her backside in her jodhpurs, Holder felt a gentle but pleasing twitch in his groin. Not that he would ever seek to do anything about it. For all his obvious character defects, Vernon had been a faithful husband for more than forty years. Early in his career, he had made a clear decision not to mix business and pleasure. It was a rule he had never broken. His family was his one saving grace. He considered a stable, loving home life a major reason for his longevity in the unstable, unloving criminal world in which he had chosen to operate.

'I like to be hands-on. I always stick to what I know. Which means London clubs.' And London girls. 'That's why I'm such a good business partner.'

Dalby-Cummins could feel the old lech's eyes on her rear but chose to ignore it. She had called this meeting and she was determined to exploit her home advantage. 'Not so good recently. I've been looking at the latest numbers from London. It makes pretty grim reading.'

'Harry never did have much of a long-term plan.'

'Harry's been out of the picture for a while now. You're the one in charge. There is nothing in the data that suggests we'll be able to reverse the recent declines.'

'There have been a few short-term issues,' Holder conceded.

'Is that all they are?'

'What else would they be?'

'If that's the case, I'm quite happy to take a long-term view.' She waved a hand in the direction of the Monfils Valley, looking its best under a surprisingly warm sun. 'After all, my family has farmed this land for more than five hundred years.'

'Good.'

'But if the problems go deeper, we'll need to rethink our strategy. There's a difference between short-term ups and downs and a long-term trend. At its peak, this farm was more than forty thousand acres. That was something like a hundred and twenty years ago. The property is less than a quarter of that size now. We've only just got to grips with more than a century of steady decline. Things are picking up again, but it's taken a long time to turn things round and a lot of hard work to change some of the things we do.'

Tuning out of the business-school tutorial, Holder tried to remember the last time he'd been on a farm. It was probably when he was still at school: a fourth-form trip to the countryside. Throwing stones at the sheep. Ellie Johnson giving him a messy hand-job on the back seat of the bus in exchange for a couple of cigarettes.

Happy days.

His hostess mistook his expression for a sign of appreciation of his surroundings. 'Not bad, is it?' She lifted her face to the sun. 'It's the only place where I've ever felt truly at home.'

'Uh-huh.' If Holder hadn't come all this way for a business lesson, he hadn't come for a confessional either.

'Harry might have been a useless little shit, but at least his London business has managed to subsidise this place for the last decade.'

And now you want more. Holder wondered about killing her

on the spot. He could probably choke her to death in a couple of minutes. Dump the body just about anywhere you like. No one would ever know. The woman had no kids, no heirs as far as he knew. He would slip back to London and take control of her share of their business.

Simple.

Maybe the countryside wasn't so bad, after all.

'With a bit of luck, the farm should be able to break even in the next three to five years. The idea is it'll be self-sustaining after that.'

'Fingers crossed.' Farmers always seemed to be losing money. It was a miracle that there were any of them left. Reaching into his pocket, Holder pulled on a pair of gloves.

'It's not that cold.'

'I have a bit of arthritis.' Flexing his fingers, he was about to lunge for her throat when he heard a car engine. The vehicle was coming towards them. A few seconds later, he spotted a van bar-relling down a narrow country lane. On the side was the legend VDC Organic Foods.

Organic? The very word made him shudder. He knew a con when he saw one. His daughter had gone through a period when everything in the fridge had to be organic. Always will-ing to bow to the tyranny of political correctness, Val had made sure everything that appeared on their plates had the necessary paperwork to prove it had lived a happy, healthy life. Holder had never before eaten so badly. Worse still, the cost of all that middle-class stupidity had been extortionate. There had been many evenings around the dining-room table when he'd felt he might as well have flushed twenty-pound notes down the toilet.

The van pulled up at a series of dilapidated sheds about two hundred yards from the main farmhouse. A middle-aged couple wearing matching green fleeces got out and waved at

Dalby-Cummins. Each had a shock of silver hair and a ruddy complexion, indicative of a bucolic existence.

'You're branching out?' Reflecting that the window of opportunity for offing his business partner might have closed, Holder tried to feign interest in her hobby business.

'We started going organic years ago now.' Dalby-Cummins waved back. 'We've been selling to local businesses for more than a decade. Now we sell direct to the public at local markets.' The couple disappeared into one of the buildings. 'Cedric and Jinty Hamilton run the farm for me. They wanted to convert to an entirely organic system, and it turned out to be a pretty shrewd move. Once we finally got the organic classification from the Soil Association, we were able to up our prices by more than a hundred per cent. Costs are lower too – no more chemical fertilisers and we've stopped feeding the animals antibiotics. Now, we just rely on muck and common sense.'

'Muck and common sense. I like it.'

'Not a bad philosophy, is it?' She set off down the road. 'The farm is more profitable now than it's ever been. Or, at least, we're not losing as much as we used to.'

Holder followed her. 'That's all very interesting, but why did I have to come all the way up here?'

'You know I hate coming down to London – such a dirty place, such nasty people – and some fresh air will do you good.' She shoved her hands deep into the pockets of her Barbour jacket. 'C'mon, I want to show you my pigs.'

THIRTY-THREE

A group of pigs milled about aimlessly in a barn that was open at both ends. 'We only started with these a couple of years ago,' Dalby-Cummins explained, 'but they've been another great success. We currently have seventy-eight adults and sixty-five piglets. The number is going up all the time. The demand for free-range pigs is incredible. People are so sick of factory farming, animals kept in cages, pumped through with antibiotics. The whole thing is just wrong on so many levels.'

A bacon roll for breakfast wouldn't go amiss. Holder held back, not wanting to get too close to the beasts.

'Providing we don't compromise on quality, the sky's the limit. Our aim is to have two hundred sows on the farm with twenty boars, breeding a mix of Saddleback, Large Black and Domestic pink pigs – all of them fed properly, given freedom to roam and not pumped full of drugs.'

A pig's a pig. Holder eyed an empty trough running down the middle of the building. 'What do they eat?'

'Anything that's natural, basically.' An amused look passed across her face. 'We have an apple orchard especially for the pigs and we try to keep their food as simple as possible. We want them to stay well away from anything processed.' She pointed to a prefabricated shed further down the road. 'We kill them here, too. Jinty's a butcher, so we built our own butchery to ensure that the pork starts and finishes on the farm and quality is not lost.'

A butchery? Interesting. 'Can I take a look?'

'Sure. It's not in use at the moment, but I can show you around.'

Letting her lead the way, Holder considered his options. If he was going to do Vicky, the old couple wouldn't be much of an additional problem. If the place had its own slaughterhouse, disposing of the bodies would be a doddle. A sly grin crossed his face as he scanned the ground in front of him, keen to avoid stepping in more shit.

Pushing open a small door, Dalby-Cummins invited Holder to step inside. 'The animals go in the back.' She pointed over her shoulder. 'We like to keep everything out of sight of the guests.'

'I can understand that.' Holder found himself in a narrow corridor, with white tiles on the walls and the floor. Wiping his feet on a mat, he moved forward. I'll hang you on a hook, he decided, then go for the others.

At the end of the corridor, he pushed through a second door, entering a large, windowless room, illuminated by a single strip light hanging from the ceiling. A series of high-pressure water hoses were lined up against the back wall. The floor had recently been washed down but the place retained the stale odour of death.

Three large metal tables stood in the middle of the room. The first two were piled high with empty cardboard boxes. On the third sat a double-edged meat cleaver, gleaming malevolently under the artificial light, and a device that reminded Holder of a ray gun from the science-fiction movies he used to watch as a kid on Saturday mornings at the Odeon. For the briefest moment, he was transported back to tales of Flash Gordon, Buck Rogers and the Merciless Ming.

'This is Sandro.'

'Huh?' Holder jerked from his reverie to see a tall, wiry young man standing in the doorway at the far end of the room. He wore a navy cap, with a matching tunic and an apron that reached down to his ankles.

'Sandro's been a great help to me since Harry's unfortunate demise.' Stepping out from behind him, Dalby-Cummins took up a position by the far wall. Folding her arms, she waited for the action to proceed.

'I bet he has.' Holder realised he should have throttled his troublesome business partner when he'd had the chance.

'Well, you didn't expect me to sit up here all alone and rot, did you?'

'No. I suppose not.' Holder watched Sandro reach for the cleaver. 'Whatever she's paying you, I can double it. Triple it. Add a couple of noughts.'

Vicky started to laugh. 'I wouldn't waste your breath. He doesn't speak any English.'

'No?' Lifting a hand, Holder rubbed a thumb and forefinger together.

Sandro did not respond.

'He came from Syria,' Dalby-Cummins explained. 'Spent three weeks adrift in the Mediterranean on a ghost ship organised by people-smugglers. After making shore in Italy, he was dumped in a refugee camp for more than a year. After he'd made good his escape, it took him four months to get to England. God knows how he ended up here. Cedric found him one morning trying to kill a piglet with a rock. We fed him and – as you can see – he scrubbed up well. I decided to keep him. I knew that any man with such a strong survival instinct would be useful. And, with nowhere else to go, his loyalty is not in question.'

What was Italian for money? Holder tried to think back to the days of Enzo Schifo, an Italian accountant in his employ back in the eighties. '*Soldi.*' He rubbed his fingers together again. '*Soldi.*'

'Forget it, Vernon.' Dalby-Cummins ran her tongue along the underside of her top lip. 'You can't compete with my offer. I'm sorry, but it's for the best.'

'For the best?'

'I need to make some changes.' A look of determination settled on her face. 'I need better cash flow. I need to introduce fresh blood.'

'By spilling mine.'

'I know times are tough, but the London business has been suffering more than was necessary. The quality of the service has been slipping. There have been too many complaints, I'm afraid.'

Holder edged closer towards Sandro. He was conceding three inches in height, but on the other hand, he carried at least four stones in weight. If he could get close enough, there had to be a reasonable chance he could take down the foreign bastard. 'Who complained?'

'I spoke to Karen Jansen, not long before you had her killed. She was worried about you.'

'Scared, more like.' Out of the corner of his eye, Holder watched Sandro bouncing on the balls of his feet.

'Scared too. But, then, she had good reason to be, didn't she?'

Holder's brain screamed at him to attack. He tried to ignore it and stay calm. 'Karen did a runner. She was going to shop me. If I'd gone down, you would have, too.'

Dalby-Cummins shook her head. 'All she wanted to do was to go home to Australia. You were too pre-emptive. It was the same with that cop you had killed.'

'Ronnie Score would have dropped us in it for sure.'

'You don't know that.'

'I wasn't going to wait around to find out.'

'And poor old Ashley Cotterill. What was the point of that? Ashley worked for me, too, you know. Finding another accountant as . . . *flexible* is going to be a monster pain in the backside.'

It is rather a long list, Holder reflected. Then again, getting rid of people was an important part of what he did.

'There have been too many bodies,' she persisted. 'Far too many. This isn't America, you know. Murder draws too much attention to everything.'

'That's not going to stop you creating one more, is it?'

'Don't worry, you'll be the last.'

'One thing I've learned over the years,' Holder observed wearily, 'is that murder is never final. Sooner or later, there's always another wanker that needs putting down.'

'Whatever happens next won't be your problem.'

'That's not much of a consolation.'

'Let's get this done.' Dalby-Cummins pointed to the ray gun, still lying on the table. 'We can make it painless. Just close your eyes and Sandro will give you a tap with the bolt stunner. After that, you won't know anything about it.'

This is what it feels like to be a bloody pig, Holder thought. If, by some unbelievable miracle, he managed to get himself out of there, he'd give serious consideration to becoming a vegetarian.

'It would help if you were on your knees.' She pointed at the floor. 'And stay still. If you move at the last minute, there will be a terrible mess.'

Like hell. Realising it was now or never, Holder threw himself at Sandro, arms outstretched. There was a blur of limbs and he felt a searing pain as the blade sliced into his upper arm. 'Arrgh. Fuck.'

Enjoying the spectacle, Dalby-Cummins shrieked with delight. 'Finish him, Sandro,' she cackled. 'Do him.'

Holder was fantasising about cleaving Vicky's head straight from her shoulders, when the second blow bit into his neck. A spray of blood sent his attacker dancing backwards. Losing his footing, Holder crashed to the floor. Slowly, he pushed himself up onto his knees, only to be knocked down again by a succession of blows, each more brutal than the last.

'Finish him off,' Dalby-Cummins squealed. 'Hurry up. The pigs are hungry.'

Holder watched his dark, criminal blood spreading serenely across the tiles. I'm going to end up as a pork chop, he realised glumly. And a bloody organic one at that.

THIRTY-FOUR

Obeid Idris stared at the empty swimming pool and scratched unhappily at his trunks. Gabriella, still smarting at his unscheduled disappearance, was keeping him on a tight leash. Sensing his boredom, she looked over the top of her Kindle. 'You were going to take me to Disneyland.'

'We could go to Disneyland.' The prospect filled him with dread.

'The concierge can organise a trip for us.' It sounded like a threat. 'It's gonna take about four hours but the limo is air-conditioned.'

'If you fancy it . . .' Idris picked up a nearby newspaper and began flicking through the news pages.

'Shall I sort it out, then?' his girlfriend asked, peeved by his obvious lack of enthusiasm.

'Sure.'

'They've got an International Garden and Flower Festival.' Gabriella adjusted her bikini top and slipped on her flip-flops.

As she shuffled towards the hotel, Idris had a minor epiphany: I'm going to dump you when we get back to London.

The casual realisation that their relationship was over did nothing to ease his frustration. The root of his unease was simple: he wasn't working. Lying around made him feel guilty. His father, a shoemaker, had instilled in his son a ferocious work ethic. When he had embarked on his own singular career, Idris had quickly grasped that taking down rich targets was all about the preparation. The job itself was always something of a disappointment and afterwards, well, it was just a case of moving on to the next thing. His undoubted success was based on the fact that he never stood still.

A headline caught his eye. *Prince Set for New York.* The short story underneath revealed that Prince Bader Goyalan had been appointed as Saudi ambassador to the United Nations. A spokesman denied that this was a consolation prize after the prince was passed over for the throne. *'The prince,'* Mansour Hayek insisted, *'thinks he can achieve a lot in this job. There is much to do.'*

New York? Idris had never done a job in the United States. On the other hand, he was facing a new start. Maybe a new city should be part of that.

Attached to the bottom of the story was a separate item, a News in Brief:

Human rights groups have expressed outrage after Gregory Cosneau was executed live on Saudi TV. Mr Cosneau, a former employee of the International Corporate Bank of the Red Sea, had been sentenced to death after being found guilty of stealing $5m from the Royal Family. He was beheaded after King Ziyad Alarab rejected pleas for clemency.

Poor sod. Out of the corner of his eye, Idris caught Gabriella walking towards him. She wore a determined look and was waving a pair of tickets. Disneyland it is, then. Tossing the paper onto the sun lounger, he dived into the pool in search of a momentary stay of execution.

*

The hunt for a new colour scheme continued. Folding his arms, Carlyle scrutinised the mess in front of him. Half a dozen different colours had been daubed on the wall. It looked like a bunch of demented five-year-olds had run amok in his office.

Maybe I could get Dom to lend me something to put up there, he thought. A nice black-and-white photograph, perhaps. At any rate, something big enough to cover up the mess.

'What d'you think?' Appearing at his shoulder, Linda pointed at the row of small tester pots lined up on his desk.

'They all look pretty much the same to me.'

Stepping over to the wall, his PA reeled off a list of unnecessarily complicated names as she tapped each different smear in turn.

'What you're saying,' Carlyle concluded, 'is that they're all different shades of grey.'

'Basically,' Linda agreed. 'Wasn't that what you wanted?'

'I suppose.' The commander pointed at the original daubing, located at the centre of the mess. 'The first one we tried, what was that called?'

'Cool Grey Silk. That's the one that is currently at the heart of the standard colour palette for our holding facilities.'

What we put on the cell walls. 'On further reflection, I think maybe I *do* like that one the best.'

'You've changed your mind? Again?' Linda stifled a groan. 'You want the Cool Grey Silk?'

'Well . . .' Carlyle felt almost paralysed by indecision '. . . I'm not really so keen on the grey any more, but if it's going to be grey, that one's as good as any, I suppose.'

'You have to make your mind up. The Paddington Green Redecoration Programme ends soon. If it doesn't get sorted now, there's nothing we can do about it for the next seven years.'

Tilting his head, Carlyle considered the possibility of staying with the status quo.

'You can't leave your office looking like this,' Linda remonstrated.

'Oh, I dunno. I quite like it.' The commander scratched his chin. 'It looks a bit like a Kessling.'

'Eh?'

'Sigmund Kessling. He's a Canadian artist. His work goes for millions.' He scrutinised the blank look on Linda's face. 'Never mind.'

'Cool Grey Silk,' she repeated.

He had a flash of inspiration. 'Alternatively, let's just go for white.'

The look on Linda's face suggested she wanted to strangle him. 'What kind of white?'

Thrown by the question, the commander frowned. 'There are different types of white?'

Linda reeled off another set of names. 'Ghost White, Baby Powder, Snow, Ivory—'

'Ghost White.'

'Ghost White?' She was surprised by his sudden decisiveness. 'Are you sure?'

'Let's go for that.'

'I'm glad we've got that settled.' Linda headed towards the door, keen to escape before he reconsidered. 'I'll let you know when the painters are due in, so you can avoid the office for a couple of days.' She paused. 'Not that that should be much of a problem for you, given that you're never here at the best of times.'

'No,' Carlyle agreed.

'Speaking of which, DAC Glass is expecting a call from you today. Do you want me to see if I can get him on the line now?'

'DAC Glass?'

'Thomas Glass is Michelle Mara's replacement. I expect he wants to talk to you about the latest performance statistics – your poor meeting-attendance record.'

Carlyle felt a spasm of discomfort. 'I'll call him later,' he muttered. 'Email me his number and I'll do it this afternoon.'

Linda looked unconvinced.

'What do the stats say?'

'The numbers don't lie. And they don't look good. In terms of organisational efficiency, you are deep in the bottom quartile of commanders in London.'

Taking that as his cue to flee, Carlyle edged past her, heading for the exit. 'Don't worry,' he said. 'I'll definitely speak to him. Just send me the number.'

By the time he reached the ground floor, Carlyle had forgotten all about DAC Glass. Walking purposefully across the lobby, he was dismayed to be intercepted by a giant elderly bloke, dressed like an undertaker, with gaunt features and a shock of white hair.

'Commander Carlyle?'

Carlyle hesitated before confirming his identity. 'That's me.'

The man handed over a business card. 'Conrad Stockhausen, general counsel at the Investigation Unit.'

The Investigation Unit. Bernie Gilmore's mob. Trying not to look or sound guilty, Carlyle studied the card. 'I knew your Mr Gilmore a little. I was very sorry to learn about what happened.'

'That's why we're here.' A small grey-haired woman appeared from behind the lawyer, jabbing the air with a pair of red-framed spectacles. 'I'm Francesca Culverhouse, the founder of the Unit.' She didn't offer her hand.

Carlyle nodded. 'Is there something I can do for you?'

'Bernard Gilmore was a fine journalist, one of a dying breed.'

'Yes.'

'The Unit will be launching a campaign in his memory.'

Oh, God. Carlyle stared at the floor. Someone had spilled some coffee next to where they were standing, leaving a congealing mess. 'I know he would have appreciated that.'

270

'And we will be making sure that his outstanding stories are seen through to their appropriate conclusion.' Culverhouse gave him a knowing look.

'I was just heading out.' Carlyle glanced hopefully towards the door. 'I need to—'

'We know he was on to you,' Culverhouse hissed.

Feeling more than a little shifty, Carlyle looked around. The last thing he needed was someone to catch him having this conversation in the middle of the station.

'The Met needs a proper shake-up.' She paused. 'Someone like Chief Inspector Andy Wick is a disgrace to the police force.'

Eh?

Culverhouse scrutinised him. 'I think we can both agree on that, don't you?'

'Yes,' Carlyle stammered, 'that's right. From what little I understand, it's a very sorry tale.'

'Our in-depth investigation into police corruption will be a fitting tribute to Bernard's memory.'

'It will be thoroughly researched and one hundred per cent accurate,' Stockhausen chipped in, 'based on a range of reliable and verifiable sources.'

There was a lengthy pause before Culverhouse added, 'And, as you would expect, we will be steering away from the more outlandish type of claims and accusations that are invariably floated in situations like this.'

Carlyle reached for the olive branch. 'Everyone's got an axe to grind,' he remarked sadly.

'We are completely committed to responsible reporting,' a reptilian leer crossed Culverhouse's face, 'and, as such, would appreciate some senior help when it comes to sorting the wheat from the chaff, so to speak. On deep background.'

'As long as it is completely non-attributable, I will be happy to help where I can.' Carlyle edged towards the door. 'I agree it would be the right way to remember Bernie.'

A look of understanding passed between the policeman, the journalist and the lawyer.

Culverhouse placed the spectacles on top of her head. 'I appreciate that, Commander. Thank you.'

THIRTY-FIVE

'How many people in the room have a problem sleeping?'

Not me. Sitting in the back row of the Huxley Theatre, Carlyle stifled a yawn. When my head hits the pillow, I go out like a light. His mother used to say that was a sign of a man with a clear conscience. The memory made him chuckle.

'Dad,' Alice whispered, 'for God's sake. Be quiet.'

No one can hear us, we're up in the gods. Still, Carlyle did as he was told. The Imperial College open day was completely Alice's gig. His job was to keep his mouth shut and be as helpful as possible. That meant looking interested in a lecture on the impact of sedatives on brain function. The aim was to provide would-be students – and their parents – with an insight into the type of research they could get involved in, should they decide to study at the university.

On the distant stage Brian, a spotty postgraduate student in a Metallica T-shirt, grabbed the lectern tightly. Behind him, on a cinema-style screen, was a massive picture of a mouse. 'Don't worry,' he laughed nervously, 'you won't be volunteering for anything. I just want to get a sense of who can relate to this particular problem.'

After several seconds of rather embarrassed silence, a couple of middle-aged women near the front of the audience reluctantly raised their hands.

'Good.' A look of relief passed across Brian's face. He tapped a keyboard on the lectern and the mouse was replaced by an image of a woman sitting up in bed. 'Lack of sleep is a big problem for many people. If you are suffering from stress or if you have irregular work shifts, it can affect your physical and mental health.'

Tell me about it, Carlyle reflected. The only thing that had ever seriously interrupted his kip over the years had been night shifts, pounding the streets of the East End when he had been a young constable working out of the Mile End station. Happily, those days were long gone.

'Various drugs are readily available,' Brian continued, 'but none of them offer rest as good as natural sleep. Our research aims to help lead to new ways of dealing with this problem by chemically switching on different parts of the brain. If we switch on the preoptic hypothalamus, for example, it triggers a deep sleep.'

Struggling to keep his eyes open, Carlyle watched Alice scribbling in a spiral notebook.

'The action is very similar to the way sedatives work on the brain,' Brian continued, 'and the new findings may lead eventually to better treatments for insomnia and more effective anaesthetic drugs.'

The large lecture hall was about half full. By a rough estimate, around two-thirds of those present appeared to be either Chinese or Indian. Wondering how well Alice would fit in, Carlyle reached for his phone. Trying to be as inconspicuous as possible, he tapped at the screen. A text from Alison Roche nestled in his in-box.

Forensics confirm Emmanuel Bole as Cotterill killer.

Manny Bole was a known associate of a flamboyant little gangster called Bob Biswas. Ostensibly an Antwerp diamond trader, Biswas had been on the fringes of various high-profile crimes without ever feeling the cuffs snap on his wrists. Carlyle tried to work out a possible connection between Biswas and Vernon Holder. When nothing came to mind, he laboriously typed a reply to Roche with his index finger.

'If you don't sleep for a long period, your body shuts down,' Brian continued, from the stage, 'almost as if you had taken a drug . . .'

Carlyle was trying to pull up some background on Biswas on his phone when Alice gave him a dig with her elbow. 'Sorry,' he mumbled, 'work.'

His daughter pointed to a large sign on the wall: *Mobile phones to be switched off in the auditorium.*

'Back in a minute.' Stepping into an empty corridor, he hit Roche's number. The sergeant answered on the first ring.

'What do you think?' she asked, energised.

'What's Manny Bole doing in all of this? I can't immediately see what the link might be with Vernon Holder.'

'We need to find out. I called Holder's office, but his PA said he was out.'

'Where?'

'She wouldn't tell me.'

'He won't have gone far,' Carlyle observed. 'I don't think he's ever left London in his life.'

'Oh, I don't know. Last time we saw him he had quite a tan. You don't get that in Archway.'

'You do if you go to Boulant's Solarium,' Carlyle ventured, mentioning a notorious spa on the Holloway Road. 'We're going to have to pay him another visit.'

'Want to go up there now? I can just about do it before I have to go to the nursery to pick up David,' she continued. 'I'd get Alex to do it, but he's in a big Andy Wick case meeting. I don't think things are going very well for the chief inspector right now.'

'Oh?' Carlyle wanted to dig deeper but now was not the time. 'Let's not worry about trying to get up there today. We're not in a monster rush. Vernon isn't going anywhere. He likes sitting in his grotty office, watching the police running round in circles. He gets off on it. And why not? He's got a hundred per cent success record so far.'

'So far.'

'Ashley Cotterill'll be his undoing.' Carlyle pawed at a hole in the linoleum flooring. 'By the way, did you find anything useful in those papers Cotterill gave you?'

'Not a thing.' Roche groaned. 'That was a complete fiasco. The consultant we hired had only got halfway through the papers when Thomson pulled the plug on the grounds that we couldn't afford any more of his time. I should have insisted on the accountants sending us someone more senior who could go through the material more quickly. That's five grand up the spout. In hindsight, going for the junior guy was a false economy.'

'Don't beat yourself up about it.'

'We got nothing and now the inspector is on my case for wasting her budget.'

'It happens.'

'Thomson didn't want me to hire anyone in the first place.'

'You were only using your initiative.'

'They don't like that in the Met,' Roche observed sourly, 'do they?'

No, they most certainly do not. 'Do you want me to have a word with her?'

'That would probably only make things worse. She doesn't like you very much.'

'That hardly puts her in a minority of one.' Carlyle couldn't have cared less. 'How did she get on with Karen Jansen's parents?'

'She handed over the body and packed them off back to Australia as quickly as she could.'

276

Carlyle gave an approving nod. 'Professional detachment.'

'A worrying lack of empathy,' was Roche's verdict. 'She doesn't seem to care that Ashley Cotterill died for that file. She's counting the pennies so we can't even manage to read it properly.'

'Don't worry about it. For all we know, the information in there doesn't add up to much anyway. Manny Bole sounds like a good lead. And we'll put some pressure on Vernon. Overconfidence will get him in the end.'

The sergeant sounded less than convinced. 'I could see if the nursery will keep David for a little longer. I don't want to hold things up.'

'You're not. I'm tied up for the rest of the day myself.' Carlyle considered the illuminated sign that read '*LECTURE IN PROGRESS*'. How long could Brian keep talking about mice and sleep? Probably quite a long time, he decided. The sound of approaching footsteps echoed down the corridor. Turning away from them, he instinctively lowered his voice. 'What about tomorrow?'

'Earlier would be better,' Roche suggested. 'Before Thomson finds me something else to do.'

'In that case—' A hand landed between his shoulder blades, pushing him into the wall. Dropping his phone, the commander was spun around, allowing a fist to smash into his face. Blood filled his mouth and he was overwhelmed by nausea. As his legs gave way and he slid towards the floor, he registered a second blow. Followed by a third. Without the strength to fight back, he simply let go, waiting for unconsciousness to take over.

THIRTY-SIX

Carlyle woke with a start. He was sitting on the floor, his feet bound with plastic restraints, as were his hands, which were tied so tightly behind his back that his shoulders burned. His head throbbed. At some point in the proceedings, he had vomited down the front of his shirt. To say he didn't smell too good was something of an understatement.

'What a time to have a kip,' proclaimed a familiar voice.

They were in the back office of the Molby-Nicol gallery. About five feet away, similarly bound, Dominic Silver had raised himself onto a stack of old catalogues. Dom had clearly been subjected to a serious beating: there was a deep gash above his left eyebrow and his right eye was almost closed.

Carlyle tried unsuccessfully to raise enough spit to rinse the sour taste from his mouth. 'Need I ask what happened?' he croaked.

'Alain Costello turned up with some muscle. They smacked me about a bit, tied me up and left me here. A while later they came back with your dear self.' Dom looked towards the closed door. 'I'm just glad Eva wasn't around.'

Carlyle wondered if Dom's wife might call in some reinforcements. 'You're not expecting her, by any chance?'

'Nah. She's gone to see her mum. By the time she gets back, we'll have all this sorted.'

278

Yeah, right. Carlyle tried to piece together what had happened back at Imperial. After the first or second punch, however, there was nothing but darkness. He wondered about Alice. Was she still in the lecture about the mice? 'How long have I been here?' he asked.

'About an hour, not much more than that.'

They were interrupted by the sound of voices in the gallery.

Carlyle lowered his voice. 'What's the plan?'

'I haven't seen an order of service, but I imagine Costello has a spot of torture in mind, followed by a bit of whining about what we did to his dad and then violent death.'

'How could he know what we did to Tuco?'

'He *assumes*. You know what they say: *always assume*. It helps make life go faster. Anyway, as far as the little psycho's concerned, there isn't really any downside in being wrong.'

'I suppose not.'

'Not that he is, of course.'

'No.' Carlyle looked towards the ceiling. 'Where's Hunter?'

'I gave him the day off.'

'You gave him the day off?' Carlyle cried. 'What the fuck did you do that for?'

'Keep your voice down,' Dom hissed, nodding towards the door. 'The longer those boys stay out there the better, as far as I'm concerned.'

'But the guy hasn't even been working for you for a week,' Carlyle protested, albeit more quietly. 'How could you give him a day off?'

'What can I say?' Dom chuckled. 'I'm an enlightened employer.'

'You're a mug,' was the commander's verdict.

'Spoken like a man who's never been any good at managing people.'

Carlyle didn't waste any time arguing the point. He recalled the conversation he was having with Roche when he was attacked. Could the sergeant be looking for him? It was a long shot.

'We don't really need him until the Kessling paintings arrive,' Dom explained.

'You might as well get your money's worth,' Carlyle responded, channelling his inner Calvinist.

'Daniel's already more than paid his way. The insurance company has reinstated my cover and agreed a reasonable premium. Well, not exactly *reasonable*, but affordable. Just about.'

'That's good to know.'

'We've got a firm shipping date, by the way. The paintings should be here in a fortnight. From the images I've seen, they're really quite something.' Dom shifted on his pile of catalogues, trying to find a more comfortable position. 'I've got very little doubt that they'll go down in history as some of Sigmund's greatest works.'

And we'll go down in history as worm food, Carlyle fretted.

'Once they get here, we'll get them hung. I'm thinking we'll reopen ten days to a fortnight after that. There'll be a big party to celebrate.'

'Shame we won't be here to see it,' Carlyle groused.

'Now's not the time for your bloody negativity,' Dom snapped.

'I'm not negative.' Carlyle wondered if Dom might be in shock.

'Not negative?' Dom let out a harsh laugh. 'You're the most pessimistic guy I've ever met. Always have been. Even back in the day you couldn't enjoy a line of whizz when we were rotting on those damn picket lines for fear of getting caught. Always looking over your shoulder. Always fearing the worst.'

'I'm just pragmatic.' The commander wasn't really in the mood for a forensic dissection of his character. He badly needed to pee. Wiggling his toes, he tried to take his mind off his aching bladder.

'That's one way of putting it. You always were the quintessential glass-half-full kind of guy.'

'It's helped keep me alive.' Until now. 'It just seemed to me to be a sensible way to approach things.'

'Maybe,' Dom conceded. 'But I always looked at the *possibilities*. You just looked at the dangers. Even when I offered you a job, you were too scared to take it.'

'Too scared to take it? You were a drug dealer, for God's sake. I'm a cop. There's only so far across the line I wanted to go.'

'Once you've crossed it, you've crossed it.'

'But if you go too far, you can never come back.'

'I came back.' Giving up on the catalogues, Dom eased himself onto the floor. 'I did what I did for a while and then I came all the way back.'

'You did what you did for a hell of a long time. Decades.'

'I still came back,' Dom repeated. 'And, as you know, I was never convicted of anything. Not even close.'

'So, we're both going to meet our Maker with a spotless record.' Carlyle snorted. 'I don't know about you, but it doesn't make me feel any better about things right now.'

'Always the pessimist.'

The sound of a siren on Cork Street caused Carlyle to catch his breath. It rose to a crescendo, then fell away. 'Fuck.'

Dom looked at Carlyle. 'You know, the times when I was furthest on the wrong side of the law, the darkest times, you were there, by my side.'

Embarrassed, the commander coughed. 'I know.'

'We made a good team.'

'I don't know that we were a team,' Carlyle felt the words stick in his throat, 'but we were always on the same page.

I always knew you had my back. Even in the worst situations I knew you wouldn't cut and run.'

'Likewise.' Dom paused, conscious that the conversation was descending into schmaltz. 'And it was Costello who killed Bernie Gilmore. He was boasting about it earlier. Bernie must've legged him over.'

The journalist's death seemed ancient history to Carlyle. 'Bernie's boss came to see me. The Investigation Unit wants to do a number on Andy Wick.'

'Old news,' was Dom's verdict.

Carlyle disagreed. 'For the media, Andy Wick is the gift that keeps giving. Francesca Culverhouse made it clear that they're quite happy to put any story about us on the back burner if I play ball.' He gave a weak smile. 'I told you they'd trade.'

'That might change when we're found in here, bound and gagged and shot in the head.'

'Well, we'll be past caring by then.'

'After they find your battered and bloodied body, you're going to be a bigger story than Andy Wick. For a while, anyway.'

'Fame at last.'

Dom started to laugh.

'What's so funny?'

'You don't get a sniff of a promotion for almost thirty years and then you get promoted three rungs in one go.'

'Four.'

'Four rungs in one go – it's totally bloody unheard of. And then—' Dom cut himself off. 'John bloody Carlyle.'

'Shit happens.'

'Only you could manage such a spectacular fall from grace.'

'I'm not sure I've ever enjoyed a state of grace during my time on the Force.'

'No, I suppose not.' A pained look passed across Dom's face. 'Any regrets?'

Carlyle finally generated enough saliva to spit on the floor. 'Nah. Apart from going out like this, obviously.'

'Obviously.'

'I mean, what's the point of regrets?'

THIRTY-SEVEN

There was the sound of voices, followed by a gentle thud. Staring at his feet, Carlyle listened to footsteps on the wooden floor. Your death, he told himself, is going to be banal and anti-climactic. No point in worrying about it. You certainly won't be bothered in a couple of minutes from now. The door creaked open and he screwed his eyes shut.

This is it. Game over, Rover.

Fuckedy, fuckedy, fucking, fuck.

'About bloody time,' Dom growled.

Carlyle opened his eyes to see a grinning Daniel Hunter filling the doorway.

'I'm not interrupting, am I?'

'Get us out of here.' Dom kicked out at the desk. 'There's a pair of scissors in the top drawer. Hurry up.'

On the other side of the door, Carlyle could make out a prostrate body. He squinted at Hunter. 'Didn't you have the day off?'

'I did, but I ran out of cash.' Hunter moved behind the desk and pulled open the drawer. 'Three quid sixty for a cup of coffee – it's totally ridiculous.' His outrage reverberated in his voice. 'London's so bloody expensive. How can anyone afford to live here?'

'Don't worry,' Dom croaked, 'you've just qualified for a monster bonus, my son. Enough to keep you in lattes for the rest of your life.'

'Sounds good.' Coming up with a large pair of red scissors, Hunter quickly released his boss. 'Who are those guys in the gallery, by the way?'

'Some very unwelcome guests.' Struggling to his feet, Dom vigorously rubbed his wrists as Hunter cut Carlyle loose.

'Are they dead?' the commander asked hopefully.

Hunter advised not. 'When they wake up, they're going to have a hell of a headache, though.'

Extending an arm, Dom helped Carlyle to his feet. 'Are we going to call the cops?'

'I am the cops.'

Dom eyed his friend carefully. 'You know what I mean.'

'I'll deal with them. But first I've gotta have a slash, or I'm going to fucking burst.'

Standing on the pavement, phone clamped to her ear, Nayla Thomson was engaged in animated conversation. Carlyle watched the inspector through the window, wondering who she might be talking to. He had come too far to be brought down by a callow management trainee showing too much of an interest in what exactly had happened here. Compared to Alain Costello, Thomson didn't seem that much of a threat, but he knew he would have to remain watchful.

At the back of the gallery, Dom was enjoying a reviving whisky. Hunter had disappeared upstairs. After a while, Roche wandered in from the street.

'Here you go.' The sergeant tossed Carlyle his phone. 'Alice picked it up outside the lecture theatre. You gave her a hell of a fright.'

'Yes.' Carlyle wondered how he was going to credibly spin this latest fiasco when he got home.

'She's a smart kid – pulled up the call log and rang me. I took her home and spoke to Helen. They know you're okay.'

'Thanks.'

'Imperial, eh? Good luck with those fees.'

Carlyle stared at the phone. '*If* she goes there.'

'She seems very keen.'

'Just wait till it's your turn.'

Roche's expression grew solemn. 'You were very lucky here. If it hadn't been for Hunter –'

'I know.'

'– I'd never have found you in time.'

'Better to be lucky than smart,' Carlyle quipped.

'Seriously, John, those guys are animals.'

Whenever anyone called him 'John', it was clear that he was in line for a severe scolding. Carlyle quickly moved the conversation along. 'Where've you taken them?'

'They're at Paddington. The hope is that they'll be deported imminently. Costello's violated the terms of his pardon so he should go straight back to prison. And his associate has several warrants out for his arrest.'

'So, we'll toss them back to the French and let them sort it all out?'

'That's the plan.'

'Dom says they killed Bernie Gilmore.'

Roche looked at him carefully. 'You want us to keep them?'

Maybe, before Thomson had arrived, the prisoners could have been made to disappear, just like Tuco. Not now, however. 'As long as they're behind bars,' Carlyle declared, 'I don't really care where they do their time. Let's just hope the Frogs keep them inside this time.'

'I'm sure the French judiciary won't make the same mistake twice.' Roche gestured at his phone. 'Don't you want to call home?'

'I should talk to the girls face to face.'

'In that case, you'd better head off. We'll need to get a

statement but that can wait. Give me a call tomorrow and we can sort things out.'

Carlyle nodded. 'It looks like the same gang came back for another hit on the gallery.'

'Something like that,' Roche agreed. Carlyle, Dom and Hunter would get their story straight and she would turn it into 'fact' with a minimum of fuss.

'Thanks, Ali.' Standing up straight, Carlyle was aware of just how badly his body ached. You're getting on, he reflected, too old for this nonsense. Once he had explained himself to Helen, he would need a hot bath and a very large whiskey, followed by a long, dreamless sleep.

'That's enough adventures for a while, okay? You scared the hell out of me, too.'

'Deal.' Carlyle gave her a gentle pat on the shoulder. 'Thanks for riding to the rescue.'

Roche blushed slightly. 'Hardly.'

'And sorry I made you miss nursery pick-up.'

'Don't worry. I got that sorted. Everything's under control.'

'God bless Alex.'

'Yeah, God bless good old Shaggy.' She pointed him on his way. 'See you tomorrow.'

Heading along the street, Carlyle felt the phone vibrating in his hand. Hitting receive, he lifted the handset to his ear.

'John Carlyle.'

'This is Andy Wick.' Despite the relatively early hour, the disgraced chief inspector sounded more than a little intoxicated. 'I've got a bone to pick with you.'

Uh-oh, Carlyle thought, here we go.

'I hear you've been slagging me off to the media,' Wick snarled. 'What the fuck d'you think you're playing at?'

You want an argument, sunshine, I'll give you one. Carlyle

287

launched into a tirade of abuse, focusing, among other things, on his colleague's alleged parentage. Only when he stopped to cross the road, did he realise that the call had dropped.

Staring at the screen in disgust, Carlyle watched the phone spring back into life. The fucker was clearly a glutton for punishment. 'As I was saying—'

'Inspector Carlyle?' The woman on the line was clearly not Andy Wick.

'Yes,' he barked, not bothering to correct her on matters of rank as he crossed New Bond Street. 'Who am I speaking to?'

'My name is Vicky Dalby-Cummins.'

'Harry's widow?'

'Among other things,' came the cool response.

What could the woman want from him? Carlyle's mind skipped through a few possibilities, dismissing all of them as less than credible. 'I hear you're running the show now.'

Dalby-Cummins did not demur.

'How's Vernon?'

'He's a sleeping partner. Pretty much retired.'

That didn't sound much like Holder to Carlyle. 'I'd like to speak to him.'

'That might be difficult.'

Carlyle did not press the point. 'What can I do for you?'

'I was wondering if we could meet up. There are things we could usefully discuss.'

'Talk away. I'm happy to listen.' Navigating his way through the oncoming pedestrians, he came to a halt in the entrance to Burlington Arcade.

'In my experience, these things are better done face to face. I was wondering if you might like to come and see my operation.'

The farm near the Welsh borders? Carlyle instantly recoiled. 'That's a long way to go for a chat. Will Vernon be there?'

'Maybe.' She chuckled. 'We can certainly offer some great

hospitality. We source all our food locally and our animals are slaughtered onsite. Plus, there's lots of fresh air and some great views.'

'Hm.'

'You could get out of London for a couple of days – bring your wife, have a little break.'

When was the last time he and Helen had been away anywhere? Carlyle couldn't remember. A trip to the countryside wasn't his idea of a good time but it wouldn't kill him. And Helen would be up for it. The possibility of winning some Brownie points at home gave him pause.

'Okay,' he relented, 'why not?'